BASIN 63

PHILIP CHANDLER THRILLERS
BOOK 1

SCOTT MCINTOSH

Paperback ISBN: 979-8-9941792-0-8
Digital Book ISBN: 979-8-9941792-1-5

ALSO BY SCOTT MCINTOSH

Philip Chandler Thrillers

Basin 63

To find out more about Scott's books, visit:

WriterScottMcIntosh.com

1

———

I felt the blow before I saw it coming.

As a reporter, I had been attacked before for something I had written, both verbally and online. But this was the first time I had ever been attacked physically—and for something I hadn't even written yet.

At that time of night, Fremont's Main Street was quiet, except for Cowboys Lounge down the block, the front door open, emitting a wedge of light and muted sounds of laughter, music, the click of pool balls and clinking glasses. I was thinking about heading down for a drink, when I heard a dog bark in the distance.

Even though the sun had set, it was still hot, sticky hot, unusual for Idaho's arid climate, and unusual for September. A cold beer would taste good right now.

As I fished in my pocket for my keys and fumbled with them in the front door lock, something nagged at me. The smell of cigarette smoke. The dog barking.

I started to turn, but it was too late.

I felt the whoosh of air behind me, saw a glint out of the corner of my eye, then felt the jarring impact on the back of my head that snapped my neck forward and to the side. My vision started to close at the edges but opened back up when my knees hit the sidewalk.

I instinctively started to look back and up, but a set of large meaty hands pushed my shoulder blades forward, throwing me down to the ground. A hard toe kick to my thigh sent a shock of pain up and down my leg, numbing it. Two more kicks to my right side took the wind out of me, and I gasped for air. One hand pushed down on my left shoulder, and another grabbed a fistful of my hair and pushed my face into the sidewalk.

A raspy voice accompanied by bad breath whispered in my ear, "Be careful what you write about. You know what I'm talking about."

The hands let up, and another kick to my side curled me up in pain.

"Stay down," the voice said. "Don't get up. Don't look back."

Through squinting eyes, I glanced back but not quick enough to get a full look at the figure that rounded the corner and walked away.

I stumbled to my feet and tentatively made my way to the corner of the building, peering cautiously around the edge, in case my attacker was waiting. He wasn't.

The dog barked again, then a car started in the distance, and I saw a black SUV drive away.

I felt a rush of dizziness and braced myself against the building's wall.

I made my way back to my office, unlocked my door and went in. I locked the door behind me and eased myself into my chair.

Just three days earlier, I was sitting in that very spot, depressed and bored, contemplating my life choices, a familiar, lonely cloud settling over me. I had been in a rut, a laid-off cops-and-courts reporter from Boston wallowing for the past two years in a small town outside Boise, Idaho, writing about city council meetings, school boards and Friday night football games. I missed the action of crime scenes, homicides and police chases.

But since the murders three days earlier, I was out of the rut, following leads like a searcher using a dim flashlight down a darkened tunnel. Getting punched in the head outside my office told me a lot. That I was on the right track. What was at the end of the track, though, I still didn't know. But I was getting closer. That much I did know.

If I was being honest, despite the pain, for the first time in months, I was happy.

2

———————

News of the murders broke the monotony of a typical Monday night.

I was putting the finishing touches on a routine city council article about a land deal that would turn eighty acres of farmland into a subdivision of houses and apartments, a common sight in Fremont, a once-rural dusty Idaho farm town that used to contain five hundred people but was rapidly transforming into a suburban city of fifteen thousand.

It was just before midnight, and I was sitting alone in my storefront office, which at one time had seemed magnificent and novel but now felt shabby and familiar in the two years since I had become the sole owner, editor and publisher of the *Fremont Herald*.

Static from the portable police scanner on the corner of my desk served as soothing white noise, typical for that time of night. Typical for a sleepy small town. Nothing like the bank of scanners in the middle of the newsroom in Boston, always crackling with activity.

That was why the voice coming over the scanner startled me.

"Fremont Fire to dispatch."

I recognized the voice of Rod Pearson, an old-timer with the Fremont Fire Department.

"Go ahead, Fremont Fire."

"Can you send the coroner out to 55729 South Swan Falls Road. We've got a double homicide."

Having spent every week for the past two years hand-labeling each subscriber copy of the newspaper, I recognized the address. The image of their label popped into my mind instantly and automatically: Wanda and Vern Thompson, 55729 South Swan Falls Road.

I checked to make sure the PDF of that week's issue of the paper had gone through to the printer. I grabbed my jacket, locked up and got in my car. Down the street, people were shuffling out of Cowboys Lounge and heading home. No drink tonight. But at least the cloud had lifted.

I turned my beat-up Honda Civic off Main Street and south onto Swan Falls Road, an eighteen-mile stretch of asphalt that lay like a chalk line snapped on the desert floor before it descended sharply into a canyon to the Swan Falls Dam, where the Snake River was flowing at about 540,000 gallons a minute, just enough to move the turbines to power a few thousand homes.

As I drove, my phone buzzed.

"Philip Chandler," I said.

"It's John." Fremont Police Chief John Hernandez insisted on using his first name with me, and I insisted on addressing him as "Chief," a formality I maintained as a reminder that this wasn't a friendship, it was professional.

"I'm down at the Thompsons' place." His voice quavered at the couple's name. "You might want to get down here. They've been shot. Killed."

"I'm already on my way," I said. "I'll be there in about ten minutes."

Vern and Wanda Thompson were in their seventies, lifetime residents of Fremont. Vern was a farmer who grew potatoes—or "taters," as he called them—along with alfalfa, wheat, sugar beets, and corn. He was a quiet, unassuming man, always in faded jeans, a rumpled T-shirt, a nylon windbreaker and a sweat-stained trucker's hat covering his scraggly gray hair. If the weather was cold, he added a plaid fleece-lined flannel hoodie. Years in the field had weathered Vern's face to a brown leather. His teeth were ground down to gray nubs.

That someone would kill the Thompsons was unimaginable. A robbery? Did the Thompsons stumble upon a burglar breaking into their house? It couldn't be murder-suicide. Family dispute? I ran through the possible scenarios I had accumulated in my fifteen years as a reporter, and none of them added up. Not the Thompsons. Not in Fremont.

Some sort of psycho serial killer? Doubtful. In my line of work, I had so rarely come across a true serial killer. Once, in fact. A rapist who drove around the Boston suburbs in a white cargo van and abducted women in mall parking lots. But that was the only one I had covered. Murders, in my experience, usually were committed by drunk husbands, people on the losing end of a drug deal, someone who owed someone money.

As I drove out of town and farther into the desert, I was already thinking about the lede on my story: "Longtime pillars of the Fremont community Vern and Wanda Thompson were found shot and killed in their home Monday night."

My brain automatically began calculating how I could put the story in that week's issue of the paper. Get rid of the feature at the bottom of the front page, move everything else down, kill the teasers at the top of the page and run a short, no-jump, hold-to-cover story striped across the top with the big headline "Local Fremont couple shot, killed." Sixty point, bold. Resend a PDF of page one, tell the printer to swap out just the front page, and I'd have the biggest story on the newsstands that afternoon before the first news conference. Better up the press run by a couple hundred copies.

Part of me felt guilty for thinking that way about the murder of two people I knew and respected. But it was automatic. I'd been in the newspaper business for fifteen years, and I was wired for deadlines, headlines and selling papers.

3

The familiar flashing blue-and-red lights of the police cars, which served almost as a salve, lit up the night sky as I approached the Thompsons' house.

About a half dozen police cars, Fremont's entire fleet, were parked along the road when I pulled up. The empty driveway was surrounded by yellow police tape.

Chief Hernandez stood on the front lawn talking to an officer, illuminated by the porch light and the flashing police car lights. I pulled over on the right shoulder across from the house and checked my watch. 12:20 a.m.

I knew enough to hang back for now and not crowd Hernandez. All the lights in the house were on. Hernandez disappeared inside.

Hernandez often called to tip me off to a story. We had developed an affinity for one another, even though we came from different backgrounds. While I was from "back East," Hernandez had grown up in Idaho and was Mormon, which included about a third of the population of Fremont. But we were about the same age, mid-thirties, both young for our respective prominent roles in a community dominated by old white men, or pale stale males, as I called them.

From my position at my car across the street from the Thompsons' house, I grabbed my camera, a trusty Nikon D70 I always kept in the trunk, and took some photos of the scene.

I marveled at the Thompsons' house. I had always imagined Vern and Wanda living in a small, dilapidated old farmhouse with an oak tree out front complete with a tire swing and white picket fence. The sight of a modern suburban house was shocking.

It was a two-story proper colonial, something you'd see in a Connecticut suburb, but out of place in the West, with a sprawling, well-manicured lawn, a new barn and shop out back as big as the house and several mature trees on a lot, perhaps an acre, that stood in stark contrast to the surrounding desert landscape.

I looked anxiously at the house, willing Hernandez to come out to give me just enough information for my five or six paragraphs, just enough to get a story on the front page of that week's issue. Across the street, Dan Wilde, one of the Fremont police officers, nodded at me.

"Phil," he said curtly.

"Dan."

"Chief'll be out in a minute," he said, as if reading my mind.

I had developed a professional, if strained, relationship with the small Fremont police force that consisted of eight officers. To them, I was an outsider, a city slicker who had graduated from one of those ivy-covered institutions of higher learning, and they reminded me all the time that "You're not in Boston anymore."

It had been two years since I got laid off from my job as the cops-and-courts reporter at the *Boston Examiner*, a job I loved with a boss I didn't love. I missed the smell of car exhaust and bakeries, the vibe of a still-quiet city at dawn with a coffee in hand, the sound of car horns, and the din of a neighborhood bar at happy hour on a Friday evening.

Of late, I was beginning to wonder if buying a small weekly newspaper in Idaho hadn't been a mistake.

In Boston, I could schmooze with the cops, find their regular watering holes near their precinct stations, buy drinks and get scoops, such as my story about the diary the van-driving serial rapist and killer had kept. I was the only reporter in Boston who had those details and I found out later the editor of the competing *Boston Globe* was pissed as hell I had gotten the scoop. But perhaps more importantly was the stuff I didn't report, the things the cops at the bar said and did that, in a hungover stupor the next morning, they wished they hadn't told me or done in front of me, only to find out I hadn't put it in the paper. How many times had I gotten a call from one of these cops thanking me for keeping something quiet? I kept a running tally of favors owed.

But the cops in Fremont were different. They were Eagle Scouts who didn't drink after their shift was over. When I first came to Idaho after buying the paper, I looked for them in the bars after their shifts ended at eleven, suffering the derision of the locals who laughed at me for not knowing all those cops were already home, tucked into bed with their wives and six kids fast asleep in their bedrooms.

I occupied a limbo state of being both an outsider and an insider, just as I had felt throughout my entire life. Maybe that's why I became a reporter in the first place, always an outsider with a front row seat to the action but keeping the world at arm's length.

After a few more minutes, Hernandez came out of the house, stopped to give instructions to Wilde, then crossed the street to talk to me.

Hernandez's solid build, his close-cropped black hair and brown skin contrasted sharply with the pasty-white doughy officers in his charge. Hernandez had married the daughter of a local dairyman, who also happened to be the local stake president, the highest position in the LDS Church at the local level. I often wondered if Hernandez's religion superseded his race in achieving his position as police chief. I suspected Hernandez was a reluctant Mormon, converting after meeting the girl of his dreams and learning they couldn't marry unless he converted. I also suspected Hernandez's race in a white-dominated world was why he took a liking to me; he knew what it was like to be an outsider.

"It's bad," Hernandez said, shaking his head. He was clearly unnerved, something I had never seen from him before. Of course, Fremont had never had a murder before, let alone a double murder, let alone a double murder of good, upstanding citizens they knew. This wasn't some bar fight gone wrong. It must have been even more devastating to have members of your own church murdered.

Hernandez gathered himself, cleared his throat and switched to official mode as if in a press conference. I pulled my reporter's notebook out of my back pocket, a signal we were on the record now.

"We've got two deceased individuals, husband and wife, Vern Thompson, age seventy-eight, and Wanda Thompson, seventy-seven. They were located in the residence together, each with gunshot wounds. There were no signs of forced entry, no signs of robbery."

"Who called it in?" I asked.

"Neighbor. Henry Vanderlinn. He was driving by, noticed the garage door was open, all the lights were on. He decided to check in on them. Knocked on the front door, no answer. Front door was unlocked, as it usually is around these parts, so Vanderlinn opened the door, saw the bodies, called police."

Henry Vanderlinn was a local dairy farmer just up the road, owned probably two thousand acres of land himself.

"What time?"

"Approximately 10:30 p.m. Monday."

"Murder-suicide?"

"No. No gun found."

"Where were the bodies?"

"Living room. In the front."

"You know what type of gun? Caliber?"

"No, not until...well," Hernandez sputtered, but I knew he meant not until they pulled the bullets out of the dead bodies. "No, not yet. But looks like small caliber, like a pistol."

"How many shots?"

"Two in each."

I stayed silent, shaking my head and scribbling in my notebook, giving Hernandez an opportunity to either say more or conclude the interview.

"Got what you need?" Hernandez said finally.

"Yep." I put my notebook in my back pocket, indicating we were now off the record.

Hernandez's shoulders dropped, and he visibly changed from police official to human being. We looked at each other and shook our heads.

"This is awful," I said, genuinely moved at the thought of losing Vern, a man I considered a friend. "I can't think of two better people in this town."

"I know," Hernandez said. "They were real pillars in the church, too. Just really great people, hard-working, reverent, good, good people. I just can't believe it."

"It explains why Vern wasn't at the city council meeting," I said.

"Yeah, I should have known something was wrong when he wasn't there. He's always at city council."

"He was just in my office the other day telling me about some land sale he heard about."

Hernandez smiled and chuckled at that.

"He knows everything going on in this town," Hernandez said, and I noted the use of present tense.

We were silent again, stealing glances at the house, lit up against the dark sky. A warm breeze drifted over the farmland, carrying the faint scent of sage and Vanderlinn's dairy down the road.

"No other evidence?" I asked incredulously.

"Nothing."

"No signs of forced entry, no robbery. A safe? Anything?"

"Nope, nothing," Hernandez said. "I'm telling you, it's strange."

"I just can't believe it. You think there'd be some sort of clue as to why someone would do this."

"You don't believe me? See for yourself."

I hadn't consciously intended the effect of my words, but it worked just the same. Part of Hernandez's reaction was casual, just talking. Part of it was a challenge. Hernandez was indignant that I would question his abilities. And part of it seemed like an invitation, as if I might be able to spot something he had missed.

"Sure," I said.

"All right," Hernandez started but then paused, thinking better of it. "But you can't write anything from this. This is all off the record."

"Of course."

"Or take pictures." Hernandez was now scolding me, as if I had tricked him into something.

"Okay."

"Or touch anything."

"Got it."

Hernandez shook his head a little bit. "I can't believe I'm doing this. Come on, before I change my mind."

4

———

Hernandez entered the house first, and I followed, keeping it clear who was in command.

Officer Wilde gave an odd look in acknowledgment this was not protocol, shook his head and turned away, as if not wanting to be a witness.

"This how they do it in Boston?" he said in a low enough voice that only I could hear.

The front door opened to a small foyer with a staircase wrapping around it and a coat closet under the stairs. To the left, I could see a study. To the right was the living room, where the bodies were still lying. Police were done taking measurements and notes.

"Keep your hands in your pockets," Hernandez ordered.

Seeming to want to avoid the living room for now, Hernandez led me to the study, which held a wall of books on one side, a large writing desk and executive leather office chair in the middle. Facing the desk were two padded armchairs. The smell in the room reminded me of church. I imagined Vern sitting at the desk in his windbreaker and jeans, or "dungarees," as he called them. The desk was strewn with papers and a ledger but in a normal manner. Next to an electric typewriter, Vern's sweat-stained trucker hat sat on the corner of the desk, filling me with sadness, and I resisted an urge to reach out and touch it.

"You can see nothing's been tampered with in here," Hernandez said. "There's even a locked desk drawer that's been left alone. Nothing was gone through in the drawers. That filing cabinet in the corner was left alone."

I walked around the desk, hands in pockets, surveying the room.

"Those windows locked?" I nudged my head to the facing windows.

As Hernandez looked over the windows, I looked down at the desk.

"Yep, all locked, no broken glass, no forced entry."

I looked at the ledger on the desk. A series of a half dozen numbers running down the left column didn't seem to be money. 63-14972. 63-63891. Another column to the right was labeled "CFS" with another series of numbers, 0.6, 1.4, 0.5 and so on.

Hernandez moved back out to the foyer, and I followed him.

"The front door was unlocked, but we think they probably kept their door unlocked like most people around here," Hernandez said.

I shook my head. The concept seemed foolish and naive.

Hernandez entered the living room. I stayed a half step behind him. The room was surprisingly modern, spare and tidy, reminding me of a funeral parlor, a grim thought, considering the circumstances. I had expected a country cottage farmhouse or something, cluttered with glass cabinets filled with knickknacks and tchotchkes.

Now I could see the bodies.

The first dead body I had ever seen was when I was working the night shift as a nursing home security guard to put myself through college. I was asked to help move a dead resident's body into the home's cooler. I was shocked by the in-between state of the body, looking human but not alive, an arm that had slipped off the side of the gurney, feeling cold and stiff, like a piece of meat. Since then, though, I had seen several bodies in Boston, while covering homicides, a victim's body still lying uncovered in the middle of some random street in some random neighborhood in Jamaica Plain or Dorchester.

This was different.

I peered into the living room. Vern was facedown in front of the fireplace and he was holding a poker in his right hand. Wanda was also lying face down but toward the back of the room, facing the opposite direction. Pools of dark, thick liquid surrounded each of the bodies. I could smell the sweet metallic odor of blood and the faint whiff of gunpowder. It helped that I couldn't see their faces.

"Best we can tell—and remember you cannot write a word of this, totally off the record," Hernandez said. Wilde glanced at me.

"Of course."

"Best we can tell, Vern and Wanda and the suspect were in the room together, and Vern decided to grab the poker from the fireplace and go after the shooter. But the shooter pulled out a gun and shot and killed Vern," Hernandez said, pointing at Vern with a pen. "Wanda started to run away toward the back of the house"—he pointed to Wanda—"and the suspect shot her in the back as she was fleeing."

I nodded, thinking and looking around the room.

"And nothing out of place?" I asked.

"Nope."

"Nothing rummaged through or stolen?"

"Nope."

I stayed silent.

"Only thing we found was a piece of paper on the floor where we figured the shooter was standing," Hernandez said. He motioned to Wilde. "Dan, hand me that paper."

Wilde hesitated, then produced a clear plastic evidence bag containing a piece of paper from what looked to be a plain white notepad. Hernandez held it up for me. I still had my hands in my pockets and I leaned forward to get a better look. On it was written Vern Thompson, the Thompsons' address and then some numbers at the bottom in a hasty scrawl: 63-14972, 63-86167, 63-92962. I reflexively glanced back at the study, thinking the numbers matched the numbers in the ledger, but I couldn't be sure. I considered saying something but then thought better of it. I tried to commit the numbers to memory. I was dying to pull out my notebook but kept my word to keep this off the record.

Hernandez quickly pulled the paper away and handed it back to Wilde.

I looked into the living room and decided to try to saunter in to get a better look. Hernandez put a hand on my chest and started to look nervous.

"I think that's not a good idea," Hernandez said. "Better stay in the foyer."

Hernandez looked at Wilde, and Wilde looked away, as if not wanting to be a party to this breach of protocol.

"Let's go," Hernandez said to me. "I think that's enough for tonight."

I led the way out of the house. We stopped in the front yard.

"You going to try to get this in the paper this week?" Hernandez asked.

"Going to try."

"I'd better let you go, then."

"Thanks, Chief. I appreciate it," I said and turned to go. We shook hands, and I said a tentative, "I'm sorry." These were, after all, Hernandez's people, not mine.

I truly felt like an outsider now, which is a good place for a journalist to be.

"Philip," Hernandez called after me. I stopped and turned. "Remember, you can't write anything about this part, right?"

"Absolutely," I said.

As soon as I got in my car, I pulled out my notebook and furiously began writing what I had seen. Even though it was all off the record, I wanted to get down on paper as much as I could remember. I knew Hernandez was going way out on a limb, and he was putting a lot of trust in me. I was flattered by the confidence he put in me, and I didn't want to betray that trust. Hernandez had given me more information than he should have, and I was now getting anxious to get back to the office and get a brief story in this week's issue.

Back at my office, I reworked the front page of the paper, stripped out the teasers at the top, wrote up six paragraphs, put on a headline and re-sent the front page to the printer. I sent an email to my printer explaining the new front page.

Under the 60-point, bold headline, "Local Fremont couple shot, killed," my story began: "Two longtime pillars of the Fremont community, Vern and Wanda Thompson, were shot and killed Monday night in their home on Swan Falls Road."

5

____

If you saw Vern Thompson on the street, in his tattered windbreaker and twenty-year-old Ford F-150, you would think he was dirt poor, but some said he was possibly the wealthiest man in Fremont. He owned unknown thousands of acres of farmland, and people said he was one of the smartest businessmen around. He'd go all in on alfalfa, and the prices would skyrocket. He doubled his wheat one year, and there was a drought in Nebraska. He tripled his corn acreage another year, and Iowa farmers had a run on corn for ethanol.

The previous year, I had asked Vern, "What're you planting this year?" —a phrase I had picked up from farmers talking to one another down at the coffee shop.

"Oh, I figured I'll do quite a bit of sugar beets this year," Vern responded. About two months later, a hurricane leveled Haiti and other Caribbean islands, destroying that year's sugarcane crop. Sugar prices spiked, and the local sugar factories scrambled to find—and pay top dollar for—any and all sugar beets not already under contract.

While most residents of Fremont held me at arm's length, Vern Thompson, for some reason, had taken a liking to me from day one. At my very first city council meeting, Vern had given me a tip about a new well the city wanted to drill because an old well was failing, but Vern remembered that years ago, the city had let developers tap into the city's drinking water to irrigate lawns, causing the old well to do double duty. I dug up old records and past meeting minutes, verifying everything Vern had told me. I wrote a story about it, spurring the city council to simply replace the old well pump and force the developers to hook into the irrigation system.

It seemed odd at the time, but I sensed the mayor was upset with me that I had ruined the city's plans to drill another well, even though it was saving the taxpayers money. Something struck me about the importance of water and getting more of it.

Vern would stop by the office from time to time, ostensibly to pay a bill or take out an ad or drop off an announcement. He would linger. I knew to wait.

"You know," Vern would start out and then go on to give me some news tip or story idea.

The last time I saw him, Vern had said something about a land deal out in the middle of the desert he was looking into and something about senior water rights. I was on deadline and I admitted I didn't know what Vern was talking about, but I knew Vern was always worth listening to.

I was flattered that Vern had confided in me, someone who was both an outsider and a reporter. Vern was born and raised in Fremont, and he must have harbored a natural suspicion of anyone not from Idaho. When most everyone else had treated me like an outsider, Vern had treated me like an insider.

As a reporter, I was good at compartmentalizing, separating my work self from my real self, and that was what I had been doing with the news of the Thompson killings. Now, though, for the first time since the call came over the scanner, the news instincts had worn off, and I had a chance to mourn the loss of my friend.

6

I awoke Tuesday morning after just a few hours of sleep, threw on some clothes, made a cup of coffee, retrieved the *Idaho Statesman* from the front porch and sat down in my breakfast nook.

My rental, a two-bedroom house on Fourth Avenue, was just three blocks from my office on Main Street in downtown Fremont. For $300 a month, I got pretty much what you'd expect: a modest dump that hadn't been updated in forty years, which, honestly, was just fine with me. I kept it clean and spare. I had sold or given away most of my belongings back in Boston, and what little was left, I was able to pack into my car. It made for an uncluttered existence. The house had character, though: narrow-plank hardwood floors, arched doorways, crown molding, built-in bookshelves and a wood-burning fireplace. The kitchen had a breakfast nook often found in houses of that era. The house was owned by an older retired couple. The wife had been a teacher and was now working on becoming a painter, and the husband had been in construction and was now working on being an alcoholic.

The house came modestly furnished with a mid-century sofa, armchair and a small oriental rug. Against the wall separating the main room and the kitchen was a simple, large two-drawer desk I had set up as a writing station when working from home. Outside, a short white picket fence surrounded a postage-stamp-size lawn. It was the perfect home for someone in lonely self-exile.

I had gotten into the habit of parking my car in front of my house and walking the three blocks to my office, an amazingly short commute compared with what I went through to get to work in Boston. On the way, I would pass Harvey Taylor's place, a similar house but in a more deteriorated condition. It was surrounded by a chain-link fence that contained Roscoe, Taylor's aging bloodhound who would always bark at passersby, even me, no matter how many times I had walked past.

As I read the paper and sipped my coffee, I noted the *Statesman* didn't have anything on the Thompson murders because word hadn't gotten out until after their deadline. I smiled, knowing I would have the story on my front page that day while the competition had nothing.

As was my custom, I read the paper front to back, devouring every section, local, state, national, international, sports, features, classifieds, everything. *Someday*, I thought, *the public is going to be sorry we don't have newspapers anymore.*

Arguably, my favorite section, all the way in the back, was the legal notices: bankruptcies, name changes, foreclosures, annual budgets, ordinances, fee changes, delinquent taxes, development applications.

Many of the notices merely satisfied curiosity. Adam Jones was changing their name to Andrea Jones to match gender identity. Frederick Smith was being foreclosed on. Tim Thornhill hadn't paid his bill on his storage unit, and the contents were to be auctioned off.

Sometimes I got scoops, like seeing a notice the county was declaring a sole source procurement for software made by a company whose owner, I discovered after I looked it up, had donated to the reelection campaign of one of the commissioners. Always looking where others weren't looking. Noticing what others didn't see.

I was scanning that day's legal notices when I spotted it.

It jumped out at me and shocked me so much that I took in a sharp breath and bolted upright in my chair.

It was like a flashlight shining on the numbers.

I was looking at a legal notice from the Idaho Department of Water

Resources for water rights applications. The numbers for each application were in bold: 63-93821, 63-41653, 63-59174.

I immediately recognized them as similar to the numbers Vern Thompson had written in the ledger that was on his desk and the piece of paper police had found in the living room. I also recognized the notation "CFS," which Vern had written at the top of one column. In the legal notice, each application had a CFS number, or cubic feet per second, indicating allotment. Under each application number was a name and address, point of diversion, or where the water was being taken from, and proposed use, such as irrigation or stock water.

I couldn't remember the exact numbers in Vern's ledger, but I was certain they must have been water applications. Vern was a farmer, though, I told myself, and must hold water rights, and the ledger could have been just a list of his own water rights.

Still, the matching numbers on the piece of paper found in the living room gnawed at me. I didn't hold much stock in coincidences.

I looked at my watch and knew I had to get out to my printer and pick up the copies of that week's paper and deliver them around town.

By eight a.m., the story of the murders was all over the news. Hernandez had sent out a press release, which got picked up by every TV station and paper. Hernandez had scheduled a press conference at the police station for that morning. If I hustled, I could pick up the papers and make it back in time for the press conference.

I had already posted the story on my website and sent out an email news alert to all of my subscribers. My site admittedly didn't get a lot of traffic—my readers preferred the printed copy of the paper. I checked my site's analytics and saw 10,429 people had read my story, which was a record, even better than when I had done live updates from the state playoff game the Fremont football team had played in the previous year. People were searching for "Fremont murders," and my story was coming up first on a Google search.

When I arrived at my printer's shop, the papers were ready and waiting for me, and I sped back to Fremont with the papers in the trunk of my car.

By the time I pulled up at the police station, which was in the same building as City Hall, a converted church on the south side of the tracks, reporters from the three local TV stations and two newspapers were lining up Hernandez in front of the Fremont City Hall sign. The TV reporters were clipping their microphones to Hernandez's shirt and attaching their transmitters to his belt, trying to hide the wires.

Hernandez repeated the exact words of the press release, which reporters hated because they already had that information. And then when the reporters began to ask questions, Hernandez declined to comment, citing the ongoing investigation.

I smiled, knowing I had more information than everyone else.

After the other reporters left, rushing back to file their stories, I lingered.

"You got a minute?" I asked Hernandez.

"Sure, come on in," Hernandez said as we entered the police station.

I sat in a chair across the desk from Hernandez. I asked what more information he could give me and what from our conversation from the other night I could use in my story the following week. Hernandez threw me a couple of bones, things no one else had yet.

"Hey, do you have photos of the scene?" I asked.

"Of course," Hernandez said.

"Can I have a look at them?" I tried not to sound too eager, but I was champing at the bit to confirm the numbers as water rights.

Hernandez hesitated, thought about it, glanced down at an iPad on his desk, then glanced back up at me. He shrugged.

"Sure, but you can't use anything without asking first," he said. "You got it?"

I recognized again that Hernandez was going out on a limb and could simply tell me no. But Hernandez had gone out on a limb before, and I hadn't burned him. The chief knew he could trust me, a vital currency in my profession. A reporter can build just as much trust by what he doesn't write. Hernandez opened the iPad, touched the screen a few times, then turned the iPad over to me without saying anything. I scrolled through the photos. I had my notebook on my leg below the level of the desk, an old trick I used, so Hernandez couldn't see if I was writing anything. Then I thought better of it.

"Mind if I take notes?" I asked.

"No, just as long as you don't use anything without asking first."

"Got it."

I swiped through the photos, moving quickly past the gruesome photos of the bodies. That wasn't what I was after.

Hernandez's phone rang and he took the call, which relieved me so I didn't feel like I was being watched.

I finally got to it. A photo of the piece of paper found on the floor in the Thompsons' living room. 63-14972. 63-86167. 63-92962. I copied the numbers in my notebook, quickly glancing up at Hernandez, who was still talking on the phone, his back now turned to me, and looking out the window. I got what I was after, and I quickly swiped through the other photos to make it look like I hadn't been looking for anything in particular.

I swiped past a photo of the desk in Vern's study and swiped back. I noticed a photo of the ledger. I zoomed in on the open ledger on the desk. I was able to make out the numbers in the far-left column: 63-86167, 63-14972, and so on. I looked over at my notebook at the numbers he had written down from the piece of paper found on the floor; three of the numbers matched. I quickly wrote all the numbers down. I looked over at the column next to them. It was labeled CFS—the letters I had seen in the legal notice for allotment. I quickly wrote down those numbers, too.

Hernandez got off the phone and turned to me.

"See anything?" Hernandez said.

"No," I lied in a disappointed voice as I casually swiped through the photos. "Nothing. It's weird, right?" I was putting it back on Hernandez to be the teacher.

"Yeah, it is," Hernandez said, shaking his head. "I've never seen anything like this. It's just sad. They were the good ones. I can't imagine why anyone would want to harm them."

I continued scrolling through the photos perfunctorily when one of them caught my eye.

"What's this?" I said, holding up the tablet.

"Tire tracks on the Thompsons' driveway," Hernandez said. "Wilde spotted it. I don't know how he saw it in the dark like that. The Thompsons had their lawn sprinklers on earlier that night, and some of the water pooled at the end of the driveway, and we think the shooter drove through the mud and then onto the driveway. Caliche clay, thick stuff. The tracks were still wet when we got there."

"Can you tell what kind of car?"

"No, but we were able to figure out what kind of tire from the pattern of the tread, which helps."

"What kind is it?"

Hernandez flipped the pages in a notebook on his desk. "It's a Pirelli Scorpion all-season plus, 225 millimeters wide. Which means it goes on an SUV or crossover or pickup truck. A nice one. Not some beater. Those aren't cheap. Doesn't narrow it down a whole heck of a lot, but it's something."

I nodded and started to write it down in my notebook.

"Nope," Hernandez said sharply. "Don't even write it down. Totally off the record, Phil."

"Okay, okay," I said, holding up my hands. I repeated in my head, *Pirelli Scorpion, all-season plus, 225 millimeters.*

"All right," Hernandez said, holding out his hand for the tablet, which I returned to him.

"Well," I said with an air of finality, anxious to get going, "thanks for letting me do this."

"Sure," Hernandez said. "But remember, you can't use anything without asking first. I'm trusting you here."

"I got it."

When I got in my car, I pulled out my notebook and wrote down "Pirelli Scorpion all-season plus, 225 millimeters."

7

____

As the owner, editor and publisher of the *Fremont Herald*, I did everything:
wrote the stories, shot the photos, covered city council, school board, high
school sports, designed the paper, even did the weekly deliveries. Only
recently had I hired someone to hand-label the copies of the paper for me.

Delivery day, Tuesday, was my least favorite. It was a tedious and tiring
process and it usually took most of the afternoon, especially if I had to wait
in line at the store behind a bunch of old boys getting off work from a
construction site and buying a case of Keystone Light. I often thought about
how different this life was from the one I had left behind in Boston.
Delivery was taking longer and getting more difficult, too, since I had grown
circulation from eight hundred copies when I first bought the paper to
nearly two thousand now. Bundles were getting heavier from the increased
numbers of copies and pages, and I had doubled the number of places
where I sold the paper.

This week, I did my deliveries as quickly as possible, skipping a couple
of locations so I could make my way back to the office to confirm whether
those numbers in Vern's ledger were indeed water rights. Fortunately, I beat
the after-work crowd buying Keystone Light.

Back at my office, I called the phone number in the legal notice for the
Idaho Department of Water Resources.

"Water Resources, Jerry Hansen," answered a deep voice that sounded like Sam Elliott.

"Hi, Jerry. This is Philip Chandler from the *Fremont Herald*."

"Hi, Philip," he said pleasantly, a good sign. Government employees were not always enthusiastic when taking a call from a reporter.

"I had a couple of questions about water rights."

"Sure, fire away."

I asked him a few general questions about filing a water rights request, and Hansen explained the process of filling out an application, paying a fee, specifying place of use, point of diversion and purpose of use, whether for irrigation, stock water, commercial, ag, residential.

I asked him what CFS stood for, and he told me cubic feet per second, essentially how much water an applicant was proposing to use. One cubic foot per second was the equivalent of seven and a half gallons per second, or 450 gallons per minute. Point of diversion was where you were taking the water from and was listed as longitude and latitude coordinates. Irrigation was a complete mystery to me, but Hansen was patient.

"How do I look at one of these applications?" I asked.

"It's all online," Hansen said. "We're one of the few state agencies that's digitized everything. Sometimes it takes a while to get online, but it gets there eventually. You got a number for what you're looking for? I can look it up for you, make sure it's in the system."

I hesitated, calculating the risk. I flipped the pages of my notebook to the list of numbers from Vern Thompson's ledger. I picked one.

"Sure. It's six, three." I heard Hansen begin to type. "One, four, nine, seven, two."

"All right, let's see what you've got here," Hansen said and sighed as he waited for the computer to do its work.

There was a pause that seemed to take too long, and I could hear a folder opening and papers shuffling.

"What did you say you're working on?" Hansen's voice had changed. It was still polite, but colder, suspicious. I was kicking myself for giving one of the numbers on Vern's list. I wished I had given Hansen another number, a random one from the legal notices.

"I heard Fremont might need a new well, so I was just trying to figure out how that worked," I said. Time to play dumb. "I really don't know anything about any of this. It's really confusing."

"Sure, sure," Hansen said. I sensed a change. "Well, it's there, for sure. I'm looking at it right now. So, all you have to do is go to our website and click on water rights." He was talking much faster now. "And from there, there's a button to click to search for individual water rights. Just punch in your number, and you're good to go."

"Okay, so just –" I said as I was writing that down.

"If that's all," Hansen interrupted. "I've got to get to a meeting. Let me know if you have any questions. Thanks for calling."

The line went dead.

8

I hung up the phone, typed in the web address for the Department of Water Resources and clicked on the link for water rights applications. I was given a prompt to type in basin and water right number, and I typed in 63 and 14972, the one I had just given to Hansen. A screen opened with a list and icons for four PDFs in descending order.

At the top was 63-14972_file1 first, then 63-14972_file2 below that, then file3 down to file4 at the bottom. It was a pretty rudimentary system and looked to be homemade by someone who maybe knew a little something about computers, and the department decided to just do it in-house.

I clicked on 63-14972_file1. It was the initial application with applicant's name, address, location, use, point of diversion and CFS. The applicant was F9 Development, representative Ted Dunlap, with a downtown Boise address.

I scribbled the point of diversion, place of use and purpose in my notebook and then printed out the file. I noted the application wasn't for a new water right; it was a transfer of ownership. The initial water right was from 1937.

I stopped when I saw the name of the previous owner.

It was Dan Perry.

Sometimes, I imagined my brain working like a spinning Rolodex, constantly rolling through the facts in my head. At times, the Rolodex seemed to self-organize, stopping and opening to the most important cards.

At that moment, the Rolodex stopped at the last conversation I had had with Vern Thompson. It was about Dan Perry's farm south of town.

Perry ran a small, forty-acre farm far out into the desert. It was an old-school farm: a couple dozen dairy cows, a field of alfalfa and fields of potatoes, sugar beets and corn. He never grew large enough to compete, and the farm had become unsustainable financially. Perry's wife had died, and his kids didn't want to take over the farm, so Perry sold out. Vern had asked if I knew who Perry had sold his land to. I didn't. He asked if I had heard of any development applications out that way. I hadn't. He asked if I knew why someone would buy Perry's farm without developing it. I didn't. He was asking about water rights.

I wasn't sure where Vern was going with his line of questioning, and I remember wishing he would just get to the point and give me whatever scoop he was trying to give me. I recalled with guilt that I had been impatient and was perhaps short with Vern, telling him I had to get back to work. I felt regret now at the memory.

But the conversation nagged at me for another reason. What was the story Vern was trying to put me on? Was it possible that it was somehow connected to his murder?

The first water right on Vern Thompson's list was the land deal that Vern had asked me about just before he was killed. It was also one of the water rights on the piece of paper found in the Thompsons' living room.

My hand was shaking a little with excitement as I opened file2, which was a five-page water study done by a company called PFS Resources. The water study was confusing and technical, showing detailed specifications of soil composition, water-bearing levels and rock layers. I took some notes, then hit print.

I tried to open file3, but when I clicked on it, I got an error message "file in use."

I closed the message window and opened file4. File4 was a proof of publication affidavit showing the legal notice as it appeared in the *Idaho Statesman*. I printed that, too.

I went back to file3 to try to open it and got the same "file in use" message.

I thought maybe I had locked the file by accident, so I refreshed the page. When the page reopened, the PDF files were out of order. File3 was at the top, then file1, then file2, then file4.

I tried to open file3 again, and it was still locked.

Something occurred to me. I went back and tried to open file1, and it was now locked. I realized someone else was looking at the files at the same time. Jerry Hansen must have been opening the files and locking them just as I was looking at them.

Hansen was looking at the files when we were on the phone together. Maybe he just hadn't closed file3 yet, I figured. But that didn't explain why I was able to open file1 before then.

I refreshed the page again. This time the files were back in order: file1 on top, then file2, but then file4. There was no file3. Hansen must have deleted it.

What was in file3 that Hansen didn't want me to see?

9

———

The Idaho Department of Water Resources Western Regional Office was in a low-slung, nondescript brick building near the airport. In fact, it was less than a hundred yards from the hotel where I had stayed when I first came to Idaho after buying the *Fremont Herald* two years earlier. I hadn't even noticed the building at the time.

I entered a narrow hallway with faux wood paneling that hadn't been updated in thirty years. The dingy matted carpet in brown, orange and yellow swirl patterns perhaps looked bright at some point in time. A sliding glass service window was immediately on the left, but no one was stationed at the counter. Budget cuts, probably. The whole office had the reek of budget cuts. Idaho didn't want to make it too easy for its government agencies to enforce regulations.

I could see into the office, a messy room cluttered with papers, logbooks and shelves of tall, narrow plat books. The same paneling extended into the office, punctuated by pinned-up, yellowing maps of Idaho, curling at the corners. Metal blinds on a bank of windows on the far wall reminded me of my elementary school, and the heavy metal-and-vinyl office furniture was reminiscent of an ancient doctor's office. Next to the service window was the door to the office inscribed in black-and-gold letters and the Idaho state seal. It, too, was unlocked, and I walked in.

I stepped into the musty office and looked around but didn't see anyone. Several smaller office doors were off the main room, and I read the nameplate for Jerry Hansen next to one of the smaller offices.

A slight man with a thick mustache emerged from a break room. He was wearing the Idaho uniform: plain white dress shirt, blue jeans, belt buckle, square-toe western work boots. He was whistling and dunking a tea bag in a mug and pulled up when he saw me standing there.

"Oh," he said and looked around the office as if looking for others. "I didn't hear you come in. Can I help you?"

"You must be Jerry," I said pleasantly, recognizing the Sam Elliott voice, which surprisingly didn't match the stature of the man before me.

"I am. Can I help you?"

"I'm Philip Chandler from the *Fremont Herald*."

"Oh yeah," Hansen said with a slight smile of initial recognition that quickly went away upon further remembrance. "What can I do for you?" He stole a quick glance at his office, which I inferred held the missing file of the water rights application I was looking for.

"I wanted to take a look at that water rights application we were talking about on the phone," I said, nodding in the direction of Hansen's office, a subtle way of letting him know I knew where it was.

"You didn't have to come all the way out here. It's all online, like I said," Hansen said. "Didn't you find it?"

"No, not all of it." I pulled out my reporter's notebook from my back pocket and with it a piece of paper folded in half lengthwise. I decided to play dumb, a reporter's technique I learned long ago. "I figured it'd be easier if I just came down here and looked at the originals. You know, I'm a paper guy, obviously, being in newspapers. I like to look at the real deal, hard copies, you know."

I handed Hansen the piece of paper.

"What's this?" Hansen said, unfolding it.

"Oh, that's a public records request for a few applications I want to take a look at. I figured you're a by-the-book kind of guy, so I thought it'd make it easier for you if I had the records request all ready. That way if your boss asked you about it, you'd be able to tell him you had no choice. You had to provide the records, because the state's public records law requires it."

We stared at each other for a couple of seconds. How Hansen handled the situation from there would tell me a lot. Hansen broke the stare by looking down at the records request. I detected a slight smile. Hansen looked back up at me as if evaluating me.

"Sure," Hansen said and pointed at the conference table in the middle of the room. "Have a seat. You can look at them here. I'll go get them."

I sat down while Hansen went to a long row of filing cabinets first on the far side of the room. I watched as Hansen looked down at the numbers on the records request, located the proper filing cabinet, pulled out the correct files and placed them on top of the cabinet. When he was done, he gathered the files with both hands, crossed the room and set the files on the table in front of me. Hansen continued to his office, grabbed a file off his desk, then emerged with the file 63-14972, the application we had discussed on the phone.

Rather than pore over all the documents there in the office, I took out my phone and photographed every page of every file, being careful to mark the beginning of each file by photographing a close-up of each application number from the tab. Hansen watched me.

In general, the files were divided into four or five sections, with several pages either stapled or clipped together.

The first section was the main application, containing the application form and usually an engineer's report filled with technical details. The sections were of varying lengths depending on the complexity of the application. Another section headed "Notification" contained proof of the applicant sending letters or emails to affected parties. A third section headed "Letters of community analysis" contained responses from the parties and other protests. I noticed, as expected, Vern Thompson had filed a protest in each application. In each case, the letter used the same short wording, two paragraphs printed on Thompson Farms letterhead, stating his protest of the application.

I got a chill and shuddered, looking at Vern's words, imagining Vern sitting at his desk in his study, typing out these letters on his typewriter, entering water rights numbers and CFS values in his ledger. It was as if Vern was speaking to me from the grave.

Depending on the complexity of the application, a fourth section contained further analysis and follow-up to the protest. A final section contained proof of publication of the legal notices like what I had seen in the *Statesman*.

When I got to the file for 63-14972, the one for Dan Perry's farm, the one that had the missing file online, I photographed all the pages and recognized that the section that had been missing, the section Hansen must have deleted, was the section on protests. At a cursory glance, I didn't notice anything out of the ordinary. Hansen sipped his tea and watched me.

When I was done, I gathered the files, tapped them on the table to make them neat, then stacked them together in a pile. I sat down and looked at Hansen.

"What's this section on protests?"

"That's what we call it when someone objects to a water rights application. Whenever someone fills out an application, a legal notice goes in the paper, and we wait and see if there are any protests."

"Do protests ever work?"

"Oh, sometimes. Usually when someone has seniority."

"Seniority?" I thought of my last conversation with Vern, who was asking about senior water rights. "Like senior water rights?"

"Yep. First in time, first in right. The person who got the water rights first has priority over everyone who comes later."

"How can you tell who's got a senior water right?"

"It's listed right there." Hansen leaned over and pointed to a box on the application. "Those water rights you got there are all pretty old rights, mostly senior rights."

"But these are new applications."

"They're new applications for old water rights. They're transfers. All of those applications are someone purchasing someone's senior water rights." Hansen opened one of the files and pointed to a spot in the middle of the first page. "See here? 1937. This water right was first acquired in 1937." He opened another file. "This one's 1907. That's really old. Those all pretty much have seniority."

"It seems like the protest letters from 14972 were missing in the online file," I said.

Hansen furrowed his brow. He seemed to be deciding whether to feign ignorance or spill what he knew.

"I have the whole file now," I added, starting to get impatient. "You might as well tell me."

Hansen seemed resigned.

"One of the protesters had called me before you did and asked me to remove his protest. I told him I couldn't do it, that it had already been filed on record. But he was pretty insistent, sounded kind of desperate."

"Was it Vern Thompson?"

"No, it was someone else, a local developer, young kid just starting out. I was actually thinking about pulling his protest when you called. When you gave me the number and it was the exact same one, I got nervous. So I pulled the file online temporarily, just to give me time to decide what to do."

"And what did you decide to do?"

"I left it in there. It's there," he said, nodding toward the file. "It's back online, too. Even though I like the guy, it's already been recorded. I'd be breaking the law if I tampered with it." It always stunned me when I realized how much discretion public officials used when disclosing—or not disclosing—public records, as if they had the latitude to make the call. It always made me wonder how much more was being covered up by government bureaucrats. At least Hansen was honest.

"Did the developer say why he wanted to withdraw his protest?"

"Not really. Just said he changed his mind. He sounded a little bit urgent about it. It was odd. It's not the kind of thing you just change your mind about."

"Hmm," I said.

"What's the story you're really working on?" Hansen said.

I smiled and relaxed.

"I'm not really sure right now," I said. "I feel like I'm walking around a big, dark room with a small flashlight. Don't worry. I'll consider all of this background for now. I'm not planning on writing any of this yet."

"That's good to know," Hansen said, visibly relieved. "I don't want to get this guy in trouble."

"What's this guy's name?" I said.

Hansen winced.

"I'm not going to write about him," I said. "But I do want to talk to him."

"It's Nick Ashley. Local guy in Fremont. Independent, small operation. Builds five or six houses a year. Nice ones, higher end. Not mansions, just a step up from the cookie-cutter houses you see around there. He's planning his first subdivision. He bought forty acres in Fremont, planning on building eighty houses there. He's a good guy. Don't get him in trouble."

"I won't," I said. "Don't worry."

I turned back to the top page of the application for 63-14972 and pointed to the company listed as the applicant.

"Who is this F9 Development?" I asked.

Hansen looked over my shoulder at the application. "Looks like just some shell company."

"Shell company?"

"Developers create a shell company specific to a development. Protects the bigger business from any losses, I guess."

"So it's a developer?"

"I just assume so. Don't know of any farmer who bought the property. Plus, one other thing."

"What's that?"

"Farmers don't create a shell company to hide behind."

"Right," I said, getting up from my chair and extending my hand. "Well, thanks, Jerry. I appreciate it."

"Any time. Let me know what you find out."

"Will do." I turned to go, then paused. "One more thing. What's the first number in all these water rights applications? 63."

"That's the basin."

"Basin?"

"Each part of the state has its own basin, where all the water drains into," Hansen said, holding his hands together like a cup. "All of the water in Boise comes from that basin."

"Basin 63."

"Basin 63."

10

I drove to Fremont City Hall to see how I could find Nick Ashley. I hadn't heard of him before, and he didn't have an office in town.

"Hiya, Phil," Amanda greeted me at the counter of the city's planning department. "What can I do for you?"

Amanda was in her early thirties, a little younger than me, had long brown hair, high strong cheekbones, full lips and deep brown eyes. On warm summer days, an arm tattoo would peek out from under a short-sleeve shirt on her toned bicep. She wore a single stud earring in each ear, but I noticed old markings of several piercing holes all along both ears. I heard she had a rough past, but she must have turned her life around just in time and gotten on the straight and narrow. She was clerking for the planning department and studying to get a degree in urban planning. I was reminded, as I always was whenever I saw her, that I'd like to hear Amanda's story one of these days over a glass of beer at Cowboys Lounge.

It had been more than two years since Laura had left me, and I was thinking maybe it was time I got over her.

"You know a local developer by the name of Nick Ashley?" I asked her.

"Sure. Good guy. I actually went to school with him. He's from Fremont. He builds nice houses. He's building that Mineral Springs subdivision off School Street. It's his first subdivision."

"Does he have an office somewhere?"

"No, I don't think so. I think he mostly works out of his house. Although he built a model house in Mineral Springs. He might keep an office there. You might try that."

"Thanks, Amanda. You're the best."

"Anything for you, Phil," she said, and I paused and thought of asking her about getting that beer. I opened my mouth, but nothing came out.

"Yes?" Amanda asked, as if in invitation.

"Have you ever heard of F9 Development?" I asked instead of asking her out.

Amanda furrowed her brow and thought. "F9 Development. No. I don't think so. Who are they?"

"That's what I'm trying to figure out. I saw their name on a water rights application."

"Oh, it's probably just a dummy business name. Developers do that all the time."

"So I've heard."

"Anything else?" she said, again opening the door for me.

"You know Dan Perry's farm?"

"Dan Perry's farm?" she said, disappointed.

"Yeah."

"I think so. Way out of town. Way, way south, out in the middle of the desert."

"That's the one."

"Yeah, I know it."

"Has anyone come in with a development application for it?"

"No, I'd remember that. And that's too far away from Fremont to even come into the city."

"Okay, just checking."

"You know, Vern Thompson came in asking about Dan Perry's farm, too. Just a couple of weeks ago, before he… before, well…" She trailed off.

"I'm not surprised. Thanks, Amanda."

11

I made my way through downtown past the library and turned right on School Street. Mineral Springs was tucked away off to the left, fronted by a wrought-iron fence and a brown stone monument announcing the subdivision. Two houses could be seen off in the distance in an otherwise empty field lined with a few streets, curbs, gutters and sidewalks. As I drove closer, I noticed the foundation for a third house. Next to it was a twenty-foot construction trailer. The first house I came to—a sprawling one-story residence with stone accents matching the entrance monument—had a sign out front: model home and sales office. I parked my car and went inside.

The house had that comforting, new-house smell, a combination of new carpet, drywall and plaster and fresh paint. I could tell immediately that this was not a typical cookie-cutter Fremont house. Flagstone tile in the entryway led to hardwood floors in the hallway and continued into a formal dining room. As I entered the main room, I was greeted by wooden beams in a vaulted ceiling, a massive stone fireplace, granite countertops and stainless steel appliances and rangehood in the adjacent kitchen, and a large covered patio already outfitted with sofas and chairs surrounding a gas fire pit that looked southwest out to the Owyhee Mountains in the distance.

A young man emerged from a side room off a darkened hallway to the left of the kitchen. He was mid-thirties, handsome, with short blond hair and a square stubbled jaw, and he was wearing a black Carhartt hooded sweatshirt over a white T-shirt, dark-blue jeans and well-worn Red Wing steel-toed work boots.

"How's it going?" he said, extending his hand. I hoped I wouldn't disappoint him too much when I told him I wasn't there to buy a house. "Nick Ashley."

"Philip Chandler with the *Fremont Herald*," I said as we shook hands. "Nice to meet you."

"Oh yeah, I know you. I love the *Fremont Herald*, read it every week. Love what you're doing with it. It's a real paper now."

"Oh, thank you. I appreciate that."

"You looking to buy a house?"

"Well, no." I watched the look of disappointment turn quickly to guarded curiosity. I let my gaze move about the house. "But if I were, this is what I'd be looking for. This is real high quality."

"Thanks, yeah." Nick looked around, too, clearly proud of his work. "I try to build more than just starter homes, something different, a little nicer, something you can't usually get around Fremont." He paused. "So what are you here for?"

"I'm doing a story about water rights," I said tentatively. Ashley nodded, his expression unchanged. "Do you deal with water rights a lot?"

Ashley scoffed. "Sure. Have to in this business. You can't build houses without water."

"What about protests?"

"What about protests?" Ashley said a bit defensively, guarded.

I decided to just shoot straight. I instinctively liked Ashley, and I didn't want to jerk him around.

"I saw that you had filed a protest on a water rights application just outside Fremont." I pulled out my notebook from my back pocket, flipped a couple of pages. "It was an application for a company called F9 Development."

"Yeah, I did, but I withdrew it."

"How come?"

Ashley paused, looked down at the floor, then at the notebook, then back up at me.

"On the record?"

I nodded.

"I filed a protest against a competitor just to slow down the process a little bit. When I realized it was a good project, I dropped it."

I wrote all that down.

"That's it?"

"Off the record?"

I put my notebook in my back pocket and clicked my pen closed. I didn't like going off the record. Off the record meant I couldn't use anything that was said. My general rule was that my job was to write stories, not talk about them. But this was different; I wasn't sure what I was chasing or what I was even writing about quite yet. I needed information. If I didn't agree to go off the record, I'd have nothing to go on.

"Sure."

Ashley motioned for me to sit at the dining table. He pulled out a chair and sat down, and I did the same.

"I watch these water rights applications pretty closely as they come in," Ashley said. "This one seemed a little odd."

"How so?"

"Its location. It's way out in the desert, middle of nowhere, not really near anything. It'd be really difficult to build a subdivision out there."

"How so?"

"Well, it's more than just water. You've got to build sewer, too. And those roads out there are barely two-lane country roads, far away from the nearest main road or freeway."

"Okay, so what do you think's going on?"

"I don't know. That's why I filed a protest."

"So why did you really drop it?"

Ashley paused and looked sideways at me as if to confirm this was still off the record. I nodded.

"I got paid a visit," Ashley said.

"Paid a visit by whom?"

"I don't know the guy. He didn't give his name. It was kind of threatening."

"Threatening how?"

"He said he worked for the people who were applying for that water right, and those people wanted to know who was protesting it."

"F9 Development?"

"I assumed so, although he didn't say specifically."

"What did you tell him?"

"Just what I told you before—I'm a competitor and just wanted to slow it down."

"What did he say to that?" I asked.

"He said, 'Drop it,'" Ashley said. "Said it just like that."

"What did this guy look like?"

"Big guy, burly, like a bodybuilder, big arms, big chest, bald, flat nose, wearing some sort of Black Rifle Coffee Company T-shirt, distressed jeans with the embroidery on the back pockets."

I nodded and considered.

"So you just agreed to drop the protest?"

"Well, then he made a real threat," Ashley said.

"How so?"

"He said if I didn't drop my protest, another protest would be filed against my water rights here. He said my sewer permits would get held up. My building permits would get slowed down. Basically, he'd tie things up enough that it would kill my business. And I can't afford that. I've got a family. I've got a son who's two years old, and we've got another baby on the way. I've risked everything to make this subdivision happen. This is my whole business. I've sunk everything I own into this subdivision, and honestly, I... I'm hanging by a thread right now. I just need a couple of sales, just need a couple of people to walk through that door just like you did, or else..." He trailed off. "I'm not some big developer. I don't have a few hundred houses going on at one time. I can't just walk away if one of my subdivisions doesn't work out."

Ashley looked expectantly at me.

"I get it," I said. "I would have done the same thing. I don't blame you."

"Well, really, it's not that big a deal. Honestly. I didn't have a problem dropping the protest. I don't really care that much about it. Heck, these protests are filed all the time. It's almost routine. I don't get why some goon tried to strong-arm me into dropping it. It's like they were making a bigger deal out of it than it really is."

"Yeah, I guess that is strange," I said. "Do you know anything about this F9 Development?"

"No, it must be some shell business to hide who's really behind the application. Happens all the time."

"Okay, well, thanks, Nick."

"So," Ashley said in a guarded tone, "you're not gonna write any of that, right?"

"No," I said. "Strictly off the record. I appreciate you telling me all this. It's really helpful. It's just between you and me for now."

"Thanks, I appreciate it."

I gave Ashley my business card, thanked him for his time and the information and reassured him again that this was all just between us.

On my way out, I said, "You have an ad for your houses?"

"Yeah, but I can't afford to advertise right now," Ashley said.

"Is it camera-ready?" That meant it was already built and could be placed on the page without any work.

"Yeah."

"Email it to me," I said, pointing to my business card in Ashley's hand. "I'll run it a few times in the paper. No charge."

"Thanks, Phil," Ashley said, smiling. "That's great. I'll do that. Thanks."

"You bet."

I turned, exited through the beautiful, dark-stained heavy oak door with wrought-iron hardware and let it close smoothly, the latch sliding quietly and neatly into place. I walked down the perfectly level flagstone walkway bordered by an immaculately trimmed golf-course-worthy lawn.

That's when the explosion went off.

12

The concussion of the explosion hit me first, making me reflexively duck my head and put up my arms, as the sound followed almost immediately after the blast of air. Time seemed to go in slow motion then, as I hunched my body over, instinctively protecting my vital organs. Then came the sound of shattering glass just before chunks of wood, glass and metal went flying past me.

Time sped back up to normal speed, and I noticed my ears were ringing now. Sensing that the explosion had come from my left, I moved almost automatically to my right, toward the center of the house and closer to the driveway. Without turning back, I began to jog then run away from the explosion, my hands now covering the back of my head, and my body still hunched over.

After about a hundred feet, I stopped and finally turned around to face the house, which appeared normal. A plume of black smoke rose to the sky behind the house.

Nick Ashley ran out the front door and around the corner toward the black plume of smoke. After a few seconds, Ashley came back around the corner of the house, talking into his cell phone that was held to his ear, walking rapidly toward me.

By the time Ashley reached me, the ringing in my ears had subsided a bit, and I could hear that Ashley was talking to a 911 dispatcher about the explosion.

"No, I don't think so," Ashley said into the phone, then turned to me. "Are there any injuries? Are you injured?"

"No, I don't think so," I said, and it sounded like I was talking underwater.

"No, no injuries," Ashley said back into the phone. "Okay. Okay. Thank you." And then he hung up the phone.

To me, he said, "Police and fire are on their way," just as I heard sirens start up in the distance.

"What happened?" I asked. Even though I was still in shock and was concerned about another explosion, I began to walk toward the side of the house to see for myself. Instinctively, I took out my cell phone to take some photos and video.

"It was my tool shed," Ashley said, following me around the house. "It just blew up."

On the side of the house, I first noticed two blown-out windows on the first floor, and as I walked farther, I could see what was left of Ashley's tool shed, just a jagged collection of charred pieces of wood sticking up from a blackened concrete slab surrounding a column of smoke and dying flames in the center.

It took only a couple of minutes for three Fremont fire engines, two police cars and two ambulances to arrive on scene. Hernandez arrived shortly after.

Firefighters hooked up to a hydrant and quickly extinguished the flames. Dan Wilde and another officer took measurements and assessed the damage to the house, which was limited to two broken windows and some chips in the exterior paint.

I joined Ashley and Rod Pearson, of the Fremont Fire Department, who was questioning Ashley about the explosion. Hernandez stood next to them, listening silently.

"You got any lithium batteries in that shed?" Pearson asked, taking notes.

"Sure. A bunch. Almost all my tools anymore are battery operated," Ashley said. "My drills, chop saw, nail gun. They're all on batteries."

"You keep them plugged in?"

"Of course. That's how you charge them."

"But, I mean, after they're charged. Do you go and unplug them once they're done charging?"

"No," Ashley said, looking over at Hernandez. "Am I supposed to?"

"Well, we've had some reports of garage fires because of lithium batteries. Some of them are overheating and causing fires."

I had seen a couple of press releases about this happening in Boise and Meridian.

"But not explosions," I broke in.

Pearson stopped and gave a "mind your own business" look at me.

"No," Pearson said slowly, turning back to Ashley, turning his back slightly to me. "But I assume you've got flammables in there: gas, oil?"

"Yeah," Ashley said. "Of course."

"Well, that probably explains the explosion," Pearson said.

"Probably?" Ashley said.

"It'll take some time to determine the exact cause. I've still got to get in there and look around. It's too soon to say for sure about anything right now." Pearson closed his notebook. "I'll keep you posted, Nick."

"Thanks, Rod."

Pearson walked away, and Hernandez turned to me.

"What are you doing here?"

"I was talking to Nick for a story."

"What story?"

I stole a glance at Ashley. "Just about his development here. Thinking of doing a feature on it."

"Pretty unlucky that you were here right when that shed exploded."

"I guess it depends on how you look at it. I'd say I was pretty lucky."

"Seems pretty odd that the shed blew up like that," Hernandez said, looking back at the smoldering remains.

"I had no idea I needed to unplug my batteries like that."

"If that's what it was," Hernandez said, still looking thoughtfully at the shed.

"You think it was something else?" I asked.

Hernandez seemed to startle out of his thoughts, realizing a reporter was asking him a question. "No, no. I'm sure Rod's right. He'll get to the bottom of it, anyway. He's probably the best fire investigator in the valley."

Ashley and I said nothing.

"Well," Hernandez said abruptly, "glad no one was hurt and everyone's okay." He turned to Ashley. "If you need anything, you can give me a call any time, Nick."

"Will do, thanks, Chief," Ashley said.

Hernandez walked back to his car, taking one more glance at the tool shed before leaving.

Ashley turned to me, expecting me to say something.

"You didn't say anything about the threat you got," I said.

"You think they're related?"

"Kind of coincidental, don't you think?"

"Yeah, but I don't want to go around making crazy accusations if it is just a coincidence."

I didn't say anything.

"And I don't want to bring any attention to that threat if that's really all it was."

"Still, though."

"Let's see what Rod comes up with. If it is intentional, I'll tell the police about the threat I got."

"That's probably smart."

We stood quietly for a moment, looking at the still-smoldering shed.

"Are you all right?" Ashley asked me.

"Yeah, I'm fine," I said. "I guess it could have been worse."

"For sure. You could have gotten hit by something bigger. I found a couple of pretty big chunks of two-by-fours in the grass over there, and one piece of siding flew through the house window."

"How about you?"

"I was well inside the house when it went off."

"I mean in terms of the loss of your stuff?"

"Oh, yeah, that was most of my tools in that shed. I've got some at home, but that shed held just about all my work tools."

"I'm sorry. I know you said you were cutting things close, moneywise."

Ashley smiled. "Fortunately, my wife convinced me to keep a healthy insurance policy, which should cover this. Good news is I'll probably get to do some shopping and get all new tools."

"Well, that's something good to come out of this."

I headed back to my office, a little shaken and a little more nervous but perhaps even more determined now to figure out what the hell was going on.

13

I had two signs on my office front door. One was a "closed" sign with a clock, showing when I expected to return. The other was a paper printout taped to the inside of the glass door informing customers they could leave any checks, classified ads, messages or photos in the secure dropbox to the left, pointing toward a mail slot in the wall.

Upon entering my office, I checked the dropbox first and found the usual assortment of subscription renewal checks, a couple of classified ad submissions, a birthday announcement with a photo and a large manila envelope without any writing on it.

Inside the manila envelope were two printouts of business licenses from the Idaho Secretary of State office. One was for F9 Development LLC, and the other was for Coyote Flats LLC. Both companies were on Vern's list of water rights applications.

Both businesses were registered to a man named Brad Childs.

I looked inside the manila envelope to see if anything else was inside. There wasn't. I looked all over the front and back of the envelope to see if there were any markings that could be a clue. There weren't. I even smelled the papers and the envelope to see if there was a scent on them. There wasn't.

I looked back inside the dropbox. Nothing.

I went back over the water rights applications, especially in light of the envelope I had just received.

None of them mentioned Brad Childs anywhere. They were all signed by someone named Ted Dunlap. On each of the applications, the company that filed the water report was PFS Resources in Boise, signed by Oscar Mason.

So all of the water applications had Ted Dunlap and Oscar Mason of PFS Resources in common, but that could just be because PFS did a lot of water rights applications. But now, because of the business licenses someone dropped off for me, I knew at least two of the applications could be traced back to Brad Childs.

A ridiculous notion crossed my mind that somehow Vern had left the manila envelope for me. I wasn't superstitious, and I didn't believe in ghosts, but it wasn't the first time I sensed that Vern was somehow guiding me, just like he had always done when he was alive, ever since that first time we met at the city council meeting and Vern had tipped me off about the new city well.

I looked out of my office window and onto the street and sidewalk outside, as if someone might be watching me open the manila envelope. I shook my head at my own paranoia.

I picked up the phone and called the Secretary of State office and asked for Kenneth Millar.

Millar was a chief deputy in the office, which dealt mostly with elections but also handled all of the business filings in the state. I had written a story the previous year about a Fremont city council election recount, and Millar had helped me with some of the details of the state law.

"Can you look up a couple of business filings for me? I know I can go through the front desk, but they always make me fill out a public records request form and send it in and it usually takes a few days. I was hoping to get it a little more quickly."

"Sure. Shoot."

I went down the list of companies associated with the water rights on Vern Thompson's list.

"How about Mayfield LLC?"

I could hear Millar typing.

"Brad Childs. Want the address?"

"Sure."

"4468 Chinden Boulevard."

I wrote the address down.

"Orchard LLC."

"Brad Childs, same address."

I read the names of the other companies. Meadow, Arbor View, Sage Butte, all registered to Brad Childs, all the same address.

"All right. Thanks, Ken. I sure do appreciate it."

"Anytime. Need anything else?"

"Nope, not now. You know, you really need to get these records online."

"I know, I know."

"Maybe when you're in charge."

"That'd be nice."

"Say, when are you going to run for secretary of state? Isn't it your turn yet?"

"Not this time around. The old man's going to run one more time. That'll give me a little more time in the chair, try to put my name out there a little more. Thinking next time around."

"All right, well, let me know. Give me the scoop, will you?"

"Sure. You bet."

"Thanks, Ken."

I hung up and looked over my list.

I let out a low whistle, confirming now that all the application numbers on Vern Thompson's desk were related and connected to one man, Brad Childs. And that Childs was hiding his association with the water rights by putting them under different shell companies.

Looking at the list of applications, I confirmed what Hansen had told me, that they were all transfers of old water rights, dating to 1937, 1945, 1921, even one from 1903. I spent an hour looking up the locations based on the applications' listings of township, section and region numbers. The water rights were spread out all over the desert.

Each one was small by itself, but when I tallied up the amount of water in all of the applications put together, it was significant—8.2 CFS. That's the equivalent of more than two cities the size of Fremont. That would be a city of about 11,000 houses, or about 30,000 people.

I let out another low whistle. I wasn't sure if I had stumbled onto the reason Vern and Wanda Thompson were killed, but I knew that at the very least I had stumbled onto a really big story.

I called Jerry Hansen.

"Hi, Jerry. Did you drop off a manila envelope in my dropbox here at my office?"

"No, sure didn't."

"You know those water rights applications we were looking at?"

"Yep."

"Someone dropped off the business licenses for two of those companies."

"Huh. Interesting."

"Yeah, you know a guy by the name of Brad Childs?"

"Sure. Big developer. Probably the top home builder in the valley now."

"All those applications I asked for this morning? All of those businesses are registered to Brad Childs."

"His name wasn't on any of the water applications."

"I know."

"Let me do some looking, and I'll let you know if I come up with anything."

As soon as I hung up with Hansen, my phone rang, and it was George, the manager of the local grocery store.

"We're sold out of papers," he said. "Can you bring some more?"

"I just dropped off this week's papers a few hours ago," I said.

"I know. You're sold out. Everyone wants to know about the murders."

"I'll be right over."

Fortunately, I had ordered an additional five hundred copies of the paper. It had cost me a little bit extra, but it looked like it was going to pay off.

I dropped off another two hundred copies at the grocery store. I decided to check out my other locations.

"Oh good," Jean, the clerk at the Chevron, said when she saw me. "We just sold your last paper about fifteen minutes ago. We need more."

I left another fifty copies. This was going to be a good week. If I sold all five hundred extra copies, which it looked like I would, that would be an extra hundred seventy-five dollars. Plus, I had inserted subscription forms in every single-copy paper that week, which meant I'd likely get some new subscribers, which meant extra money that month.

I had owned the newspaper for two years, and, being a one-man operation, I had put in some long days like this before, and they usually paid off —literally. When I was working for the *Boston Examiner*, I got paid the same amount whether I worked twelve hours a day or clocked out at 4:59 p.m. I had worked too many twelve-hour days for someone else, and all I got in return was a pink slip.

Owning my own business, though, working twelve hours usually meant more single-copy sales or new subscriptions or more ads that paid the bills. For now, it was good to keep myself busy, to keep the cloud from settling in. But I knew I could do too much. The paper could be all-consuming. There was always more that could be done and no one to tell you to go home and call it a day.

The best part about owning your own business is that the sky's the limit. But the worst part, I had learned, is that the sky's the limit.

14

Downtown Fremont wasn't much to look at, a three-block stretch of sun-baked brick and faded concrete block buildings huddled along Main Street. Some sported false facades, attempts to modernize storefronts that had long since given up the pretense. There was Cowboys Lounge, a dimly lit dive bar perpetually smelling of stale beer and regret; next door, the Reliable Insurance Agency, its windows perpetually dusty; then a real estate office with peeling paint; a popular, if somewhat dingy, Mexican restaurant; a thrift store overflowing with cast-off treasures and forgotten memories; Miller's Hardware, where the floorboards creaked with every step; Fremont Savings and Loan, its imposing brick exterior a relic from a bygone era; a financial adviser's office, its tinted windows reflecting the harsh desert sun; and finally, my own storefront, the *Fremont Herald*, its slightly crooked sign hanging precariously above the door.

At one end of downtown, looming over the dusty city park, stood the skeletal remains of the old water tower, now empty and rusting, a monument to a time when Fremont was a thriving farm town, before it became a bedroom community of transplants who didn't even know Fremont had a downtown. The park itself was a sad collection of cracked concrete, a weathered bandshell, a basketball court with bent hoops, and hot-metal playground equipment that had baked under the relentless sun since the

1950s. Much of downtown Fremont felt frozen in the 1950s, a faded snapshot of a town that had seen better days. I was willing to bet that if you found a photo of downtown Fremont from 1950 and removed all the cars, you wouldn't be able to tell the difference from a current-day photo. The only things that seemed to change were the seasons and the slow accumulation of dust on every surface.

This was a stark contrast to the new strip malls and shopping plazas being built on the outskirts of town, surrounded by hastily constructed subdivisions that seemed to rise overnight. The chain coffee shops, ice cream parlors, fast-food joints and sandwich places that didn't advertise in the paper were the signs of forward progress, leaving behind the bygone days of Fremont's downtown and a sense of community along with it.

Cowboys Lounge, just a few doors down from my office, was owned by the former mayor, who notoriously used to bring developers there after city council meetings to cut deals on proposed subdivisions. It's probably where he had cut the deal to allow developers to tap into the city's drinking water system to irrigate their lawns.

I got there early, before the usual evening crowd. It was still light out, and the front door was propped open, airing it out and bathing the bar in daylight that gave the near-empty room an odd look and the feel of someone's home. I preferred a bar at that time of day to the crowded, loud, smoky nighttime. It still had the fresh smell of scrubbed floors, bleached tabletops and lemon-scented disinfectant. It held the sense of unfulfilled expectations and endless possibilities, in stark contrast to the booze-soaked disappointment and regret of the later hours.

"Phil," Charlie said from behind the bar, already reaching for a pint glass and pulling the tap for Sierra Nevada, my usual. The *Boise Weekly* had done a story the year before on the coldest beers in the Treasure Valley, surreptitiously bringing in a thermometer to fifty bars across the valley, and it turned out Cowboys Lounge had the coldest beer at just above the freezing temperature for beer, 29 degrees.

"Charlie," I said, sitting at the far end of the bar, with a view of the door and the rest of the room.

"Burger?"

"Yep."

"How was business this week?" Charlie asked me.

"Pretty good, unfortunately," I said as Charlie put the glass of beer in front of me on a coaster.

"Yeah, Thompson story, huh?" Charlie said, nodding to the bar at a copy of that week's *Fremont Herald*.

"Yeah," I said. "I've already sold out all my copies."

"Damn shame. Never seen anything like it in Fremont."

"Good people," I said.

"So I hear," Charlie said. "They never set foot in here, that's for sure."

I chuckled and nodded.

"I'll get your burger started," Charlie said and disappeared into the kitchen.

Two men made their way in, gave me a nod, which I returned, and sat on the other side of the bar. Charlie came out of the kitchen and waited on his new customers. I sat and read the *Idaho Press-Tribune*, the other daily paper from the next county over. It was smaller, more small-town local and old-fashioned, not as good as the *Idaho Statesman*. But folks in Fremont liked it better because it had farm news in it, and it allegedly wasn't as "liberal" as the *Statesman*.

After a while, my burger came, and the bar remained quiet while I ate and read and downed another beer.

Bernie Samstone showed up at the bar then, and he stood in the open doorway for a few moments, blinking his eyes and looking around, adjusting to the light, his mouth open, as if waiting for someone to greet him or show him to his seat. He was a big, beefy, dopey guy, now in his late fifties, with massive forearms that dangled at his sides. He was balding above a heavy brow that seemed to always be furrowed in thought as if his brain was struggling to process every piece of information it received. His body was clearly the product of hard farm work all his life, but his T-shirt now was tight across a growing belly that pushed down on his dirty Wranglers. Soon, I thought, Samstone would have to be one of those old farm boys who had to wear suspenders to keep his pants up.

I liked Samstone all right. He was, as they say, a gentle giant, kindly but not the sharpest. He was a bachelor who lived alone in the tiny farmhouse he grew up in, still farming the land his now-dead parents had farmed, a couple of hundred acres of alfalfa, sugar beets, potatoes, the standard.

It was his land that had gone before city council Monday night. Samstone was trying to get approval for a subdivision on eighty acres of it. By most accounts, Samstone wasn't a very good farmer, which had become obvious since his parents had died and left the farm to him. He had been struggling to make a go of it, and developing his land was his way out of that line of work. The plan included about two hundred single-family houses along with several apartments.

Samstone was trying to get all the entitlements in place and then sell the whole thing off to a developer. Actually, pretty smart of Samstone, since he'd get a much higher price for the land that way.

"Hey, Phil," Samstone said, sitting at the bar next to me.

"Bernie."

Bernie shook his head. "Boy, that's something about the Thompsons."

"Yeah."

"What do you suppose happened?"

"I don't know. What do you think?" I didn't like to "talk away" my stories. My commerce was the written word; anything else wasted my time. I preferred to do the listening, then let people read what I knew in the paper.

"Looks like it's gotta be some kind of robbery," Samstone said.

"Sure, but nothing was stolen."

"The guy must've got scared," Samstone said. "Maybe he thought the Thompsons were gone and they surprised him, so he shot them, thought someone would hear the shots, so he took off before he could steal anything."

"Mmm."

"Damn shame, either way."

"Mm-hmm."

"Can't believe that was going on while we were all at city council," Samstone said.

I welcomed the chance to change the subject.

"By the way, that was a good presentation on your development," I said.

"Oh, thanks. Kinda crazy that all those folks showed up complaining about the apartments."

"Half of them are crazy. The other half just want to close the gate behind them."

"I saw you had a story on it in this week's paper. I don't know how you do it, Phil. I mean, you got that story and the murder in the paper the next day?"

"Yeah, I had just finished writing up your story and sent the paper off, when I heard the call come over the scanner. It was a long night."

"I'll bet," Samstone said. "People around here sure do appreciate what you've done with the paper." Samstone took a long swallow of his beer.

"Do you know somebody by the name of Brad Childs?" I asked.

Samstone grunted. "Well, I can't say I care too much for him."

These were damning words from Samstone, who, like Vern Thompson, seldom said a negative thing about anyone.

"Why don't you like him?"

"He's got a bad reputation."

"How so?"

"He used to build nice houses, but then he got too big. He started cheaping out on his houses, cutting corners. He rips off suppliers, not paying them what he owes them. I guess that's what you got to do in that business. Sad, though."

"He ever approach you about your land?"

"He did, but I wouldn't put in with a guy like that."

"How come?"

"He's screwed over too many farmers around here. He'd write his contracts so that farmers don't get paid until Childs gets paid. A farmer would think he'd be able to retire on the sale of the land until he finds out he wouldn't get paid until long after he's dead and buried. They'd be lucky if their kids saw a penny of it, the way the contract was written."

"Anybody ever sue him?"

"He's got a whole team of lawyers and will take anyone to court who dares to fight him. Most farmers know by now, you see him coming, you lock the door."

"But he asked you about your land?"

"It was strange. He only asked me about my water rights. He asked what year they were from."

"What did you tell him?"

"They're old, very senior. My grandparents filed when they home-steaded here in the 1930s." I knew that Samstone's parents had moved to Idaho from Oklahoma during the Dust Bowl days.

"And he made you an offer?"

"He gave me a lowball offer with a bunch of strings attached. I wasn't interested. Besides, I wanted to develop the land myself, make more money that way, rather than get the crumbs that a guy like Childs was going to pay me. I had Lauren take a look at the contract, and she told me to tear it up."

"Who's Lauren?"

"My attorney, Lauren Broten."

"Was she the one who gave the presentation on your development at city council last night?" The woman presenting Samstone's development to the city council had stood out, attractive and young, about my age. The development industry wasn't exactly crawling with young, attractive women.

"Yep, that's her. She knows her stuff. She does a lot of real estate development work, mostly for bigger developers but sometimes for small guys like me. She's smart. She's easy to look at, too," Samstone said with an old man's leering chuckle.

"Sure."

"She said she wants to meet with you," Samstone said.

"Really?" I tried to disguise my interest by raising my glass of beer and taking another drink.

"Yeah, she came down to see me today, said she was impressed with your story about my project. She said she wanted to meet with you, you know, to talk more about the project, the apartments, the water rights, all that stuff. She said she had some information that you might be interested in."

"What about?"

"I don't know. She just said she'd be able to fill you in on the water situation around here."

"When did she want to meet?"

"Tomorrow, if you're available," Samstone said. "She said to give her a call ahead of time and let her know you're coming."

"Where does she work?"

"The Hoff Building downtown."

I knew the building in downtown Boise.

"Sounds good. I'll give her a call tomorrow," I said, finishing my beer. "Thanks, Bernie."

"You bet," Samstone said, finishing his own beer, as I stood up to leave.

I walked a block past my office, turned the corner and headed for my house, thinking about meeting with Lauren the next day. Roscoe barked his usual greeting as I passed.

15

<hr>

"When in doubt, head on out."

That was the phrase I learned in my very first newspaper job from a crusty old editor, and it was a mantra I continued to live by as a reporter. It meant "go to the scene." Whether it was a fire, a homicide, a car crash or whatever, go to the scene and see it for yourself with your own eyes. "Hang up the goddamn phone and get your ass out there," was another way that crusty old editor put it.

Whenever I struggled with a story, I knew my best bet was to go to the scene and see it for myself. That's how I thought now about Dan Perry's farm. I was having trouble understanding this story, if it was a story, and I felt deep in my reporter bones that I just needed to go lay eyes on the land to make sense of it. When in doubt, head on out.

The drive out of town was mercifully pleasant. It had been a long, hot, dry summer that stretched well into September. Because of a shortage of water, irrigation season ended in mid-August, nearly two months early. Farmers had missed out on a final cutting of hay, and yields on sugar beets, corn and potatoes were way down. It was a bad year. The entire state was in a drought, and so far that fall, no rain had fallen. Several wildfires had burned in the state, and the smoke had made its way into Boise, casting the city in an apocalyptic orange glow.

When I told my friends in Boston that I was moving to Idaho, they thought Idaho was all snow and cold, like the Canadian tundra. They had no idea that Boise was high desert. They would be amazed to know that Boise had broken a record for most days—twenty-three—over one hundred degrees that summer. I began to think we were all just a bunch of frogs, and the proverbial pot of water was starting to boil.

Finally, by mid-September, the desert nights were getting cooler, even if the days were still in the eighties. At least the smoke had cleared out. Trees in town were starting to change colors slowly and vibrantly, a real fall, like I was used to back East, and I stopped to think whether I missed it or not.

I passed one last subdivision of maybe twenty houses, ugly McMansions that I had written about before because their communal well was drying up, and the water was testing positive for uranium and arsenic. They had to issue a bond to dig a deeper well. Water fees tripled. It was a mess. And that was just twenty houses.

As I drove on, the landscape turned to desert. After five minutes, I was amid flat, dusty brown sagebrush land, punctuated by a couple of farm fields and just one or two small farmhouses visible on the distant horizon. I passed a double-wide trailer with a gate, a "No Trespassing" sign, and a Confederate flag hanging from the front of the trailer. I drove another five minutes, and the land became even more desolate. I turned south and drove another two miles, looking for Dan Perry's farm.

I pulled up in front of a tiny abandoned one-story house set back a hundred feet from the road and buried among a copse of cottonwood trees, the old-fashioned form of air conditioning. Behind the house stood a barn, its sun-faded red paint giving way to exposed gray boards. The fields around the house and barn had signs of having been cultivated at one time, but already the desert was reclaiming the unplowed land.

I shut off the car and got out. Only a kick-up of warm air that smelled of dust and sage disturbed the otherwise absolute silence. I walked out onto the desert land. Rocks and dirt crunched under my feet, and I felt like Cary Grant in the crop duster scene in *North by Northwest*.

I could now see why Vern was asking about whether anyone had made any development applications. A development this far out was unlikely.

The roads were barely serviceable. Houses out here would be too far away from any services.

Another gust of wind sprayed dirt in my eyes, and a dust devil formed in the middle of one of Perry's fields, slowly rising a couple hundred feet in the air, and a feeling of agoraphobia swept over me, and I became slightly dizzy.

That was when I heard what sounded like the racking of a shotgun. I reflexively looked toward what I thought was the abandoned house and caught a glimpse of sunlight glinting off something metal among the trees.

And then the shot rang out.

16

The gunshot echoed over the dusty land. I instinctively dropped down, one knee and one hand on the ground, and one hand over my head, as if that would do anything. I looked at the house to see if I could spot the shooter, then looked over at my car, which was a hundred feet away, with no cover in between. I continued to look back and forth between the house and my car, preparing to make a break for it, when I heard the man's voice call out.

"You're trespassing on my land," came the voice, which oddly filled me with a sense of relief. Something in the voice told me that I was safe, that this man wasn't going to kill me. Still, I heard another racking of the gun.

I stood up slowly and raised my hands above my head.

"I'm sorry, I didn't know anyone was out here."

"Well, I am. Now get off my land."

Still holding my hands up, I walked slowly toward my car. "Are you Dan Perry?"

"Who's asking?"

I made it to my car and put my hands down, now technically off Perry's land.

"I'm Philip Chandler, with the *Fremont Herald*."

Silence.

Dan Perry emerged from the trees and walked about halfway toward me. Perry pumped his shotgun, and a shell popped out onto the ground. He picked it up and pocketed it and let the shotgun point down toward the ground. I took that as a signal that it was safe to come forward. We stood facing each other in the middle of an open field.

Perry was wearing knee-high rubber boots over faded and stained Wranglers, an unbuttoned, torn and stained plaid shirt over a plain black T-shirt, and a beat-up John Deere trucker's hat. He had a scraggly black-and-gray beard and mustache beneath open and pleasant blue eyes that had a touch of something that I couldn't quite place.

"So, you're that new feller that Gus sold the paper to," Perry said, referring to Gus Haggard, the *Fremont Herald*'s previous owner. Even though it had been two years, I was still the "new feller."

"Yep, that's me."

"That Gus, he did a good job. He would tell it like it is."

I heard this from time to time and took it as a slight. Gus Haggard had seldom interviewed people other than his friends and disgruntled residents with an ax to grind, often anonymously. Under Haggard, the *Fremont Herald* was full of rumors, gossip and accusations, often false. Under my ownership, the paper had become more professional, more objective. My stories included multiple sources. I got both sides of the story. Some people, though, preferred Haggard's style of "journalism," always looking for a fight, railing against the mayor, alleging that someone was in someone else's pocket, whether true or not. By comparison, my *Fremont Herald* was boring—professional, but boring. Whenever someone told me that my predecessor would "tell it like it is," I figured they liked it better when Haggard owned the paper.

"He sure did," I said.

"Sorry about the greeting," Perry said a bit solemnly. "That was just a warning shot in the air. You gotta be careful around these parts, trespassing on a man's land."

"I'm sorry. I didn't know."

"Well, now you do." Perry looked me up and down, and I knew to wait before jumping in.

"Well, let's get out of the sun," Perry said and turned and walked toward the house. I followed. In among the shade of the trees, Perry's front porch was surprisingly cool and comfortable. Perry leaned the shotgun against the wall and sat down on a rocking chair. I sat in its mate next to him.

"What are you doing all the way out here?"

"I'm working on a story about water rights," I said.

"Yeah?"

"I heard you sold your property here."

"So?"

"Well, can I ask who you sold it to?"

"Brad Childs," Perry said with a sneer.

"I hear he doesn't have a very good reputation. Why'd you sell it to him?"

"I had no choice. No one else is going to buy my property all the way out here. My granddad homesteaded out here back in the thirties. Back then, they didn't realize how far out this was. It was just cheap land, part of the Homestead Act. They took what they were given and were thankful for it." He sneered again. "This land ain't worth a damn, pulling rocks out of this place for forty years."

I stayed silent, let him talk.

"My kids are all off doing their own thing. None of them wants to farm. Which is fine by me. I wouldn't want them to take over this place anyway. You know, our daughter is a doctor now," he said, beaming with pride. "Our one son works for Idaho Power. Our other son is an accountant."

"That's great."

"We done good," Perry said, his eyes starting to well. I knew that Perry was now talking about his dead wife. "We done good by them. They turned out all right."

"They sure did." I desperately wanted to spare the man the embarrassment of crying in front of a complete stranger, so I asked him a question that I knew would jar him.

"So how much did Childs pay you for your land?"

It worked. Perry jolted as if stung by a bee. He sniffed and ran his hand across his eye. His sneer returned.

"Not nearly enough. But I had no other choice. There weren't any other buyers. No one's going to farm this land. When Annie died, I couldn't run this place by myself. I had to sell, and Childs was the only one buying. At least he's letting me stay here for the time being."

"Is he going to develop your land?"

"Funny," Perry said.

"What's that?"

"Old Vern Thompson come all the way out here a couple of weeks ago just like this. Vern drove up in his pickup, just like you did. Of course, I didn't shoot at him because I recognized his truck." We both laughed.

I got a tingling sensation, as if Vern was confirming my hunch. "What did he ask you about?"

"He asked me about whether Childs was working on developing my property."

"What did you tell him?"

"I said if he was, he wasn't doing anything about it. He hasn't even sent anyone out to do any surveying."

"Did Vern ask you about your water rights?"

"He sure did. He wanted to know if Childs asked me about my water rights."

"Did he ask you how old they are?"

"Yep, and I told him that's what Childs wanted to know. How old my water rights were. When I told him 1937, he made an offer on the spot."

Perry chuckled.

"In a way, I think I got the better of him."

"How so?"

"My well is drying up, but he didn't ask me about that. The last few years, I've been running out of water late in the season. My well's been drying up earlier and earlier, but Childs don't know that."

"Did Vern ask you anything else?"

"That was it. After that, he just got back in his truck and left. That was the last time I seen him. Damn shame about what happened to him and Wanda."

"Sure is." I honored the code among farmers of lingering silence, giving time for Perry to say something else. Perry stayed silent, too, apparently lost in a reverie of his own, although his lips were moving, as if talking to himself, and it looked like tears were starting to well up again, thinking about Annie. I wondered how long he'd hang on, sitting out here in the house where he and Annie raised their children and lived a good life together. I glanced over at the shotgun and was overcome with sadness.

"All right, well, thanks, Dan," I said finally and stood up. "It was sure nice meeting you. I appreciate your time."

"You bet, anytime." Perry stood and shook my hand.

I checked the time. I'd have to hustle to get up to Boise to meet Lauren. I got in my car and headed back toward town, escaping that creeping feeling of agoraphobia. I looked in my rearview mirror and saw Dan Perry standing there rubbing his chin, looking down, shaking his head and talking to himself.

17

———

There could be no greater contrast than going from Dan Perry's farm to downtown Boise, and I thought to myself that this urban-rural connection was one of the things that I loved about Idaho.

On my way, once I got back into cell range, I called Lauren Broten's office. I was nervous, feeling like a high school kid calling up a girl to ask her out to prom.

"Hello, Philip." Lauren sounded genuinely pleased to hear from me, which set me at ease. "Bernie said you might be giving me a call."

"Yes, he said you wanted to talk to me about his project and something about water."

"I'd love to fill you in," she said. "I was just down in Fremont yesterday to see Bernie."

"You should have stopped by my office," I said.

"I did, but you weren't in," she said.

"Oh, I'm sorry I missed you." I said it with genuine disappointment, hoping she would catch my sincerity.

"So, I've got a meeting in about five minutes," she said, "but I should be done by eleven. Can you call me back then?"

"How about I come up to see you?"

"Even better," she said invitingly. "Do you know where my office is?"

"Hoff Building?"

"Seventh floor."

"I'll see you then."

"I'm looking forward to it," she said in a way that gave me a buzz of excitement.

The Hoff Building at the corner of Eighth and Bannock was a stately art deco edifice built in 1930, designed by architect Frank Hummel of Tourtellotte and Hummel. The original eleven-story building began its life as Hotel Boise and still had remnants of the era. The building had since been turned into offices but retained art deco flourishes.

Walking into the Hoff Building wasn't like stepping back in time, though. Rather, it was a sense of being a part of history, a continuation of it, that perhaps by waking up in the mornings, showering, shaving, eating your Corn Flakes, going to your office at the Hoff Building, making your way through the lobby, entering the narrow elevator doors festooned with Egyptian carvings and rectilinear geometric line patterns and opening your office door, you were maybe just like that person doing the exact same thing ninety years ago. Walking through the Hoff Building made you want to put on a gray flannel suit and leather-soled shoes and become a more refined person.

The building was now home to law offices, lobbyists, developers and architects, no doubt inspired by the work of Boise's original famous architecture firm. It was a stark contrast to the dusty desert farm fields I had just visited.

The Broten Law Firm shared the seventh floor with a prominent lobbying outfit that employed a former governor. I exited the elevator into a narrow hallway of half glass, half wood, so that it looked into another hallway lined with offices of the lobbying firm, each office door topped with the name of its occupant. I was disappointed there were no transom windows to complete the sense of time travel. I looked for and found the name of the former governor, whose office was unlit and apparently empty. To the right, the hallway ended at a door to the stairwell. I turned left and went around the corner where I was greeted by a large glass door on which were stenciled in gold-and-black letters, "Broten Law Firm, John Broten, Esquire, Lauren Broten, Esquire."

I wondered who John Broten was, though the name sounded familiar. I had noticed Lauren wasn't wearing a wedding ring, but maybe she just didn't wear one.

The woman at the front desk was plump, bubbly, pleasant, and greeted me with a cute dimpled smile.

"Good afternoon, can I help you?"

"I'm here to see Lauren Broten."

"Do you have an appointment?"

"Yes, she told me to come up."

"Your name?"

"Philip Chandler."

"I'll let her know you're here. You can have a seat." She pointed to a modest wood-paneled sitting area with an overstuffed mahogany leather couch, two matching leather chairs and a heavy oak coffee table. "Can I get you some water or a cup of coffee?"

"No thanks. I'm good." I sat on the couch, which was remarkably comfortable. The surroundings gave me the urge to light up a cigar and swill a glass of brandy. I did my best to look dignified in my department store blazer, no-iron button-down dress shirt, scuffed Bostonians and chinos, which I now noticed were beginning to fray at the cuffs.

Lauren Broten kept me waiting perhaps two minutes too long.

"Philip," she said as she strode around the corner to the sitting room. Lauren was attractive, slim, confident and, wearing heels, almost as tall as me. She wore a black knee-length skirt over tanned bare legs and a tight-fitting white blouse with the top two buttons undone. Her black hair was pulled back loosely in a haphazard bun. From what I could tell she wasn't wearing much makeup except for a hint of lipstick on her full lips, maybe a little rouge on her high cheekbones and mascara that accentuated her deep brown eyes. She had the beginnings of smile lines that gave her an added look of sophistication. Her black-rimmed glasses didn't seem to have much of a distortion, causing me to wonder if they were more for appearance than utility. If so, they did the trick.

"Hello, Lauren." I did my best to stand up straight and fix my posture, sucking in my stomach as I buttoned my blazer with my left hand and extended my right, which Lauren took with a downward grip, the back of her hand turned upward, giving me an impulse to kiss it.

"Good to see you," she said, smiling. "Welcome." She swept her hand across the room. "Let's go back to my office."

I stole a glance at her toned calves as I followed her down the hall.

Lauren's office was bright and sparsely decorated with sleek Scandinavian furniture of fabric and light wood, a stark contrast to the stuffy leather and oak paneling of the firm's lobby. I surmised that the decor in the waiting area was the preference of someone else, someone older with older tastes. Straight back was a wall of books behind a blonde-wood thin-top desk, free of anything but a laptop and a tidy inbox of files. Lauren led me to an informal sitting area of two armchairs, a coffee table and a sideboard.

"Have a seat," she said. "Coffee?"

"Sure. Thank you," I said as I pulled out my notebook and sat in one of the chairs. I looked again at her left hand, checking to see if she was wearing a wedding ring. She wasn't. I asked the question to which I was afraid to hear the answer.

"So I assume you and John Broten are related?"

"Yes, he's my father."

I was more relieved than I let on.

"He's had this practice for years. I joined him in the practice a few years ago."

"The name sounds familiar."

"Well, he's a state legislator, too. He sometimes makes the news. He's a state senator, used to be a county commissioner."

"Yes, that's where I've heard his name." I recalled that Broten was pretty much your typical Republican, talking about maybe running for governor someday. He used to be county commissioner for a couple of years, then a seat came open in his district in Boise, so he ran and won. A relatively quiet, reasonable legislator, unlike some of the legislators who show up every session looking to make a name for themselves by banning library books, defunding public television or trying to define marriage as between one man and one woman. There are two kinds of politicians: those who come to make policy and those who come to make headlines. Broten fit into the former category.

Lauren handed me a cup of coffee and poured herself another. She pulled the other chair across the floor a couple of inches closer to me and sat down, throwing one leg over the other casually, revealing more thigh as her skirt rode up her leg. She leaned on the chair arm that was closest to me and took a sip of coffee, leaving a hint of lipstick on the rim. Her casualness unsettled me, as I was accustomed to more formal interviews. Our closeness made the room seem bigger. I set my own coffee cup on the table, cleared my throat and trudged ahead.

"So Bernie said you could tell me more about his project, but he said something about you wanting to talk about water and water rights in general," I said.

"Sure," Lauren said. "I like Bernie."

"Yeah, me too," I said. "He's a good guy."

"It's a good project, too," Lauren said, more professionally.

I was relieved to get down to business. I liked Lauren and liked being near her, but I had work to do, too, and I couldn't afford to waste time.

"Do you think it will get approved?" I asked.

"I think so," she said confidently. "Frankly, city council can't turn it down."

"What about all the people who showed up to oppose it?"

"It doesn't really matter," she said dismissively.

I raised an eyebrow and wrote down what she said. Lauren looked down at my notebook and frowned, recognizing perhaps for the first time that I wasn't here on a social call.

"I mean, it matters," Lauren said, "but not when it comes to approving the project or not."

"Mm-hmm," I said as I wrote.

"What I mean is the project meets all of the legal requirements set by the city's zoning code and comprehensive plan. If they were to reject the proposal, it would be considered arbitrary and capricious and they'd open themselves up to a lawsuit."

I was writing all of this in my notebook and was thinking I might have a follow-up story about Samstone's development after all.

In between sips of coffee, Lauren explained the sections of city code that pertained to Samstone's project and how the comprehensive plan established the allowable densities—including those controversial apartment buildings. At one point, she opened a file that was on the coffee table and her bare knee touched my knee, sending an electric shock wave up my spine. She showed me the traffic study they had done, the soil composition test results and the water study. She had printed out sections of city code and zoomed-in printouts of the city's comprehensive plan map that showed the density designations for Samstone's land. I took careful notes.

"What about water? One of the neighbors showed up to testify, saying her well had run dry," I said. "Bernie said he has enough water for the project already?"

"Yes, thank God," she said. "He has senior water rights dating back to when his grandparents homesteaded there, and it should be plenty for his project, which is a good thing because there's a bit of a run on water rights right now. That's probably the story you should be writing."

"What story?"

"There's been so much growth in Boise, so much construction, new subdivisions going up, there's real concern we're going to run out of water. What I've heard is that some developers are buying land just for the water rights."

"I've heard that, too. I was just out at an old dairy farm out in the desert that looks like it's just for the water rights," I said, not wanting to give away too much of what I was working on. "How does that even work? What happens if the developer doesn't develop that land? What good are those water rights?"

"That's a good question," Lauren said and put her hand on my forearm, sending another electric shock through my body. "I'm no expert, Philip." I liked hearing her say my name, and I liked that she called me Philip instead of Phil. "I'm just telling you what I've heard. I deal with more conventional development. Someone like Bernie Samstone wants to develop his land, I look at land use, city codes, the existing water rights and put together a development that fits all the parameters. If someone is buying land just for the water rights, I don't know what they're up to."

Lauren's face was turned toward the file on the table, but her eyes were glancing sideways at me, giving me the odd sense that she was waiting for my reaction.

"So where would I start? Who should I talk to?"

"You could start with the Department of Water Resources, look at applications for water rights transfers, see who they come back to," Lauren said.

"I kind of already got a start on that," I said. "I was able to find a few applications already."

"Oh, good," Lauren said a little too quickly.

"Seems like these developers register business names under phony names and use someone else as a registered agent."

"Yes, I've heard of that." Again, she glanced sideways.

"Makes it kind of difficult to track."

"But it sounds like you've got a good start."

"Just a start. It's not making a lot of sense to me right now."

"It will," she said in a tone that struck me as odd. "You know, there was someone who was referred to me the other day, a water expert you could talk to. Here in Boise. Let me see if I can remember," Lauren said, glancing over at her desk. "I think I had it written down somewhere."

She got up, and I watched her as she walked toward her desk. She leaned over the desk and grabbed a file.

"Here it is," she said, pulling out a piece of paper that had a sticky note attached to it. "Oscar Mason."

The name sounded familiar. "Who's that?"

"He's a water expert. With PFS Resources." She sat back down and crossed her legs, handing the note to me.

Seeing the name in writing, I remembered. Oscar Mason of PFS Resources had been the one who filed the water rights applications on behalf of Childs's companies. I was struck by the coincidence.

"Does he do work for Brad Childs?"

"Who's that?" she said, and I thought I detected a smile.

"Brad Childs, Summers Builders. He's a developer in town. A pretty big developer," I said, finding it hard to believe that she hadn't heard of him. "Bernie told me Brad Childs approached him about his water rights. He apparently is behind the land deal out in the desert."

"Oh, sure, Summers Builders. Yes, I know them. Well, PFS does a lot of work for developers. They're a pretty big outfit. Oscar Mason is an expert. You should talk to Oscar Mason."

"Okay. I'll give him a call." I started to think of other questions to ask, but Lauren interrupted my thoughts.

"Well," she said, uncrossing her legs and slapping her hands on her thighs, "I hate to say it, but I've got another meeting in about five minutes."

I stood up, caught off guard, left with the feeling that I hadn't gotten to all I wanted to get to, but somehow Lauren had. "Well, thanks for your time. I appreciate it."

She stood up and shook my hand.

"My pleasure. If you have any more questions, let me know. Happy to help anytime."

"Will do." I turned toward the door and grabbed the handle, reluctant to leave.

I made my way to the elevator, passed through the lobby and emerged onto the city sidewalk where the crisp fall-like morning was giving way to another hot, dry day.

18

———

The website for PFS Resources was slick, with a section on major water projects all over the West, with photos of headworks, canals, wells. I looked it over during lunch from a table at the Java coffee shop on the corner of Sixth and Idaho. Under a section headed "Media," there was a list of links to articles in which PFS Resources was included. I noticed that Oscar Mason had been quoted recently in a story about minimum water flows on the Snake River required for operation of the Swan Falls Dam.

I called PFS Resources and reached Mason. I told him I was working on a story about minimum water flows on the Snake River required for the operation of the Swan Falls Dam. I gave Mason the impression that I had only a rudimentary understanding of "how all this water stuff works." Mason said he was available. "Come ahead," he said.

Oscar Mason's office was on the twenty-first floor of the US Bank Building in downtown Boise. The windows behind the office's reception desk provided a spectacular view of the Treasure Valley to the south, all the way to the Owyhee Mountains. A visitor would have to get up close to the window to even see the city streets below.

The reception area was well-appointed in a modern and spare design with metal-and-glass tables festooned with copies of *Architectural Digest*, *The Wall Street Journal* and *The Economist*. Sleek, low-backed black leather sofas and chairs were flanked by glass-and-silver end tables holding up colorful arrangements of zinnias in silver vases. Apparently there was a lot of money in water consulting, and they weren't ashamed of it.

I made my way to the smiling attractive receptionist who reminded me of an eager young camp counselor greeting frightened children being dropped off by their parents at camp for the summer. She sat cheerfully at a long sleek desk that was fronted by the PFS Resources logo, complete with large shiny black letters and a blue-and-white painted metal rendition of water waves backlit by a blue-and-green light. I couldn't help but juxtapose this office with the shabby office of Jerry Hansen at the Western Regional Office of the Idaho Department of Water Resources. Although the state government held all the power, money like this can buy you a lot of influence.

"I'm here to see Oscar Mason," I said.

"Do you have an appointment?" the woman said, still smiling.

"I called ahead and he said he'd be available if I came up."

"Your name?"

"Philip Chandler with the *Fremont Herald*."

After alerting Mason of my presence, the receptionist directed me to one of the seating areas.

"He'll be with you shortly," she said.

The low-back leather sofa proved to be awkward and uncomfortable, and the leather chair wasn't much better. So I stood and paced around the office, making my way to those windows behind the reception desk and looking down at the city.

I wasn't really sure what I was expecting a water engineer to look like, perhaps more like Jerry Hansen than George Clooney, so I was surprised when Oscar Mason emerged looking more like the latter than the former. Mason was tall and thin, fit like a triathlete, wearing a tight-fitting polo shirt bearing the PFS Resources logo over a well-defined left pectoral. He was wearing immaculate Wranglers over brown engineer boots. His facial features were chiseled and sharp, and his eyes were husky-dog blue, under perfectly coiffed thick gray-and-white hair set against tanned, smooth skin. He looked like one of those aging models that cologne brands will drag out of their Rolodexes in an effort to appeal to the fit-and-over-forty crowd.

"Phil?" Mason said with a too-white set of teeth as he strode magnificently toward me, and I suddenly felt shabby and tried to stand up a little straighter. I noted the use of the familiar "Phil," which grated on me when used by someone I didn't know well. I had, after all, introduced myself on the phone as "Philip." I picked up on the overconfidence and thought I could use it to my advantage.

"Oscar," I said, extending my hand.

"Nice to meet you."

"Thanks for agreeing to meet with me on such short notice," I said.

"Sure, come on back."

We made our way to his corner office where the views of the Boise Foothills to the east and the Owyhees to the south were even more spectacular. Mason's office was decorated in a similar fashion as the lobby, but on the walls were several photos of Mason in various places: the top of the Grand Canyon; the top of Mount Borah, Idaho's tallest peak; kayaking in the ocean; kneeling by a raging river; exotic locations that I didn't recognize. In each of the photos, Mason was alone. *Imagine covering the walls of your office with selfies*, I thought.

"Have a seat," Mason said, directing me to a leather chair, as Mason sat down in the chair behind his desk, which I noted was remarkably devoid of any papers. "So you want to know about the Snake and water flows at Swan Falls?"

"Yes." I pulled out my notebook from my hip pocket and the pen from my shirt pocket. As expected, Mason loved to hear the sound of his own voice, and for the next twenty minutes without me asking a single question, Mason explained the history of water rights, the Snake River Plain adjudication and power generation at Swan Falls. I was looking for an opening to try to tie the conversation to Childs's water rights applications.

"So how do groundwater rights relate to surface water?" I asked.

"Excellent question," Mason said. "We've come to understand that groundwater, at least to some extent, contributes to surface water, that a fuller aquifer will mean better flows on the surface water systems, all the creeks, streams and rivers. It's all interconnected," he said, weaving his fingers together.

"So conversely, the more that's pumped out of the ground," I said, "the more the aquifer is depleted, and the lower the flows in the Snake."

"In theory, yes," Mason said.

"What do you mean in theory?" I asked.

"Well, you have to understand that some uses of water actually recharge the aquifer. It all depends on the use—domestic, irrigation, storage. You see, when a farmer irrigates a field, some of that water seeps into the ground and fills up the aquifer underground. It's called aquifer recharge. The East Snake River Plains aquifer over in eastern Idaho is estimated to be about the size of Lake Erie. We do detailed studies of the aquifer every year to determine the water level."

"What about our aquifer here?" I asked.

"Our aquifer?"

"Yes. Basin 63," I said.

Mason paused. "We have plenty of water here."

"You said the East Snake River aquifer is the size of Lake Erie. How big is the aquifer in Basin 63?"

"Huge."

"How huge?"

"Not really sure," Mason said.

"We don't know?"

"Nope."

"You said the East Snake River aquifer gets detailed studies every year. What about a study of Basin 63?"

"Haven't done one."

"Why not?"

"Haven't really had to," Mason said. "Haven't had any issues here. We've had plenty of water."

I noted the imprecise answer from someone who seemed to give precise answers.

"The water table over in east Idaho was dropping, so we had to do a study. Over here, we're fine."

"I thought we were in a drought. Irrigation season ended in August because we ran out of water."

"Temporary," Mason said, waving his hand dismissively. "We always have these periods of drought. It's cyclical. Good water years, bad water years. They come and go."

"But with all the development and growth, it can't last forever," I said.

"We'll have water for a long, long time here," Mason said, again imprecisely.

"But how do we know that if we're not studying the aquifer?" I asked.

Mason swiveled in his chair and pointed to the Boise Foothills.

"Those mountains? You've seen them in the winter covered with snow every year. All that snow melts and feeds the entire basin."

He stood up and pointed to the east. "There, you can see the Boise River. Every year, we have to release water to avoid spring floods. No, Basin 63 is going to have water for years and years and years."

"How many years?" I asked.

"Many," Mason said definitively, as if to end that line of questioning.

Mason gave me a quizzical look, perhaps realizing we weren't talking about river flows at Swan Falls Dam anymore. I decided to quickly change the subject.

"So does PFS work for the state or cities or who?" I waved my arm, sweeping the office. "There's obviously a lot of money in water engineering. Who do you work for?"

Mason smiled, probably pleased that I had noticed his ostentatious display of success.

"Some government but mostly private clients," Mason said. "Government work doesn't pay much. We typically work for clients who are looking for water. We do detailed studies of the topography, geography, hydrology of certain areas to determine water-bearing layers, water flows, well depths, things like that."

"So you must do a lot of work for developers, then."

"Yes, that's most of our work," Mason said, now looking at his watch, and I knew he was about to call our meeting to an end.

I decided to play a hand.

"So do developers ever buy land just so they can own water rights speculatively?"

"Speculatively?"

"Yeah, just buy land out in the middle of the desert just for the sake of holding a water right."

I detected Mason shifting in his chair.

"No," he said hesitantly. "Can't say that I have heard of that." I noted the way he answered the question.

"That's just what I've heard, you know, around the coffee klatch," I said a bit dismissively.

"Right," Mason said with a smile and a chuckle. "Probably just rumors."

"Must be," I said.

"Well, I'm afraid I've got another meeting to get to," Mason said, tapping his wristwatch and standing up. "When is your story coming out?"

I stood up as well. "I'm not sure," I said. "I've still got a lot of learning to do on the subject. Maybe a couple of weeks from now."

We walked to the door and started down the hall.

"Well, let me know when the story comes out. Do you have a website? I'm afraid I don't subscribe to the *Fremont Chronicle*," he said, not even remembering the name of my newspaper.

"Yes." I pulled out a business card, which included my office address, phone number, email address and website, and handed it to Mason. As we reached the lobby, I stopped, deciding to play another hand.

"I was thinking it would be a good idea to talk to a developer for the story," I said. "You know, they deal with water rights and electricity. Do you know any developers that would be good to talk to? Maybe someone you work with?"

"Hmm, I'm not sure," Mason held up my business card and looked at it as if he were holding up a rotting fish. "But if I think of someone, I'll let you know."

"Oh, that would be great," I said. "Thank you. You know, someone local, not like a national company."

"Sure. Sure," Mason said. "I'll think on it." He was practically pushing me out of the office now.

"Someone had mentioned Summers Builders to me. Brad Childs," I said.

Mason stopped cold. He looked down at me, squinting, his mouth half-open. I could see him doing the calculations, trying to figure out my game, weighing how much to confirm. If, after all, I had dropped that name to provoke him, I must know more than I'm letting on and to deny any affiliation with Summers would have been easily disprovable by a little bit of research. I could practically see the gears turning in Mason's head. After a few moments, it became clear that Mason had decided his course of action. He closed his mouth, stood up straight and smiled.

"Sure," he said. "Summers. Terrific company. I do a lot of work with them. Brad and Fred Childs. They build great houses. Good people. I'll certainly let them know you're interested in speaking with them. I'm sure they'd be happy to fill you in from a developer's perspective." He held up my business card again. "I'm sure they'll be in touch."

Did he say that ominously?

I left the office with a slight feeling of unease that I had overplayed my hand. But I needed to shake some trees to get a sense of whether I was on the right track or just on a wild goose chase.

19

I made my way back to the coffee shop, ordered a double espresso and snagged a table in the corner. I picked up my phone as a way to clear my mind and opened X to mindlessly doomscroll.

I kept my direct messages open so that I could receive news tips from people I didn't follow or who didn't follow me. It worked well for the most part, and I didn't receive nearly as much spam or hate messages as I thought I would.

When I opened X, I had a notification for a message request. I looked at the sender, MarkFelt08081974.

Why did the name sound familiar? I googled the name and smiled at the reference.

Mark Felt was the notorious "Deep Throat" who helped Bob Woodward and Carl Bernstein of *The Washington Post* uncover President Richard Nixon's involvement in Watergate, culminating in Nixon's resignation. Woodward and Bernstein had kept their promise to keep Felt's identity a secret until after Felt died. It turned out that Felt was an FBI special agent who later became deputy director. It also turned out that Felt was from Idaho.

I looked more closely at the sender's handle and thought the numbers didn't look random. I realized it was a date, 08-08-1974. August 8, 1974, the day Nixon resigned. Clever reference, someone who knew something about journalism.

I read the message: "Look into this study of Basin 63." The message included a link, which I clicked on.

The link went to a contract on the Idaho Department of Water Resources' website from two years ago for a study of Basin 63. It was a short contract, just two pages, laying out an agreement between the Department of Water Resources and a firm called Advantage Land and Water to conduct a comprehensive study of water levels and depletion and recharge rates of Basin 63.

I clicked on the X account of MarkFelt08081974 and saw there was no avatar photo, no profile photo, no followers, not following anyone, no tweets and they had joined X that month. Clearly a fake account set up solely for the purpose of messaging me.

I replied, "Who is this?"

I then went back to the contract and scrolled to the bottom. The contract was signed by the director of the Department of Water Resources and a man named Alan Garry of Advantage Land and Water.

I looked up Advantage on my phone and saw they had an office on River Street, just about ten blocks away.

Advantage was located in an old warehouse that had previously been converted into one of those jumphouses for kids, complete with trampolines and ball pits. It must have been a short-lived fad among the North End parents who would have playdates and birthday parties there, because the jumphouse was now gone, replaced by the offices of Advantage Land and Water.

The office space was industrial, with thirty-foot-high ceilings featuring exposed ductwork and steel trusses spray-painted black. The floor was polished concrete. A woman sat at the front desk of metal and light wood. Behind her was a tall plain wall that held the Advantage logo. A metal staircase led to the back in a cut in the wall on the right.

"Can I help you?" the woman behind the front desk asked.

"I was wondering if I could see Alan Garry."

The woman started as if hit with an electrical shock in her chair.

"And you are?" She said it politely but with a sense of wariness and something else. Disbelief?

"Philip Chandler with the *Fremont Herald*."

"Can I ask what this is about?"

No reason to be coy. "I noticed that Advantage had a contract to do a study of Basin 63, and I wanted to ask Mr. Garry about it."

"Just a moment," she said as if she had said it a million times before, which she probably had. She clicked a button on her phone and spoke into her headset.

"Hi, I'm sorry to bother you, but there's someone here from the media asking for Alan." She looked up at me. "Your name again and who you're with."

"Philip Chandler. *Fremont Herald*."

The woman repeated it to the person on the phone.

"And what were you looking for again?"

"A study of Basin 63."

Again, she repeated that into the phone, and as she listened, she stole glances at me.

"Okay. Will do." She hit a button on the phone and looked up at me. "Mr. Eastman will be with you in a minute. You can have a seat over there." She pointed to a row of attached metal-and-vinyl seats that looked like they had been taken from an abandoned bus terminal.

"Thanks. Is Mr. Garry not available?"

The woman behind the desk looked annoyed and again something else. Sadness? She reflexively looked behind her. "No, he's not."

"Does he still work here?" I didn't want to waste my time.

"He... I'm not... He isn't... Mr. Garry isn't—Mr. Eastman can fill you in."

"It's just that Alan Garry was the one who signed the contract to do the study, and I was hoping to talk to him directly. If he doesn't work here anymore, I just don't want to waste anyone's time," I said, hoping to make it clear I was including myself in the part about not wanting to waste anyone's time.

The woman didn't say anything.

"Do you know where Mr. Garry went? How I might be able to find him?"

Now, the woman was annoyed and nothing else. She let out a sigh.

"Mr. Garry is dead."

20

———

Mr. Eastman—Geoff Eastman, I later learned—came down the metal stairs and crossed the lobby, extending a hand to me. He was wearing hiking shoes, khaki pants and a blue quarter-zip shirt with the Advantage logo on the chest. He was young, in his early thirties probably, much younger than I expected.

Eastman brought me back to his office, which was a glass-enclosed glorified cubicle looking out onto an open space that contained several desks and long worktables that held maps and rock samples. The room was empty, but there were signs of activity. I noticed the office next to Eastman's had a nameplate for Alan Garry.

"I'm sorry about Mr. Garry," I said as we sat down in Eastman's office. "I didn't know."

"It's all right. We're still in a bit of shock here. It just happened a few weeks ago."

"What happened? If you don't mind me asking."

"Car accident. Alan was out in the field doing some research, and his car went off the road and rolled and just exploded, went up in flames. It caused a huge plume of black smoke, which someone saw. Otherwise, probably no one would have known about it."

"Why is that?"

"He was out in the middle of nowhere taking samples. I don't know if anyone would have found his car."

"South of Fremont, out by Dan Perry's farm, by any chance?"

"Who? No, no, this was out east of here, out by the Elmore County line, just north of the freeway."

"Oh, okay, never mind."

"But you were asking about the Basin 63 study."

"I noticed that Advantage had a contract with the Department of Water Resources to do a study of Basin 63."

"Yeah, that was huge for us. Alan and I are a small outfit, and we won the contract to do that study. He and I went to the University of Idaho together, studied hydrogeology. We were looking for jobs our senior year, and there were quite a few jobs all over the country, all over the world, really, but Alan and I both wanted to stay in Idaho. You'd be surprised, but there aren't a ton of water outfits in Idaho. There's a couple of small firms in north Idaho and eastern Idaho, but they don't pay much. We both looked at PFS Resources and realized they were the only game in town. That's when we kind of looked at each other and said, 'Let's start our own firm.'"

"That's great."

"We struggled at first, for sure. It was tough to break in, especially with PFS looming over everything. We were David to their Goliath. And they're not the nicest people."

"How so?"

"They're underhanded. I mean, I guess it's just business, and they do what they gotta do. But I just think some of the things they do are unethical."

"Like what?"

"Well, they would swoop in and underbid on jobs when they saw we were bidding on something. They could afford to take a loss or break even on certain jobs, you know, if it meant screwing us out of a deal. We also heard they went around bad-mouthing us to a couple of developers, trying to sour them on using us for water work. I just don't like those guys."

"But you got the Basin 63 study?"

"Yeah, it was kind of crazy. It was a huge win for us. It wasn't a lot of money, but it was a lot of money for us at the time, and it would have put us on the map, given us legitimacy. It would have let us hire a couple of engineers, led to bigger jobs. We spent weeks putting together our proposal, cutting it as close as we could to bring in our bid as low as possible, knowing that PFS was going to try to outbid us."

"But clearly they didn't."

"That was the weird thing. They never even put in a bid."

"Really? Why do you think they didn't?"

"At the time, we didn't really know. We were suspicious. Obviously, they were an underhanded firm, we thought they would underbid again. We thought maybe it was just an error, they forgot to put in a bid or something, or they made a mistake on their bid, made them ineligible. But then it became clear."

"What happened?"

"The contract got canceled. I think PFS knew it was going to get canceled, so they didn't even bother putting in a bid. They were probably laughing at us the whole time, working our butts off to put together a winning bid. We even got a bottle of champagne and drank it in the office when we won the bid."

"But then it got canceled?"

"Yeah, out of the blue."

"Why did it get canceled?"

"I don't know. It seemed to be political. They just called us up one day and said, 'We're sorry, but we lost our funding for the study.'"

"Can they do that?"

"Apparently. The contract was contingent on funding approval, which we knew. So, fortunately, we didn't do anything until it was finalized. Alan had gotten started on the study, did some samples, put together a hydrology map of the whole basin. A lot of the work was already done as part of putting together our bid, and Alan wanted to get started on it right away. He was like a kid in a candy store with that study. He was ready and raring to go. We didn't go out and hire a bunch of people or anything like that. Otherwise, we would have sued for breach of contract."

"When did it get canceled?"

"It was just a couple of months later. It was when the legislature came back into session. They said something about the budget committee not approving the funding."

"That's too bad."

"Yeah, I mean, we were pretty disappointed, especially with all the work Alan had already put into it. But it turns out just winning that contract kind of put us on the map. We started getting more calls from developers and ranchers, and work really picked up. We ended up hiring a couple of engineers after all, and business has been really good since then."

"So do you still have the work you did on the Basin 63 study?"

"Definitely. I mean it's kind of strange that you're asking about it right now."

"Why's that?"

"Alan kind of never let that study go. He was always going back to it, bringing it up, he'd be sitting in his office"—he pointed his thumb behind him at Garry's office—"and he'd yell out, 'Hey Geoff, come and check this out.' I'd go over and see what he was looking at."

"And he was still working on it?"

"That's the sad thing. That's what he was doing way out in the desert when he got into the car accident."

"Really?"

"Yeah, he said there's a massive aquifer out there –" Eastman stood up. "Let me go grab the study. It's still in Alan's office."

Eastman returned with a three-inch-thick plastic binder and a cardboard tube. He laid them out on a conference table in his office. He uncapped the cardboard tube and unrolled a stack of maps onto the table, using a clip to the table on one end and the weight of the binder on the other. He opened the binder and flipped through several pages until he found the section he was looking for.

"I won't bore you with the details," he said. "But essentially, Alan had looked at the geology of this area out here." Eastman pointed to a section of the laid-out map. I could see it was well east of Boise, north of Interstate 84, just as Eastman had said. Eastman then returned to the binder and flipped another page to a cross section of rock layers. "He saw that the rock layers had subsumed and folded over time, with a layer of bedrock just here," he said, pointing to a dark-shaded band on the cross section. Above it was a layer of blue, which Eastman put his finger on. "And just above that, water. Now, it's pretty deep, about seven hundred to nine hundred feet, but it's massive."

"How massive?"

He turned a couple more pages in the binder and pointed to a chart that looked like hieroglyphics to me. "Have you heard of the East Snake River Plain Aquifer?"

"Actually, someone was just telling me about it."

"Well, they say that aquifer is the size of Lake Erie."

"Yes, I've heard that, too."

"This isn't quite as big, but it's about half the size of the East Aquifer. That's enough water for about three Boises."

"Whoa."

"That was his theory anyway. He was still working on it when he died in the crash."

I thanked Eastman for the information and repeated my condolences. I had Eastman print out a few of the pages from the study, including a map of the area Garry had been studying.

On my way back to my car, I called Jerry Hansen.

"Hey, Jerry, you find anything more about Brad Childs?" I asked.

"I'm still working on it, but this is..." Hansen trailed off and his voice lowered. "I don't know. This is...."

"What?"

"Bigger than I thought," he said very quietly now.

"How big?"

"I'll know more in a couple of days," Hansen said, now in a normal voice, as if someone had left the room. "I'll have to get back to you. It's strange. It doesn't make sense."

"Ah, damn it, Jerry, you're killing me," I said.

"I'll let you know more in a couple of days," Hansen repeated, this time with an air of finality.

"All right," I said, resigned. "You by any chance create an X account called MarkFelt08081974 and send me a direct message?"

"Sure didn't. I don't do that social media thing."

"Somebody did. Sent me a message about a study of Basin 63."

"Yeah, we've needed a study of the basin for a long time," Hansen said.

"But you guys approved a study a couple of years ago."

"We put the funding for it in our department budget, but it got killed at the last minute."

"What happened?"

"I don't know. It seemed to be a slam dunk. We had $250,000 in our budget for an aquifer study, which really isn't that much. But our budget has to get approved by the legislature each year. When our budget got to the Finance Committee, one of the legislators started questioning the study, really grilling us over the need for it and making statements about wasting taxpayer money, and all sorts of things. It really blindsided us, made us look pretty bad. The next thing we knew, our budget was approved without the money for the study."

"Just like that?"

"Just like that."

"Who was the legislator?"

"A guy by the name of John Broten."

21

———————

Lauren hadn't mentioned anything about her father killing a study of Basin 63.

As I walked to my car, which was still parked in front of the state capitol from earlier that morning, I called the Broten Law Firm and asked for Lauren.

"Hi, Philip." She sounded genuinely happy to hear from me. "What's up?"

"I had a couple more questions for you. Specifically about a study of Basin 63."

"Oh, you work fast," she said, which struck me as an odd thing to say.

"I heard that the Department of Water Resources had ordered up a study of Basin 63, even put out a bid for it, but then your father had helped kill the funding for it."

She was silent.

"Why did he do that?"

She was silent some more, and I thought maybe we had gotten disconnected.

"Lauren?"

"I'm just about to leave the office. If you're still downtown, maybe we could meet up."

"I am still downtown."

"Great. How about the Grove Hotel. About fifteen minutes?"

"Sounds good."

The Grove Hotel's lobby had been converted into a bar, literally called The Bar at the Grove Hotel. It was a brilliant move by the owners, because the lobby became a casual hangout and popular meeting place, like a hotel lobby from the 1930s. Overstuffed couches and chairs were scattered about, and a couple of high-backed semicircle booths were secreted away on the other side of the bar.

When I arrived, the lobby was already buzzing, with an eclectic mix of locals having a drink before the local minor pro team's hockey game that night, the Idaho Steelheads, some businesspeople meeting up for drinks after work, some couples waiting for dinner at the restaurant that was to the left of the lobby and then a collection of hotel guests, who I guessed were mostly from California—the men given away by their too-perfect fade haircuts, trimmed goatees, fitted T-shirts, and distressed, intentionally frayed jeans over flip-flops, the women given away by their botoxed faces and Gucci handbags.

I sat at the end of the bar, away from everyone else, and ordered a Sapphire and tonic. I told the bartender that a woman would be joining me and to be sure to put her drink on my tab.

I spotted her as soon as she walked in. Men in the lobby turned and watched her as she strode confidently past them across the lobby toward the bar. She must have seen me at the bar, because she walked right to me without that awkward pause and looking around the place.

"Hi, Philip," she said and sat down next to me.

The bartender came over, and she ordered an Aperol Spritz.

She looked around the lobby. "I haven't been here in a while. It's changed, I think. It's different."

"I've never been here, so I wouldn't know."

"I don't know, the furniture or something."

"The people, maybe?"

"How do you mean?"

"I feel like I'm not in Boise, like I've been transported somewhere else. These people are not from Idaho."

She looked around again. "My God, you're right. That's what it is. Look at all these people. Who are they?"

The bartender brought her drink, and she tried to give him her credit card. "All taken care of," he said, holding out a hand, palm facing her.

"You sneaky devil," she said to me. "Well, I'll get the next one."

I raised an eyebrow. "There's going to be a next one?"

"If you play your cards right."

I smiled, trying to come up with something clever to say, to keep the flirting going. I could feel my face blushing.

"Well, thank you," Lauren said, saving me. "And cheers."

"Cheers." We clinked glasses and sipped our drinks.

A couple of young men with backward baseball caps sat down next to Lauren, one of them giving her the once-over and then a glance at me. They loudly ordered shots of Jägermeister and Coors Light.

"Why don't we take one of those booths," Lauren said, nodding to the other side of the bar.

"I thought you'd never ask."

It was quieter in the booth, and I was surprised when Lauren scooched around the circular bench to sit next to me instead of across the table from me. When I sat down, our knees touched, and neither of us did anything to move them.

I didn't want to spoil the mood, but I needed to ask about her father.

"So what can you tell me about that study of Basin 63 and why your father wanted to kill it?"

Lauren seemed disappointed and sat back, her knee no longer touching mine.

"Getting right down to business, huh?"

"That's right."

"Well, my father and I don't always share the same political views, and that's all right. He's more conservative, although frankly you can't survive in this state if you're not a Republican. Honestly, we try not to let his work as a legislator interfere with our practice."

"How is that even possible? I mean, he's a lawyer who works on water rights issues and he votes on water rights issues as a legislator?"

"Idaho doesn't have too many guardrails. We're the 'least-regulated state in the union,' in case you hadn't heard," she said, using air quotes, quoting an oft-repeated slogan by the governor. "The legislature's conflict rules are a joke. Even if a bill would directly benefit a legislator, all he has to do is declare he has a conflict, and he can still vote on it. It's ridiculous." She spoke derisively now, something extra in her voice that I detected but couldn't put my finger on.

"Anyway," she continued, "we try to keep the legislature and the practice separate, so we don't talk much about it. He doesn't say, and I don't ask. But I think with the Basin 63 study, he said pretty publicly that he thought it was a waste of taxpayer money, that we do too many studies."

"Does he really believe that?"

"I suppose he does, and he wasn't the only one who voted against it. It wasn't like he was the one who killed it. But again, like I said, we don't talk about it. We keep the two things separate. You should ask him, though."

"I'd like to. Would I be able to catch him at the office?"

"Most of the time. Actually –" she said as if something had just occurred to her. "Actually, you can catch him at the capitol tomorrow morning."

"At this time of year?" The Idaho legislature was a part-time "citizens legislature," convening every January for a session that lasted typically until March or April. Legislators weren't in session in October.

"Yes, they have interim committees that meet when the legislature's not in session. My father is on the Natural Resources Committee, and they have a meeting scheduled for eleven a.m. tomorrow morning to go over a couple of bills ahead of the session. You can probably catch him there."

"I just might do that," I said.

Lauren sipped her drink and stole small glances at me.

"How long have you been working at the firm?" I asked her.

"About ten years now. Hard to believe how fast time goes by."

"Have you lived in Boise all your life?"

"Mostly. I grew up here, graduated from Boise High, but then I went back East for school."

"Where?"

"Villanova, then Columbia for law school."

"I'm impressed."

Lauren smiled. "Most people around here aren't. I tell them Columbia

Law School, and they just give me a blank stare, as if the only law school to go to is the University of Idaho."

"Well, I'm impressed."

"Right, because you're from back East."

How did she know that? I gave her a puzzled look.

"Or I'm assuming you're from back East, right?"

"Yes, Boston."

"So you know."

"Yeah, and Villanova, too. Great school. How did someone from Boise pick Villanova? I can't imagine a lot of people from here go there."

"My mom and dad went there. That's where they met."

"They must have been happy you picked their alma mater."

"Yes, Dad was very happy. My mother died when I was younger," she said plainly, without a hint of sadness.

"I'm sorry."

"It's all right. It was a long time ago. I was fourteen and my sister was eleven."

"You have a sister?"

"Yeah," she said and looked down and gave a kind of sad smile.

"Is she in Boise, too?"

"Oh yeah, she's still here."

"What does she do?"

Lauren shook her head slightly, dismissively. "Oh, I don't even know. Lots of things, I guess."

"So she's not in the family business, too?"

Lauren almost spit out her drink, choked a little bit and laughed. "No. Definitely not in the family business." But then her face became sad, and I sensed her retreat. Lauren shifted in her seat.

"So what brought you back to Boise?"

Again, Lauren's face fell, revealing that I had hit a sore spot I hadn't intended to hit. It was as if we were playing a game: I'll tell you something terrible about my past, you tell me something terrible about your past.

"Family stuff. My father wanted me to join him in the business. He wanted to get more involved in politics, and he needed help running the firm."

"No other family to help with the firm?"

"No, just me and my dad."

"So you've..." I paused, reluctant to ask the question, but I'd started the sentence and didn't feel like turning back. The gin had taken effect, and I was feeling bold, not myself. "Never been married?"

Lauren smiled and raised an eyebrow, acknowledging that I was venturing into different territory.

"No. Perhaps if I had stayed back East, I would have met someone, but not in Idaho."

"How come?"

"It's not easy being a smart, professional, educated single woman in Idaho."

"How so?"

"I didn't notice it when I was growing up. But living back East for several years and then coming back here was a bit of a shock. It's slim pickins around these parts." She nodded toward the bar. "Those two bros with the backwards baseball caps at the bar? That's the kind of man-child that Idaho is crawling with. Either that or these entitled rich white kids who were born on third base and think they've hit a home run just because they landed some low-level job in the governor's office, when in reality, their entitled rich white father knew some other entitled rich white guy. Big fish in a small pond, and they think coastal elites are the ones living in a bubble."

I just smiled and raised my eyebrows. Lauren laughed at herself.

"Sorry. Rant over."

"I guess I never thought about it."

"Trust me. It's brutal out there."

"Well, lucky for me, then," I said, the words coming from some other place. Lauren didn't seem to mind.

"Okay, your turn."

"What?"

"Where did you go to school?" she asked, changing the subject.

When I told her the name of the school, a small liberal arts school in Upstate New York, I was surprised that she had heard of it.

"Well, now it's my turn to be impressed."

I smiled politely.

"Your parents must have been proud."

"My mother was, yes."

"Not your dad?"

"Don't know where he is. He left when I was little. I never knew him."

"Oh, I'm sorry." She had moved back closer to me, I noticed.

"That's fine. Like you said, it was a long time ago." But I loathed that look of pity in her eyes, and I wanted to change the subject, not talk about myself anymore, but Lauren pressed on.

"How about you? Ever been married."

"No," I said, falling into my own trap.

"Ever come close?"

"I was engaged."

"Really?"

"Don't sound so surprised."

"No, I'm not. So what happened?"

I took a drink, thinking about how much I really wanted to share.

"Just didn't work out, I guess. I ... I guess I wasn't ready."

Lauren could tell it was a sore subject, so she didn't push me on it.

So there we were, two people poking at each other's bruises, wanting to know more about the other but not willing to share more about ourselves.

There was a pause, and we both took sips of our drinks. My mind raced to think of what to say next.

"You know, I thought about becoming a journalist," Lauren said, breaking the silence.

"Really?" I said, relieved at the change of subject.

"Yeah, when I was a freshman in college, I wasn't really sure what I was doing. I was taking a bunch of different classes, not really sure what my major was going to be. I was taking psychology and public policy and English classes. And my second semester, there was an introduction to news writing class that looked interesting. So I signed up. During class we read *All the President's Men*, the book by Bob Woodward and Carl Bernstein about how they uncovered the Watergate scandal. Do you know it?"

"Of course, it's what got me into journalism. Although I watched the movie first, when I was twelve years old, and I knew that's what I wanted to do."

"Well, I had the same reaction when I read the book."

"So what happened? Why didn't you stick with it?"

"It's funny, in a sad kind of way. I didn't realize it at the time, but looking back, I now recognize that when I told my father that I wanted to pursue journalism, his reaction was … less than enthusiastic. I mean, he didn't discourage it, he was always supportive of whatever I chose to do, but I know now that his tepid response was a signal that I picked up on, that he wasn't crazy about the idea. He said something like, 'That's interesting.' Plus, everyone studying journalism at Villanova was, well, kind of like you. They knew early on that they wanted to be a journalist, had been the editor of their high school newspaper, already had internships lined up for that summer, for God's sake. I just felt like I was way behind already and would need to do some serious catching up."

"Oh, I'm sure you would have done just fine. It's not rocket science."

"Well, and I guess I always knew Dad was expecting me to go into law and would support me in that. It just seemed like the easier path." She paused, looked down and took a sip of her drink. Then she seemed to snap out of it, looked up and smiled. "Not that I regret it," she said confidently. "I like being a lawyer, and I'm damn good at it. Still, I think about that sometimes, what if I had tried to be a reporter."

"Well, you'd be making a hell of a lot less money," I said, welcoming the chance to lighten the mood.

She laughed but didn't say anything.

"So, what brought you to Fremont?" she asked, swirling the ice in her drink.

"Honestly? I was laid off from my newspaper job in Boston," I admitted. "Cops-and-courts beat. Loved it."

"Really? I wouldn't have pegged you for a crime reporter," she said, raising an eyebrow.

"Yeah, well, I was good at it," I said a bit defensively. "I was always good at spotting details, digging up the story no one else had." I paused, remembering the rush of chasing a lead, the thrill of a breaking story. "It was more than a job, it was...a calling."

"Sounds intense," Lauren said, her voice laced with curiosity.

"It was. But the newspaper business is tough. Advertising dried up, circulation dropped...and then I was out of a job."

"That's rough," she sympathized.

"It was a double whammy," I confessed, the bitterness creeping into my voice. "Lost my job, lost my fiancée...all within a few weeks. I was kind of lost."

"So you decided to run away to Fremont?" Lauren's tone was light, but her eyes held a hint of understanding.

"Maybe," I conceded with a shrug. "Or maybe it was just time for a change. Saw the *Herald* was for sale and figured, why not?"

"And now you're the big fish in a small pond," Lauren teased, a playful glint in her eyes.

"Something like that." I chuckled. "Although, the locals aren't exactly rolling out the welcome mat."

"Small towns can be like that," Lauren said knowingly. "Takes time."

"I'm starting to wonder how much time," I admitted.

"So what else did you find out today?" she asked.

"Well, I met with Oscar Mason this afternoon."

"Oh, good. What'd he say?"

I had the odd feeling that we were co-conspirators now, working on the case together.

"Not much, really. It was more what he didn't say. I started out asking him about minimum water flows at the Snake River Dam, and he was very specific, but then when I started asking about Basin 63 and buying water rights, he got cagey."

"Interesting."

"I asked him how big the aquifer here is, and he just said it held plenty of water for years. Said we didn't need a study of it."

Lauren didn't say anything, just nodded and took a sip of her drink.

"But then I got an odd message from some anonymous person who said there had been a study of it, done by Advantage Land and Water."

"Oh?"

"I went and saw them today. One of the engineers was still working on the study of Basin 63, even after the funding got killed. He was in a car crash just a few weeks ago and was killed."

"Oh my God, that's terrible."

"Apparently, he was driving on a desert road, actually doing work on the Basin 63 study, when his car went off the road and went up in flames."

"That's awful. How old was he?"

"Young, probably in his early thirties. I talked to his partner today. They went to U of I together, started this firm right out of college. Just really sad."

"I had no idea," she said, which struck me as an odd thing to say.

"I think I might drive out there and see what he was working on."

"Be careful."

"Of what?"

"Well, I mean, those roads out there, they must be dangerous, if that guy just drove off the road and was killed. Just be careful driving."

I laughed. "Okay, I will."

Lauren finished her drink and looked at her watch. I must have looked visibly disappointed at the prospect of ending the evening. Lauren put her hand on my forearm and moved closer so our knees were touching again.

"This has been nice," she said.

"I'm glad you asked me. I'm glad I came."

"I'm glad you came, too. I'd like to do it again."

"Me too."

I drained my drink, and we stood up to leave.

"I'll walk you to your car," I said.

Outside, the evening was mercifully beginning to cool. I liked the feeling of the two of us walking together as if we were a couple, and I resisted the urge to reach out and hold her hand.

"Next time, you'll have to tell me more about buying a newspaper and moving all the way out to Idaho."

I laughed. "Yeah, that's a good one."

We got to her car, and Lauren held out her hand, preempting any sort of awkward hug. "Thanks again, Philip. This was fun."

The gin still had an effect on me, and a fleeting thought crossed my mind to pull her in and kiss her. She looked me in the eyes, and I sensed an invitation.

"So Natural Resources Committee hearing tomorrow morning, eleven a.m.," she said abruptly, knocking me out of my dream state.

"Right. Tomorrow morning. I'll be there."

We shook hands like two business associates at a conference. We said our goodbyes, and I was deflated.

I slowly walked the few blocks back to my car. I was in no rush. I had already begun to replay our conversation in my head, hoping I hadn't said anything foolish, hoping I had conveyed my interest, regretting I hadn't been more forward, remembering the touch of her hand. And, though I couldn't place its source, something else about our conversation made me uneasy.

22

___

Hernandez was still at his office Wednesday night. He was tired. He felt the pressure to solve the Thompson murders, knowing everyone in town was expecting him to do his job. He had experienced imposter syndrome all his life, especially being Hispanic in a state like Idaho, and he always had to work harder than everyone else, be better than everyone else and never make a mistake just to be accepted. He chronically believed that some people were watching and waiting for him to slip up, proving them right all along that someone like Hernandez wasn't up to the task.

With each passing day that the Thompson murders were unsolved, Hernandez felt like everyone was watching him, looking to him, almost as if they blamed him for the murders because he had not yet solved the case after just a couple of days, like on TV.

He knew in his mind that these were not rational thoughts, but they nagged him all the same. They drove him to be better.

The day before, the director of the Idaho State Police had called Hernandez and informed him that the state police would be assisting in the case. He said the governor had directed him to "help out in any way we can."

Hernandez knew he should welcome the assistance, but mostly he was insulted, perhaps irrationally, that the big boys were coming in to save the day because Hernandez couldn't get the job done. He knew it was irrational, but still it motivated him.

So back to the office he went after dinner with his family Wednesday night to read the reports on the Thompson murders again.

He lived by the mantra that the answer was always there, somewhere, just waiting for you to find it.

Hernandez read reports voraciously, completely and repeatedly, where others just skimmed them. He believed that by slowly and patiently reading the reports and looking at the evidence over and over again, he was able to absorb details of the case and wire his brain to find the solution.

After the third shift came on that night, debriefed with the second shift and then headed out on patrol, the office was quiet, and Hernandez could concentrate.

He spent an hour or so reading the reports again and forcing himself to look at the photos from the crime scene.

He pulled out the evidence baggie that contained the slip of paper found at the scene, held it up and tried to think of a way to figure out what the numbers meant.

On a whim, he typed one of the numbers into Google. The search yielded a jumble of products that had those serial numbers, ranging from drums of glycol to electrical switches, cables and watches.

Then he added "Idaho" to the search along with the number. That only yielded a salary calculator and a couple of court cases. *Perhaps these are court cases*, he thought. But the court cases that came up didn't seem to involve Vern or Wanda Thompson.

So he added Vern Thompson's name to the search.

One of the results, the second one down, below a sponsored ad for a real estate company, was an entry of a water rights application with the Idaho Department of Water Resources. The number of the water rights application matched the number on the slip of paper but had the number "63" in front of it. In bold was "PROTESTANT: VERN THOMPSON."

"Holy …." Hernandez whispered to himself.

He clicked on the link, which took him to a water rights application filed by a company called Coyote Flats. Hernandez opened each of the four files, and in the third file, there were two protests, including one by Vern Thompson.

Hernandez excitedly downloaded each of the files, then grabbed the baggie with the piece of paper in it and typed in the next number on the list.

Again, he came up with a water rights application, this time filed by a company called SB 44. Again, a protest had been filed by Vern Thompson.

Hernandez went through the list of numbers, each one matching a water rights application, each one with a protest filed by Vern Thompson.

He wasn't sure if this had anything to do with their murders, but so far it was the best lead he had. He made a note to call the Secretary of State office in the morning and get the business licenses for the companies listed on the water rights.

The lights of the Fremont police station stayed on late into the night, and John Hernandez was still at his desk when the third shift came back from patrol.

23

By Thursday morning, the Thompson murders already were old news in the papers and on TV.

It gave me an advantage, because with additional details and photos, my story the following week would seem new to readers. Still, the speed with which the Thompson murders had disappeared from the news cycle was stunning. I had been in the news business long enough to notice the dramatic change in how reporters and editors covered events. It wasn't necessarily the internet that changed how journalists covered the news. It was the advent of social media that seemed to change everything. Gone were the days of covering smaller events like ribbon cuttings and most school board meetings. Coverage of city budgets and ordinance changes was gone. Most government coverage, in fact, had been decimated. If something wasn't going to go viral or get read by thousands of people, it wasn't worth doing anymore. So journalists stuck with chasing only the big stories that were going to get a lot of pageviews on their websites, like the Thompson murders.

Being a reporter was like setting a match to a bundle of dry pine needles. The fire burned quickly and brightly but died out just as fast.

The story flashed on Facebook and X for an hour or two, maybe a few hours, then the story disappeared. Readers voraciously consumed the story, gorged on it, and then they were done with it. Once they had their fill, they stopped clicking on it, and incremental updates were ignored. They stopped commenting, speculating, fighting, sharing. They simply moved on to the next story, and reporters knew it, too, so they moved on. Reporters stopped chasing it, knowing any effort they put into follow-up stories wouldn't be rewarded with pageviews.

I had not spent much time at the Idaho State Capitol, but I knew my way around well enough. It was referred to as "the People's House," and access to the building was remarkably open. Anyone could walk into the capitol building just about any time of day and roam around. You might even pass by the governor, secretary of state or attorney general who all had offices in the capitol. It was a traditional, classic capitol building, complete with a central dome and wings to the east and west.

To the east was the House side, and to the west was the Senate side. The governor, attorney general and secretary of state all had offices on the second floor. In debates, you were supposed to never refer to the "governor"; you referred to him as "the gentleman on the second floor."

The basement level, euphemistically called "the garden level," was where the real action happened. This was where the committee hearing rooms were, where bills went to live or die. I was struck by how little debate or information was presented on the floor of either the House or the Senate once a bill got out of committee. The legislature was dominated by the Republican Party, which meant the committees were dominated by Republican legislators, so if a bill made it out of committee—often on party lines with a "do-pass" recommendation—it was as good as a done deal.

Fitting, too, that the press room and an office for lobbyists were on the garden level.

I made my way to the east wing, where the Natural Resources Committee typically met during the session.

Inside, eight committee members, casually dressed, sat at the committee podium, and only five or six people sat in the audience. Instead of sitting at the designated press table, I took up my preferred position at the far-right seat in the front row of the audience, so I could see and hear the deliberations and also look back at the audience.

I was a little late, and a man in a gray suit was at the lectern discussing logging applications on federal land. I recognized him as Daniel Smith, director of the State Department of Lands. Smith spoke for another fifteen minutes. From what I could gather, the state wanted to expedite logging on state and federal lands to head off the disaster of wildfires amid the acceleration of climate change.

Committee members asked a few questions and mostly just nodded their heads. I located John Broten at the committee table. He was dressed in a suit and stood out among the other casually dressed committee members. Broten listened intently and took careful notes.

Looking back at the audience, I took note of a couple of other people, including one in a blue suit wearing a green name tag, denoting he was a lobbyist. Another man in the corner looked like he was on his way to Sun Valley, dressed in hiking pants and a plaid shirt with a puffy vest over it. He was young, forties, fit, good-looking, with dark hair, goatee and mustache and a high-and-tight fade haircut popular with much younger hipsters. He was leaning back, scrolling through his phone, disinterested in the logging presentation.

"Thank you, Director Smith," the committee chairman said. "Up next, we will hear from Archibald Crane for the Idaho Liberty Coalition on place of use requirements in Idaho water law."

I noticed that the man in the corner put away his phone and sat up.

"Mr. Chairman, committee members, thank you for this hearing today," Archibald Crane said as he stood at the lectern. "As we all know, water rights in Idaho are a sensitive subject. We also know that private property rights are fundamental rights that we hold in the highest regard here in Idaho, unlike in some other states."

The Idaho Liberty Coalition, I knew, was a dark money lobbying outfit that painted itself as a free-market think tank, as if its positions were simply philosophically driven to promote the well-being of Idaho through the principles of freedom and liberty. In reality, as most people knew, the Idaho Liberty Coalition was part of a network of similar nonprofit think tanks and foundations set up in states across the country to influence gullible legislators to pass laws amenable to its funders. For sure, some of the positions may have been ideologically pure, but the funders' fingerprints were all over most legislation, painting a clear picture of their motives. School voucher legislation masquerading as "parental freedom" and "school choice" was really an attempt to funnel tax dollars to private education companies. Other legislation was based on dogmatic ideals of small-government free-market solutions that tended to ignore reality in favor of a version of reality that existed only in an Ayn Rand novel.

I listened as Crane explained to the Natural Resources Committee that current state law regarding place of use for water rights was an undue over-reach of state government and an infringement on private property rights.

"The Fourteenth Amendment of the United States Constitution states," Crane went on, holding up his pocket copy of the Constitution, "'nor shall any State deprive any person of life, liberty, or property, without due process of law.'"

They loved to trot out the Constitution and twist it and mangle it to suit whatever argument they had. It seemed they could find any sort of consti-tutional justification for whatever law they wanted to pass, whether it was nefarious or not. Some of these legislators ate it up, daydreaming about living among the landed gentry of revolutionary times. The mere utterance of the year 1776 sent them into a dreamlike state of reverie. Crane and the Idaho Liberty Coalition knew that these simpletons only needed to hear the word "Constitution," and they were golden.

"The state's place of use and point of diversion laws are a violation of that Fourteenth Amendment by denying the right to property without due process of law," Crane said. I noted that he had added "point of diversion" in his presentation, adding a concerning wrinkle. "It is an affront to liberty and freedom to restrict legally obtained private property owners' water rights by further placing an encumbrance as to place of use and point of diversion. It constitutes, in essence, a taking by the government, and I submit to this committee that it is a violation of the Idaho Constitution and the Constitution of the United States of America as well as Idaho's Local Land Use Planning Act."

Well, I thought, *old Crane certainly got in all the trigger words in a very short speech.*

I noticed the man in the corner lean back in his chair. I had a thought. I pulled out my phone and did an image search for "Brad Childs Idaho." Nothing. Not a check-passing photo, not a ribbon-cutting photo. Not a feature story or a chamber award. Brad Childs's LinkedIn profile didn't even have a photo of him. Still, I was willing to bet this was my man.

"With that, Mr. Chairman, I'll stand for any questions," Crane wrapped up.

"Thank you, Mr. Crane," said the chairman, Sen. Harris Christianson, of Grace, a tiny town in east Idaho. "That was a most informative presentation, certainly very eye-opening. Are there any questions from the committee? Yes, Senator Broten."

"Thank you, Mr. Chairman," Broten spoke up. "Thank you, Mr. Crane, for your presentation today. This is more of a statement than a question. This is a really important matter for Idaho. Water use is vital for the future of our state, and how and where that water is used shouldn't be decided by the government," he said smoothly, as if reading from a script. "It should be up to the free market. The free market knows best how and where to use water. The federal government right now is trying to pass the Waters of the United States Act to regulate every ditch, canal, pond and mud puddle in your backyard, infringing on the rights of every American. That's not how we do things in Idaho. That's not the Idaho way. We believe in small government and the free market. Those ideals have carried the state to be classified as having the most freedom of any state in the union, the least-regulated state in America. This proposal before us today is a great example of how we can continue Idaho on that path to freedom."

Broten turned his head toward the chairman. "Thank you, Mr. Chairman."

Then he turned toward Crane. "Thank you."

And then Broten did something just barely noticeable but to me was significant. Broten said "thank you" one more time and nodded in the direction of the man in the corner.

24

———

"Our next order of business," Sen. Christianson said, moving on to the final item on the agenda, something about a phosphate mine in east Idaho.

The man in the corner got up and started to leave the hearing room. I decided to play my hunch and followed the man out into the corridor.

"Excuse me," I said, catching his attention in the near-empty corridor.

The man just turned and looked at me, inscrutable.

"Brad Childs?" I said.

"Do I know you?" the man said.

"I'm Philip Chandler with the *Fremont Herald*," I said, and instead of extending my hand, I pulled out my notebook and pen.

"Yeah?" I felt a little bit like the dog that catches the car. My hunch was right, but now what?

"You're Brad Childs, right?"

"Yes," Childs said impatiently.

"I'm doing a story on Canadian lumber tariffs that the president is proposing and I've been looking for a builder to talk to about the impact that would have on homebuilding." I had read a story in the paper that morning on the tariffs and thought that would be an interesting story. But how that just popped into my head, I didn't quite know.

Childs smiled a smile that was not friendly. "Canadian lumber tariffs, huh?"

"Right," I said, my pen poised above my notebook.

Childs looked at the notebook, then back up into my eyes.

"Sure. That tariff is the dumbest thing in the world," Childs said, peering back down over my notebook. "We've got an affordable housing crisis right now, and this will only make it worse. They are crazy to do something like that. At a time like this, it's just irresponsible. And you can quote me on that."

He waited for me to write that down.

"You said you were Philip Chandler from the *Fremont Herald*?"

I looked up from my notebook. "Right."

"And you're working on a story about lumber tariffs?" Childs said.

"Right," I said.

"Funny, I heard you were working on a story about water rights."

I realized that Oscar Mason must have called Childs and told him that he had spoken with me. I pivoted quickly.

"Yeah, I am," I said, feigning ignorance. "Say, is that something you'd be able to talk about?"

"Not really," Childs said.

"I mean, being a home builder, you must deal a lot with water rights."

"No, not really," Childs said, almost facetiously, as if challenging me. I sensed now that there was a kind of understanding between us, and I decided to push it.

"Well, this bill on changing place of use and point of diversion rules"—I pointed a thumb toward the committee room we had just come from—"would make it easier for you to move water rights around, wouldn't it?"

"I have no idea," Childs said, squinting, his hands now on his hips.

"That's funny," I said.

"What's funny?"

"Just that there's a bill making it easier for you to move water rights around and you saying you have no idea about it."

Childs didn't say anything, but he didn't turn and walk away, either.

"It just seems like that's why you're here," I pressed on. "You weren't really paying attention to anything else except for the testimony on this bill, and then once it was done, you got up and left. Do you have an interest in this bill?"

Childs didn't say anything but just stood there assessing me. I had learned as a journalist to live in silent moments like this. In a normal conversation, humans have a natural tendency to hate silence and rush to fill it by saying something. While interviewing people, I had learned long ago to let it linger, allowing my subject to rush to say something. Too many journalists are too quick to ask another question. Good interviewers, I knew, let the other person say something first. I was always amazed by what people said just to fill the silence. Sometimes I would just sit and nod and wait. Sometimes I would pretend to be writing in my notebook. But it seldom failed that, when I stayed quiet, the other person blinked first, and they usually said something to break the spell.

I stared back, my pen hovering over my notebook. Childs finally broke.

"No, don't know much about that stuff."

"Okay, you don't know much about that stuff," I said, dropping my hands to my sides. I decided to push my luck just a little more.

"What about F9 Development?"

Childs tensed, and I had the distinct feeling that he was holding back from punching me.

"What about it?"

"That's a company that you set up and used to apply for water rights on property south of Fremont?" I pulled my notebook back up and held my pen to it.

"And?"

"What do you plan to do with that water?"

"None of your business." Childs looked at his watch with a bored expression on his face.

"Well, I –"

"Look, I don't really know what story you're working on or what story you think you're working on, or what you're trying to insinuate, but I would stay out of my business if I were you," he said. "I'm not interested in talking to you, and I'm not interested in having any story about me in your paper. I'd advise you to quit nosing around in my business."

"I don't need your permission to do my job," I said, feeling my face flush with rising anger.

"If you write one word about me, I'll have my lawyers all over you. And I don't think you'd want that."

"Why would you need to get your lawyers involved? Have you done anything illegal?" I raised my notebook again.

"We're done here," Childs said curtly, turned and walked away.

I considered following him and asking him more questions. But I figured I had pushed my luck enough for one day with Childs. Plus, I wanted to corner Broten after the committee hearing and I wanted to get back in.

"Thanks for your time, Mr. Childs," I said to his back. "I appreciate it."

Childs continued down the marble corridor.

25

───────

Back in the committee hearing room, the manager of a phosphate mine in eastern Idaho was explaining that phosphate was a naturally occurring mineral and that elevated levels of phosphorus in drinking water was not necessarily a bad thing. I looked around the room and saw that no one else from the press was there to report on this. Broten, along with the other Republican members of the committee, nodded in encouragement, and the two Democrats just looked at each other in disbelief as if to say, "Just shoot me now."

When the presentation was over, the chairman again opened the floor to questions, and this time another Republican legislator, whom I did not recognize, made his "This is more of a statement and not a question" statement, explaining how important this issue was to the sovereignty of the state in the managing of its own natural resources and how he looked forward to hearing this come forward in the upcoming legislative session.

The chairman then adjourned the hearing, and committee members milled about, chatting, while a couple of members headed for a door behind them, allowing them an exit without having to actually confront the public.

Broten shuffled papers and chatted with the legislator next to him, glancing up briefly as I made my way to the committee table. I was practiced at the skill of conducting interviews over the transom like this, having done so dozens of times after city council and school board meetings. But I realized I was still a little shaky with adrenaline from my confrontation with Childs.

"Senator Broten?" I said.

"Yes?" Broten looked up impatiently.

"I'm Philip Chandler with the *Fremont Herald*."

"I figured that was you sitting there," Broten said. I didn't know what he meant or how to respond. "My daughter Lauren told me that you might come to the meeting today to ambush me." He let out a chuckle and glanced at the legislator next to him, who took it as his cue to leave.

Broten spoke to the legislator sitting next to him. "See you in a couple of months."

Broten then turned back to me. "What can I do for you?"

I decided to be direct. "I wanted to ask you about a study of the Treasure Valley aquifer, Basin 63."

"Yes? What about it?" he said impatiently.

"Why did you kill the funding for it?"

"Well, I didn't kill it," he said. "I was opposed to it, but I can't unilaterally kill something. That was a decision of the budget committee."

"Which you're a member of?"

"Yes."

"So why did you oppose it?"

"It's unnecessary. We've got plenty of water. We haven't had any issues. And spending money on yet another water study would simply be a waste of taxpayer dollars."

I wrote all of that down in my notebook. "How do we know there aren't any issues if a comprehensive study isn't done?"

"We haven't heard of any problems from anyone. No dry wells, no issue finding water. It'll be years in the future. Why go looking for problems before there are any?"

"Didn't the Idaho Department of Water Resources recommend a study be done?"

"Of course," Broten said, with a tinge of indignation. "It's not their money. They always want to study everything. Study this, study that, they live for studies."

I continued writing all of this down.

"What's this story you're working on?" Broten asked.

"Well, I'm not really sure, just trying to figure out the whole water situation out here," I said, playing dumb, putting Broten somewhat at ease.

Broten chuckled condescendingly. "It's pretty complicated," Broten said. "You'd probably be better off just sticking to Fremont city council meetings," he said. I couldn't tell if he was being patronizing or threatening. Or something else. I had the strange feeling that Broten was being protective of me.

"Well, still," I said. "I'd like to figure out what the water situation is and what this bill has to do with it."

"Well," Broten said and stood up, prepared to slip out the back door himself, "like I said, it's pretty complicated." He looked at his watch. "And I'm afraid I don't have a lot of time to explain it to you."

"I mean, I couldn't figure out why a developer like Brad Childs would have an interest in the issue," I said.

"What's that?" Broten let his portfolio slide from his chest to his hip.

"Brad Childs, the developer? Summers Building Company? He was sitting in the back there," I said, pointing to the corner seat where Childs had been sitting. "You gave him a little nod at the end there. I couldn't figure out what his interest in place of use and point of diversion regulations would be. I had to go chase after him in the hallway to ask him."

"What did he tell you?" Broten asked a little too quickly.

"Oh, not much," I said. "He said he didn't really know anything about water."

I knew Childs's assertion that he didn't know anything about water was preposterous, and Broten's involuntary grunt confirmed it.

I continued to hold my pen above my notebook. "Do you know why a developer like Brad Childs would have an interest in this bill?"

"No, I can't say that I do," Broten said, looking at my notebook.

"If place of use and point of diversion laws are changed, would a developer be able to take water rights from, say, anywhere, and just use them somewhere else, anywhere else he wanted to?" I asked.

"Yes, that's the point," Broten said, now impatiently. "Why should the government be able to tell the market where to use private water rights? It's picking winners and losers." Another favorite catch phrase of the anti-government types, as if the government wasn't already doing that every damn day.

"Because it's not their water, is it?" I said, trying not to sound challenging. "Doesn't the water still belong to the state? The state still owns the water but grants people the right to use it. Use it for beneficial use."

"Right, and as long as it's put to beneficial use, the state shouldn't be sticking its nose in the private market," Broten said.

I could tell that Broten was just going to keep repeating the same talking points and sound bites that he clearly had become so accustomed to repeating. He was good. So good that it seemed he had repeated the words and justifications enough times that he was beginning to believe them himself. But I knew there were real reasons behind those words, reasons that had nothing to do with beneficial use and the free market. Did he even know about the murders of Vern and Wanda Thompson? He seemed too cool and collected to be aware of it.

"So where would Childs use his water rights? If he's not going to use them where he's applied for them?"

Broten now looked impatient. "Look, I don't know what his business is. If you want to know, you should ask him. Don't ask me."

"I already –"

Broten interrupted me. "But if I were you, I would stay out of Mr. Childs's business. If he's not interested in talking to you, he's not interested in talking to you, and you should take the hint and drop it."

"With all due respect, Senator Broten, you're the one who's the public official here, answerable to the people. You helped kill a water study of Basin 63, and now you're supporting changes to place of use laws that benefit Mr. Childs. I think you owe your voters an explanation about why you're making these decisions."

"I've already given you my explanation," Broten said, more angrily. "If that's not the explanation that you want to hear, that's not my problem. As for owing my voters anything, the last I checked, my voters aren't in

Fremont," he said the last word with a sneer. "And my voters don't read your little paper."

"But you represent the entire state, not just Boise, Senator," I said. "And that includes my readers, some of whom are affected by this bill. Don't you owe them an explanation?"

"I think we're done here," Broten said coldly. "I really don't have time for this. I've got another meeting to get to. Good luck with your story," Broten said as he turned and slipped out the back door.

It was the second time that morning someone had run out on me. I must be doing something right.

26

John Hernandez decided to go see Brad Childs personally, rather than send one of his officers or someone from the state police.

He had kept the water rights applications to himself, rather than look like he was playing detective to his men or to the state police.

Besides, he knew Childs was a big player, apparently with connections, and if he wanted to keep his suspicions quiet, he'd best keep his information to himself, rather than share it with others, who might leak it to the press.

Hernandez sat on a silver metal and gold fabric chair in the front sitting area of the Summers Builders office on Chinden Boulevard and waited. For a big outfit, the Summers office was modest. It was housed in a strip mall from the seventies between a Mexican bakery and a portrait photo studio. The interior had been remodeled, with dark, hardwood floors, bright yellow paint on the walls and an open floor plan that exposed the full office from front to back, with sunlight pouring into the full space. But the office furniture was spare and old, as if original to whatever had been there in the 1970s.

A secretary at the green-metal front desk said Childs was tied up in a hearing at the capitol and was running late, but he had texted her and let her know that he was on his way for his appointment with Fremont's police chief.

Hernandez mused that a man like Childs, whose reputation Hernandez was familiar with, likely often made people wait. It wasn't really about time management or organization. Intentional or not, Hernandez knew that for people like Childs, it was all about control, sending a message, consciously or not, about who was in charge, whose time was more valuable, who would wait for whom.

Hernandez looked out the front window as a young, noticeably attractive woman in tight jeans and a tight T-shirt got out of a beat-up Hyundai Sonata and entered the photo studio next door. Something about her struck him as odd, but he let the thought drift away as he glanced back into the Summers Builders office space, wondering how long Childs would make him wait.

It was fifteen more minutes before Childs emerged, apparently having parked behind the building and entered through a back doorway. He didn't seem pleased to see Hernandez, nor apologetic for making him wait.

"I was at the statehouse for a meeting," Childs said dismissively as he led Hernandez to an office, which again, to Hernandez, was surprisingly spare and modest.

"Well, thanks for meeting with me," Hernandez said as he sat in a low chair facing Childs's desk, where Childs sat in a raised executive's chair, the only modern piece of furniture in the room.

"What can I do for you?" Childs said as he moved his mouse on his desk to bring his computer alive.

"Do you know Vern Thompson?" Hernandez asked as he pulled a small notebook and pen out of his breast pocket.

"Thompson?" Childs said, briefly glancing away from his computer screen to look at Hernandez. "Can't say that I do."

"He filed some protests against a few water rights that you had applied for."

"Okay."

"But the name doesn't sound familiar to you?"

"No. I file a lot of water applications, and there are a lot of protests."

Hernandez made a point of writing that down in his notebook and let an uncomfortable silence fill the room.

"Look," Childs said, now pulling his full attention away from his computer and giving it to Hernandez. "I file a lot of applications for lots of different things. Water rights, building permits, sewer permits, land sales. I can't keep track of every little farmer who files a protest against one of my applications."

"But you know he's a farmer," Hernandez said, noting that he hadn't shared that fact with Childs. He watched as Childs's eyes moved rapidly from side to side.

"I just assumed," Childs said. "You said he filed a protest against one of my water rights. Farmers out there are doing that all the time."

Out there. Again, Hernandez picked up that Childs knew what he was talking about but wasn't being forthcoming. He held off confronting him on that, though, not wanting to be too combative so quickly.

"And developers, too, I'd imagine," Hernandez said, trying to sound sympathetic to Childs's challenges.

"Yes, them, too. It's a competitive business. Dog eat dog. Developers will protest just to slow the competition down any way they can."

"Got it," Hernandez said, writing all that down. "But now Vern Thompson was just a farmer, not a developer. Why would a farmer file a water protest?"

"Just to make sure their water's protected, I guess."

"But you never heard of Vern Thompson."

"No, can't say that I have."

"But he filed several protests against several of your applications."

"Did he? Again, I just can't keep track of every person who files some sort of protest against every kind of application I have going."

"Even if it was several. It just seems like one or two I could understand, but if someone has filed a bunch, like seven or eight, it just seems like that's something you'd notice."

"Well, it's not," Childs said testily with a sigh. "It's not."

"Got it."

"What is this all about, anyway? What does this have to do with me?"

"Vern Thompson and his wife were found shot and killed down in Fremont last week. Maybe you saw it on the news."

"I think I saw something about that. I don't follow the news much, but I heard about that. That was his name, then? Vern Thompson?"

"Yeah, and I'm afraid we just don't have any leads to go on," Hernandez said, doing his best to sound like a country bumpkin police chief. "We're just trying to follow up on anything that might be of any significance at all, anything he was involved in. This was just one of those things we noticed and need to cross off the list."

"Well, I'd say you can cross that off the list," Childs said. "Like I said, it's just a routine exercise we're used to going through. We file an application, someone files a protest. It's just the nature of the business. Not a big deal. Hardly something someone would get killed over."

"Right." Hernandez smiled and shook his head, feigning embarrassment at even daring to suggest it. But he knew from experience that people had been killed for much, much less. "Right."

Childs stood up abruptly, signaling an end to their meeting. Hernandez got up as well and offered his hand.

"Well, thanks again for taking the time to meet with me," Hernandez said as they shook hands.

"Any time," Childs said. "You know we support the blue around here."

"I appreciate that."

They exited Childs's office, and Hernandez could now see the back door and back parking lot, which held a dark-blue BMW.

"Oh, is that your car?" Hernandez asked.

"Uh, yeah, it is," Childs said hesitantly.

"Nice, is that a B6?"

"Yeah. You know about cars?"

"Sure. That an Alpina?"

"It is," Childs said proudly.

"Wow. Don't see too many of them around these parts."

"No you don't."

"Mind if I take a look?"

"Not at all."

Outside, Hernandez gave a low whistle as he circled the car.

"Nope," Hernandez said admiringly. "Don't see too many of these around here."

He made his way to the rear of the vehicle, where he squatted and closed one eye, looking down the length of the car.

"Look at those lines," Hernandez said, doing his best to sound like a hayseed. Meanwhile, he glanced over at the rear tire. It was a Falken Azenis FK510. Not a Pirelli Scorpion.

"Beautiful car, Mr. Childs. Thanks for letting me look at it."

"Of course. Thanks."

They reentered the office and made their way to the front door and sitting area, where a bald, beefy man sat in a chair reading *Shooting Times* magazine. One leg was crossed over the other, and Hernandez saw a bulge at his ankle and the end of a leather holster barely peeking out from the hem of his jeans. When the man saw Hernandez, he shifted in his chair, put his leg down and ran a hand over his shiny head and looked away. Hernandez made a mental note.

"Well, thanks again for stopping by, Chief," Childs said as the two shook hands again, and Hernandez exited.

In the parking lot, next to the beat-up Hyundai Sonata was a black Cadillac Escalade with a personalized license plate PMPD UP, which he assumed belonged to the burly guy in the office. He could feel himself being watched as he got into his own vehicle. He pulled out and drove slowly past the Escalade, making a note of the tires.

27

———————

After leaving the Natural Resources Committee hearing, I stopped off at the press room down the hall on the garden level of the capitol building. It was an appropriately shabby affair, with old wooden desks salvaged from an earlier day and enough dingy cubicles for a dozen reporters cramped into the small, poorly ventilated space. Since the legislature wasn't in session, I had the room to myself, and I set up shop on a large oak table to the right of the door.

I called Jerry Hansen's cell phone.

"I figured you'd be calling back," Hansen said.

"So, I've got a couple more questions," I said. "I was hoping you could help me out."

"And I think I've got some more info for you," Hansen said. "How about we meet somewhere?"

"Sure," I said, hopeful.

Hansen paused for a moment. "You know the Capri on Fairview Avenue?"

I knew it. It was an old-school diner in a part of town that used to be car dealership row. The car dealerships had long moved out, to larger lots along the freeway west of the city, leaving scattered pockets of entire city blocks vacant except for weeds poking up through cracks in the pavement.

The area was starting to get discovered, and the old-time owners of buildings and lots were starting to sell out to developers putting in high-rise apartment buildings. The Capri was still a holdout, one of the last vestiges of those older days. It had a ten-foot rooster that turned on its roof and sat in front of a two-story motel that was a throwback to the sixties and had seen better days.

I looked at my watch. "Meet you there in about twenty minutes?"

"See you there."

I sat at a corner booth with my back to the wall and a view out the window to the parking lot and Fairview Avenue. Hansen pulled up in his F-150 and made his way to the booth.

"So do you have some information for me?" I asked.

"It depends on what you're asking," Hansen said. "I didn't want to talk about the stuff at the office. I wasn't alone. All right. What can I tell you?"

"How important are the state's place of use laws?"

"Pretty important," Hansen said.

I ordered a scone and coffee, Hansen a coffee and homemade cinnamon roll.

"So yeah, when you file an application, you have to tell us where you're going to use the water, and you can't change it, unless you jump through a whole new set of hoops. You can't just say, 'Oh, I'm going to take that water out of the ground here and use it over there, somewhere else.'"

"Got it."

"The thing about water in Idaho that people don't understand is that all water in Idaho is owned by the state. When someone gets a 'water right'"—Hansen made air quotes with his fingers—"that just means they get the right to use the water. They don't actually own it. It's not theirs to keep or use however they want, wherever they want. The state gets to tell you when, where, how, and how much water you get to use. In a way, the user is just kind of borrowing the water from the state."

"What about point of diversion?"

"Same thing," Hansen said. "When you get a water right, you have to tell the state where it's coming from, the point of diversion."

"So if the state were to get rid of place of use and point of diversion requirements..." I said.

Hansen chuckled and shook his head. "Never happen," Hansen said. "It's practically written in stone. It's deeply ingrained in our water laws."

"Well, the Natural Resources Committee just heard a proposal on it."

"What?" Hansen was visually surprised and angry.

"There's a proposed bill to change place of use and point of diversion laws."

"How do you know this?"

"It was just presented to the Natural Resources Committee."

"What? When?"

"This morning."

"Are you kidding me? Who brought it?" His voice rose, turning the heads of a couple of people at the counter.

"Idaho Liberty Coalition."

"Those sons of –" He cut himself short. "Of course. Was anyone else there? Was Fredericks there?" he said, referring to the Idaho Department of Water Resources director, Hansen's boss.

"I don't think so. I don't know what Fredericks looks like, but there weren't many people there. He certainly didn't testify. Just the Idaho Liberty Coalition guy."

"Those sons of –" He cut himself short again.

"But Brad Childs was there," I said, pleased that I could pass information to Hansen, hoping that he would return the favor.

Hansen sat back, looked at me and shook his head slowly. "Of course he was," Hansen said, almost to himself, as if he were putting the pieces together himself. "Of course he was."

"So those water rights I was looking at," I said. "Childs can now consolidate them and use them somewhere else if that bill passes?"

"You don't know the half of it," Hansen said. "Actually, to be more accurate..." He paused and looked up in the air, calculating. "You don't know the quarter of it."

"Okay."

"After you called me and asked me about the manila envelope you got and Brad Childs being connected to F9 Development, I did some more looking into those applications," Hansen said. "I did some reverse engineering—a reverse search—and I found about twenty-five more applications just like it."

"So, like, thirty to thirty-five applications?"

Hansen nodded.

"How much water?"

"Each one is small, only about 0.4 or 0.5 CFS per application."

"To avoid much notice," I said.

"Looks that way."

"But when you add them all up?"

"About 25 CFS. That would be enough for about 50,000 households or about 150,000 people." Now I was looking at a city the size of Meridian.

"All those applications spread out over the desert?"

"Yep."

"All under different business names?"

"Yep."

"All with senior water rights."

"Yep."

"All tying back to Brad Childs."

"Yep."

"So the idea is that Childs could take those water rights, combine them and use them wherever he wants?" I said.

"If that bill passes," Hansen said.

"Can you tell me what those other water rights you found are?" I asked.

Hansen smiled and reached into his pocket, pulled out a piece of paper folded lengthwise and slid it across the table.

"This didn't come from me," Hansen said. "You dug these up on your own."

I took the paper that contained a series of a couple dozen water rights numbers that reminded me of the list that Vern Thompson had kept. I put it in my pocket.

"Thanks, Jerry."

"It didn't come from me."

28

———

Hansen finished his cinnamon roll and left the Capri. I ordered lunch and fired up my laptop.

Another direct message from MarkFelt08081974.

The message read, "If you're interested in what Brad Childs is up to, ask Linda Davis about H-Bar Ranch development. Here's her number: 208-555-7642."

I wrote back, "Please tell me who you are. I can keep you anonymous. I'd like to meet and talk about what you know."

I set my phone down and opened my laptop. I did a search for "h-bar ranch idaho development Linda Davis."

After a couple of pages of results, I found a brief archived article from the *Idaho Statesman* from ten years earlier about a small group of environmentalists protesting a proposed development on a former working ranch, H-Bar Ranch, far outside any city limits, off Interstate 84 in the desert on the far eastern edge of the county.

A locator map accompanied the article, and I excitedly pulled out the maps Geoff Eastman had printed out from Alan Garry's study of Basin 63. H-Bar Ranch was roughly in the same vicinity as the aquifer Garry had discovered. And roughly the same vicinity as where Garry had crashed his car.

According to the article, the proposed development was a planned community, with 1,700 houses and a small commercial center, just enough for a gas station, a small grocery store, a couple of other commercial pads and a car wash.

Environmental groups had testified against the proposal at an Ada County Commission meeting, claiming the development would destroy natural sage grouse habitat and the rural, pristine nature of the area. They protested on the grounds that the roads couldn't handle the proposed traffic, new roads would have to be built, further destroying the land, and that there wasn't enough water to service the development.

The article gave a brief history of the ranch. H-Bar Ranch had been a working ranch for three generations in the Harrison family, who had moved to the valley from Oklahoma during the Depression. The last Harrison rancher, Frederick Harrison, sold his two thousand acres to a developer, after realizing that none of his children wanted to become ranchers, according to the article.

The Ada County commissioners, including Linda Davis, tabled a decision on the development until a future, undetermined date. I couldn't find another reference to the development, even though I searched a number of different ways. I searched the archives of the *Idaho Statesman* but could find no other article about it.

I looked back through the article and saw who the developer was.

It was Brad Childs.

Two entries later, there was another archived article from eight years earlier that had run in the *Boise Weekly* about how a political action committee called Idahoans for Idaho had paid for attack ads against the incumbent Democratic County Commissioner Linda Davis.

It was a brief article with few details other than a description of the ads, which featured a photo of Davis and a stream of accusations that she was a radical leftist, dangerous, bad for Idaho, that she wanted to turn Boise into Portland and Seattle, with images of homeless tent encampments and videos of riots and burning buildings. At one point in the ad, a yellow hammer and sickle on a red background popped up, accompanied by the question, "What does Linda Davis want to turn us into?"

The article quoted her opponent in the race, John Broten, who said he didn't approve of attack ads and found the ad campaign disgusting and out of bounds. He said he had no involvement with the ad and had no idea who was behind it.

"It certainly isn't part of my campaign," Broten was quoted in the article as saying. "We're running on the issues and focusing on a positive message of lower taxes, smaller government, support of law enforcement and smart growth."

The article did not say who was behind the PAC, so I went to campaign finance reports on the Secretary of State website and found the details for Idahoans for Idaho.

The name of the registered agent for the PAC was Ted Dunlap with an address in downtown Boise. There was something about the name that was familiar. I went back to my files on the water rights applications and saw it. Dunlap was listed on all of the water rights applications that were on Vern Thompson's list. That connected Childs to Dunlap, who was connected to the PAC. I suspected that the PAC trail would somehow lead to Childs.

I filtered the search of Idahoans for Idaho for the year Broten defeated Davis. The PAC had spent $96,000 on those campaign ads, ostensibly for the ads in the article.

The results page for Idahoans for Idaho included both expenditures and contributions, and lower down the page, I noticed that the Idahoans for Idaho PAC had been on the receiving end of an equal amount of money it had spent. A contribution of $96,000 had come from another PAC labeled only HBAPAC.

So I searched for HBAPAC's records for that year. Among the records was the $96,000 contribution to Idahoans for Idaho and HBAPAC's quarterly report, from which I learned that its full name was the Home Builders Association Political Action Committee. The registered agent on HBAPAC was, of course, Ted Dunlap.

So HBAPAC, fronted by Ted Dunlap, gave $96,000 to Idahoans for Idaho, also fronted by Ted Dunlap, which spent $96,000 on ads attacking Linda Davis.

I looked up the Home Builders Association.

The association had a slick website with information about construction in Idaho, photos of projects and information about the association.

On the "About Us" page was a list of building contractors who were members, and at the bottom was a list of board members.

I shouldn't have been surprised to see President Brad Childs.

29

———————

Linda Davis answered on the first ring.

After I identified myself and told her that I wanted to ask her a few questions about H-Bar Ranch, she chuckled, as if she had been expecting my call.

"I've moved on from that," she said a bit dismissively.

"Well, I don't want to dredge up the past," I said. "But I think something is happening with it now."

"I'm sure it is," Davis said. "It was just a matter of time."

"Can you tell me how Brad Childs could make this work?"

"God, if I never hear that name again," she said.

"Sorry. It's just that I think he's getting ready to develop this, but I don't understand a couple things that are going on. You were able to get the project stalled over the water rights, correct?"

"Yep," she said, almost proudly. "He can't do a thing until he can show he has the water for it, and out there, there's not a lot of water to be had, at least not cheaply."

"But let's say he's able to put together enough water rights?"

"I don't know, I've really not been following it. I got kind of ... burned out, you know?"

"I understand," I said.

"After that election and that ugly smear campaign—Brad Childs was behind that campaign, you know. Did you know that?"

"Yes, I did."

"And then John Broten approved the project. I know John. I like him, actually. He's a good person. But he looked the other way when Brad Childs ran those attack ads so he could get elected. And then he approved H-Bar Ranch, just like a good ol' boy would. Made him part of the club, I guess."

"Mm-hmm," I intoned sympathetically. At least she was talking and not hanging up on me.

"Well, he did his part and then moved on, I guess," she said cavalierly.

"Yeah, I saw him this morning at a committee hearing."

"Oh?" she said, bored.

"He was hearing a proposal to change the place of use and point of diversion requirements in Idaho's water rights law."

"Really," she said, more interested now.

"Yeah, the bill would allow a water rights holder to change the place of use and point of diversion to wherever they want."

"Jesus," she said, and I could sense her gears turning.

"So that means –" I started.

"Childs could collect water rights from anywhere and use them at H-Bar Ranch," Davis finished.

"Help me understand this, though," I said. "Childs has bought up water rights all over the desert. If he can now take those water rights and simply apply them to H-Bar Ranch, would he need to actually divert water from those other places up to H-Bar?"

"I guess not necessarily," Davis said. "If he's found enough water at H-Bar, he could just pump as much water out of the ground there as he's got rights for."

"So he could put together the 25 CFS he's already amassed and –"

"Wait," Davis interrupted. "Did you say 25 CFS?"

"Yes."

"That's ridiculous. That's the size of a couple of cities."

"I know. About 150,000 people. Fifty thousand houses. At least."

"Jesus," she said again.

"So even if he's got that many water rights, how could he even make H-Bar that big?"

"I don't know," she said, thinking. "He must have found water out there."

"But he couldn't apply for that many water rights at that one location without raising alarms."

"Right."

"But here's what I still don't understand," I said. "Even if that's what he's doing, how can he build that many houses at H-Bar, way beyond what was approved?"

"He can't. H-Bar went through the public hearing process and got approved for 1,700 houses. You can't just change that without a new public hearing, and if he thinks he's going to build 50,000 houses without some sort of public outcry, there's no way. He'd never be able to get through a public hearing process again with that many houses, especially with the water situation the way it is. No matter how many commissioners he gets elected."

"Is there some way to do it without a public hearing?"

"I don't think so," she said tentatively. "I can't think of –" She stopped herself short.

"What?"

"I wonder if those bastards wrote something into the development agreement."

"Like what?"

"After that election, I just pulled back. I needed a break from all that fighting. So I just stayed away. Didn't pay attention to what they were doing," she said. "You should go look and see what they ended up approving. Go find the development agreement and see what it says about future phases or something like that."

"Is that posted online?"

"It should be. Might take a little digging, but you should be able to find it under Development Applications. See if there's a clause about future use, future phases or future development or something like that."

"Hold on, let me look it up while I've got you on the phone."

I went to the county website, clicked on Development Services and then Past Applications. I searched for "H-Bar Ranch."

The search yielded a tangle of PDF files with a seemingly indecipherable code of letters and numbers as their names APP4397205, DA4397206, PH4397205, NM94397204.

"I don't know what all this means," I said, reading off the letters and numbers.

"APP stands for application, PH is public hearing and NM is neighborhood meeting. You want to look at the DA file, which stands for development agreement."

The file was 132 pages long, and I let out a mild groan.

"Look in the table of contents and see if you see a chapter on future use."

There was, and I scrolled to page 115.

After several paragraphs of land use jargon, I found a sentence that I was looking for. I had to read it a few times to make sure I was reading it correctly.

"Applicant is allowed to develop future phases beyond the scope of this application under the parameters that any such future development comports with the approvals, entitlements and requirements associated with this development agreement."

I wasn't 100 percent certain, but I took that to mean that Childs could develop H-Bar Ranch as big as he wanted, as long as it was developed in the same manner as the first 1,700 houses. Ostensibly that applied to the commercial aspects as well.

"Yep, that would do it," she confirmed. "Those sons of bitches."

I had learned over the years as a reporter that the answer was always there somewhere. Whether it was a document, a disgruntled employee, a line item in a budget, or a former county commissioner waiting for the phone to ring and for someone to simply ask her a question, the answer was always out there, just waiting to be found and reported on. It was just a matter of finding it.

30

———————

When in doubt, head on out. I had to see H-Bar Ranch for myself.

I finished my lunch, and within twenty minutes, I was on Interstate 84, heading east past Boise's industrial area and past Micron. A few minutes after that, I was well into the desert landscape of sagebrush and solar panels.

I exited the freeway at the Blacks Creek exit and headed north then immediately east. As I drove, I passed a couple of private gates, locked, barring passage to dirt roads that disappeared off to the horizon. I passed what looked to be some sort of power substation and another gate that led to a distant farmhouse surrounded by an unlikely copse of trees amid the brown desolate land.

Although seemingly barren, the desert was filled with its own subtle signs of life.

Massive 500kw power lines stretched across the land, their double-pillar wooden towers dotting the landscape like ancient giants marching single file across the dusty desert.

A collection of dilapidated mobile homes huddled alongside the road suggested a Fundamentalist LDS family of seven wives and fifty children, and I kept driving.

I passed a spray-painted plywood sign advertising "Land for Rent," and I couldn't figure out who the potential customer might be out here.

I slowed down as I approached another collection of what appeared to be farmhouses, junk cars and double-wide trailers strewn about on either side of the road, seeking shade under paltry willow and cottonwood trees.

The road was cracked and patched with lines of tar, the edges ragged and fading into the dirt, looking as though if unattended it would crumble and disappear into the desert clay. How anyone eked a living out of this landscape was beyond my comprehension. How or why someone would have stopped in this godforsaken land to try to farm or ranch was a testament, I thought, to how bad things must have been in the Dust Bowl days in Oklahoma.

The road continued east, deeper into the desert that now became gently rolling hills and down into a small valley that showed more signs of life.

Frederick Harrison had built a stone monument announcing the entrance to H-Bar Ranch some forty years earlier, and it still proudly stood there on the south side of the road, just beneath the original wooden H-Bar sign that arched over the ranch's driveway that Frederick Harrison's father had built forty years before that.

I pulled my car over just before the driveway, where there was a small patch that clearly had been used for a parking space or an unloading point for deliveries or farm machinery. I looked off to the distance, and it appeared that just at the foot of a butte to the south, a collection of trees may have been concealing a farmhouse. I knew the Harrisons were no longer on the property, and I wasn't keen on driving that distance to the farmhouse, if it was a farmhouse in those trees, only to find a less-than-welcoming reception. The warning shot from Dan Perry still rang in my ears.

A warm breeze carried the smell of dust and sage.

Up the road from the H-Bar Ranch, on the north side, I noticed a modest one-story green-and-white ranch house with an old gray Toyota Tundra in the driveway. The house was well-kept, the windows clean, the front porch swept, the tidy lawn newly mowed. I parked my car at the end of the driveway and walked up to the house, glancing with trepidation at the "No Trespassing" sign, which in Idaho would give the occupant of the house justification for shooting me on the spot. I stopped, stepped gingerly on the pathway to the porch, as if trying not to set off a landmine. I practically tiptoed to the front door and rang the doorbell, which set off a barking dog.

"Buddy, stop it," came a woman's voice from inside. "Quiet. Shush."

A short, squat, older Asian woman with black hair and kind eyes opened the door halfway, keeping the dog at bay. She looked me up and down and pronounced, "We're not selling."

"Oh, I'm not..." I was confused. "I'm not... I'm... Excuse me?"

"If you're here to make an offer on our property, we're not selling."

"Oh. No, I'm not here to make an offer," I said.

"You're not with Summers Builders, are you?"

"Oh, no, no, no. I'm Philip Chandler with the *Fremont Herald* newspaper in Fremont. I'm doing a story on the H-Bar Ranch," I said, pointing over my shoulder. "I was wondering if you might know anything about it."

The woman chuckled. "Dwayne," she hollered back into the house. "Someone here to talk to you about H-Bar."

A similarly short, black-haired Asian man wearing glasses and a heavily worn Carhartt jacket came to the door.

"He says he's with the newspaper, wants to know about H-Bar," the woman said. The man kept his eyes on me as he made his way around the woman and came out onto the porch, closing the door behind him.

"You with the *Statesman*?" he said.

"No, the *Fremont Herald*. I'm Philip Chandler. I'm doing a story on the H-Bar Ranch," I said, again pointing over my shoulder, "and I was wondering if you knew anything about it?"

The man continued looking at me, appraising, with only a quizzical, furrowed-brow, mouth-half-open look.

"*Fremont Herald*," the man said more as a statement than a question.

"It's a small weekly newspaper in Fremont," I said, pointing to the west, as if this man before me had no idea where Fremont was. But this far out, it was as though I had been transported to a different country, far away from Fremont.

"Gus and Janie Haggard," the man said, again offered as a statement.

"Yes, they were the owners of the paper before me," I said. "I bought the paper from them."

In my two years in Idaho, I was occasionally given a glimpse of the Idaho the way it was back in the day, when it was smaller, with fewer people, and most of those people had deep roots in Idaho and most everyone knew everyone else, when being an Idahoan meant something special and Idahoans were more connected.

The man stepped out onto the porch, and Buddy, an old black Lab, followed. Buddy, tail wagging, sniffed me, and I reached down and rubbed his ear, to which Buddy moaned with pleasure.

"Dwayne Ogata," the man said, extending his hand. "Pleased to meet you."

"Nice to meet you," I said, relieved that Ogata wasn't going to pull out a shotgun and run me off his property.

"Haggards are good people," Ogata said, stepping down the porch steps and onto a walkway through the yard.

"Definitely. Very good people," I said.

"You must be okay if they sold you the paper," Ogata said.

When Gus Haggard had sold the paper to me, he issued a formal statement. It was something along the lines of "We are resolute in our decision to turn over the paper to Philip Chandler and will not waver in our decision." I hadn't realized it at the time, but during the negotiations of buying the paper, the Haggards were sizing me up just as much as I was sizing up the business. The Haggards had been auditioning me, asking me as many questions as they answered, assessing my character and determining my fitness for the job. The fact that they had "chosen" me meant something to people around here. I had not previously recognized this code among the old Idahoans. But once this man said it, many things clicked into place for me, like finding a piece that connected two disparate sections of a jigsaw puzzle.

"I like to think so," I said, wondering if it would be too rude to bring the conversation back to the purpose of my visit. Fortunately, after a couple of moments of silence, Ogata did it for me.

"So you're doing a story on H-Bar," he said.

"Yes."

"What do you want to know?"

"Well, I guess, do you know if they're going to build houses over there?"

"I believe they are," Ogata said.

I pulled out my notebook, and Ogata looked at it suspiciously but apparently was fine with the situation, his trust of Gus Haggard extending to me.

"Been a long time coming, but it looks like it's finally going to happen," Ogata said.

"What makes you say that?"

"I've seen trucks coming and going, doing ground work out there," he said, pointing down and across the road.

"Ground work?"

"Sewer lines, water lines, curb, gutter and sidewalk. See those wooden stakes with the orange ribbons? Those mark the boundary of the development. They've got it all marked out."

I looked and for the first time noticed the small stakes, low to the ground and continuing east, where they disappeared around a bend. But I didn't see any curb, gutter, sidewalks, sewer lines or water lines.

"Where have they been doing the ground work?"

"Up on the butte there." Ogata pointed to a low-lying butte to the east. "Used to be Harrison's ranch. He'd graze cattle up there. Sad day when he sold out."

"You ever get approached about selling your land?"

"Oh sure, all the time," Ogata said.

"But you never sold."

"You'd be amazed at the schemes they came up with," Ogata said. "We used to listen to them, bring them right into the house, sit at the kitchen table with them. They'd lay out these plans for partial payment now, timed payments later, buyout clauses, escape clauses, contingency clauses. We were naive in thinking that when you sell something, you sell it in exchange for payment. These developers live in a different world. They never lay out any money until they collect from someone else. Some of these contracts they showed us, we wouldn't get paid until twenty years after we died. We never signed anything. They came into our house thinking we were a couple of hayseed farmers."

"Who was it that came to see you?" I asked, knowing the answer already.

"Fella by the name of Brad Childs."

"I thought so," I said. "He's the one developing H-Bar."

"He's the worst of the bunch. He made a deal with Greg Reynolds down there," Ogata said, pointing to one of the plots marked out with orange flags. "When Reynolds was ready to retire, he went to Childs and said he wanted his money. Childs said that wasn't the deal, pointed to a clause in the contract showing that he'd get paid when the land was developed. Reynolds couldn't handle another season, ended up selling everything and moved in with his kids in town."

"He try that with you?"

"Oh sure," Ogata said. "He was slick, real personable, real nice at first. But we saw how he treated Reynolds. When it became clear we weren't going to take one of his deals—and he laid out several different scenarios, said it would be like we were partners, but we knew better. That's what he said to Reynolds. He got real nasty, got angry. It showed me that it was a smart thing not to have him as a partner. Once he realized we weren't going to deal, he bought forty acres next to our property just out of spite. Had some bulldozers come in and grade it, rerouting the drainage so that it flooded one of my sugar beet fields. And then when that didn't work, he drilled a well about five hundred feet down right on the other side of the property line from my well and drained my well dry."

I imagined Ogata toiling under the brutal sun, coaxing sugar beets from the ground, eking out a living, only to have Childs play a mean-spirited prank.

"Can he do that?"

"Well, turns out there was an old water right on that land. A senior water right to mine. Harrison was here before my family. My parents didn't homestead here until after the war."

"Oh, was your dad in World War II?" I asked, thinking of my own grandfather, who was on a Navy transport ship on D-Day.

Ogata gave me a look that made me feel immediately embarrassed.

"No," Ogata said sheepishly. "Minidoka."

Minidoka was a Japanese concentration camp about 130 miles east of

Boise that housed 13,000 Japanese-Americans in deplorable conditions in often nothing more than tar-paper shacks, many built by the prisoners themselves. Japanese-Americans at Minidoka were taken from their homes in Washington, Oregon, and Alaska and shipped to the harsh desert winters and blazing hot summers at Minidoka. After the war, many Minidoka detainees settled in and around southwest Idaho. Ogata looked old enough to maybe have lived in Minidoka himself. I tried to do some quick math in my head, but decided to let it lie.

"Oh, I'm sorry," I said. It was a stark reminder, often lost on my generation, that we don't all share the same version of US history.

"That's fine," Ogata said quietly but dismissively. He sighed and returned to the subject of Harrison's water rights. "It wasn't much water, 0.2 CFS, but it was enough to drop the water table. Apparently, there's water farther down, a good five hundred, six hundred feet."

"How deep is your well?"

"Most of us around here, our wells are one hundred, two hundred feet down at most. Drilling new wells that deep is expensive. When Childs bought out Harrison, he had the most senior water rights, so he was able to drill a new well and pretty much take all the water. That's why all these old boys around here sold out. No more water."

"So he was able to buy everyone out?"

"Real cheap, too. Once he dropped the water table to where no one could get water out of their wells anymore, Reynolds and Thornton and Jackson lined up to sign Childs's contracts. He was buying for three thousand an acre. That's even below the price for ag land."

"How much does ag land go for?"

"Five thousand, might get ten thousand for good ag land."

"What about development land?"

"Development land out in Meridian or Fremont goes for fifty, seventy-five thousand an acre, depending on where it is. You know old lady Gustafson?"

"No."

"They had a farm out on Eagle Road, on the west side, homesteaded that place, farmed it four generations. Her husband died last year, kids didn't want to farm, sold it for 150 an acre, I heard."

"A hundred and fifty thousand dollars an acre?"

"Yup."

"And Childs is buying land out here for three thousand."

"Yep. Cheap."

"Are you the last holdout?"

"Yep, but I don't think I'm going to hold out much longer."

"To Childs?"

"Got no choice. I'll take what I can get at this point."

"Is he still offering to buy you out?"

"He hasn't in a while. Last time he sent someone out didn't go so well."

"What happened?"

"He sent some strongman to come out and threaten us."

"Strongman?"

"Yeah, some goon. Big guy, muscles, bald. He came by one day when I was out in the field, threatened my wife when I wasn't home."

"What did he do?"

Ogata chuckled.

"He didn't know my Julie very well. She reached into the coat closet and grabbed our shotgun, gave it a pump and told him he was trespassing. Idaho has got pretty good laws when it comes to trespassing, you know. She could have shot him dead on the spot and the county would have paid us to haul the body away. Anyway, he said something like he didn't think the gun was even loaded. So she pointed the gun out in the yard and pulled the trigger." Ogata started to laugh. "Right at that moment, it was just a coincidence, but a whistle-pig was running across the yard. And she blew him to pieces," he said, now shaking with laughter. "I wish I had been there to see his face. Julie said he didn't say a word, just turned around, got in his rig and drove away. She's a tough old bird, my Julie."

"She sure sounds like it," I said, laughing along with Ogata. "I'll be sure never to make her mad. Did you get his name?"

"No, he didn't exactly leave his business card."

"But you say he worked for Brad Childs?"

"I think so. He started out real nice, came to the door, introduced himself, said he was with Summers Builders. When Julie told him what he could do and where he could go, he turned real ugly, started threatening her. That's when she got the shotgun out of the closet."

"And he hasn't been back since?"

"Nope."

"Did you see what he was driving?"

"Julie said it was a Cadillac Escalade. All black. Shiny new."

31

———————

We stood there quietly, and I wrote down "Cadillac Escalade" and made a note to check what kind of tires it used.

I noticed a faint humming off in the distance.

"What's that sound?" I asked.

"What sound?"

"Out that way," I said, pointing to the south.

"Oh, that. That's the freeway."

"Interstate 84?"

"Yep, it's just a quarter mile or so that way," Ogata said.

I had driven several miles off the freeway, but I hadn't realized that I had been driving parallel to the interstate. I made a mental note of where I was and tried to envision a map of the location of H-Bar Ranch, several miles from the last exit but just a quarter mile from the interstate.

"I guess I just don't notice the sound anymore," Ogata said. "It's not that bad. I'm surprised you noticed it."

I looked up at the butte and felt the pull once again to see the thing for myself.

"Have you been up on the butte?" I asked.

"No, not since Childs bought it. It's posted now. I take trespassing pretty seriously."

Another one of those new laws passed by the legislature doing the bidding of a wealthy campaign contributor under the guise of freedom and liberty, this time a couple of billionaire brothers from Texas who were buying up thousands of acres all over Idaho and gating them off to the public. The Idaho way used to be private landowners allowing hunters, anglers and hikers to pass through their land to get to public land on the other side without batting an eye. But then, at the very end of one session a couple of years back, the brothers had gotten some legislator to propose a bill that made it a felony to trespass on someone's land, no excuses.

"Well, thanks, Dwayne, I sure do appreciate your time."

"You bet. Good luck with your story."

I got back in my car, drove down to the end of Ogata's driveway and held down the button on my tripmeter to turn it to zero. I turned left onto the road and kept my eyes on the orange markers. At six miles, I noticed a fence line running all the way to the butte, which loomed one mile in the distance. I had perhaps noticed fence lines like this before, but I never thought about their meaning, their division of property between one rancher and another, the men named Harrison and Reynolds and Ogata who toiled in desert heat digging post holes and stringing barbed wire to mark his territory from another man's land.

The orange markers continued.

At mile seven, I noticed another fence line, then another just a hundred yards or so away, flanking a thin slice of land that had tire ruts leading up to the butte, connecting to another road that I could see off in the distance switchbacking up the side of the butte to the top.

I drove another mile until the orange markers ended.

I pulled over into a clearing at a fence post and looked at my tripmeter.

Eight miles. Eight miles long by one mile wide. I did the math in my head. Forty acres is an eighth of a square mile. You can get eight, forty-acre plots in a square mile. So that's 640 acres times eight square miles. That's 5-1-2-0. 5,120 acres, so five thousand acres plus five thousand up on the butte, at least. So ten thousand acres. Three houses per acre, thirty thousand houses. On average, three people per household, ninety thousand people.

I turned my car back around and drove to the gap in fence lines and turned onto the bumpy, hard-packed dirt access road skirting an old field in the direction of the butte, which had a road leading up diagonally to the low, flat top. A large cloud of dust trailed my car as I bounced along toward the butte. I was worried about two things: whether my Honda Civic's suspension could handle these bumps and ruts and rocks that were better handled by an F-150 with nine inches of clearance and whether my plume of dust would attract unwelcome attention. After a minute, I reached the base of the butte, and I saw the first "No Trespassing" sign as the road turned west to the right and climbed up the side of the butte.

At the first switchback, another "No Trespassing" sign was posted, but I kept going, turning the car to the left and west, and approached the top of the butte.

As I crested the butte, the first sign of development appeared—a collection of pipes sticking out of the ground. Then another, and another, and another. And then, when I drove up onto the flat surface of the butte, hundreds of them, thousands of them, popped up, laid out in geometrical patterns across the landscape, all connected by miles and miles of shiny new asphalt roads and curbs, gutters and sidewalks laid out in a neat grid pattern with a few little culs-de-sac here and there.

The roads continued to the other side of the butte, which faded off into the horizon.

"Holy...." I said to myself.

I got out of my car and stepped forward onto the first street just a few yards away. My mouth was open. I couldn't believe what I was seeing. It looked similar to smaller subdivisions under construction around Fremont, just like Nick Ashley's, but on a much grander scale. A scale of one hundred or more.

Row after row of streets and pipes sticking out of the ground. It was reminiscent of a city leveled by a nuclear bomb. A massive city, without any structures. Yet.

I suddenly felt exposed up on the butte and I had the urge to get the hell out of there. Little did I know then exactly how exposed I really was.

32

———————

As I drove from Ogata's house, the sun was setting, and the desert air began to cool as I rolled down the window and enjoyed the evening drive.

The pieces were coming together, making sense as to why Childs was buying up land in the desert and applying for water rights. Land was cheap, cheaper than buying prime development land in Meridian and building a hundred houses. Childs was thinking bigger. He was ambitious, more ambitious than your run-of-the-mill developer. If he could consolidate all of his water rights and use them at H-Bar Ranch, he could buy thousands of acres for pennies on the dollar with senior water rights and build thousands of homes and make millions. What's the margin on a new house? Fifty thousand? A hundred thousand? I did the math in my head. Even at fifty thousand, that's a billion dollars' profit on thirty thousand houses. Jesus. What's the worth of an obstinate old farm couple in the face of a billion dollars?

The sky had darkened by the time I pulled my car up in front of my house on Fourth Street, and I was tired. I started toward my front door but then decided to walk to my office to check to see if the mysterious someone had left another manila envelope in my dropbox.

On the way from my house to my office, I passed Harvey Taylor's place, and old Roscoe the bloodhound barked his usual greeting.

It was a good night for a walk. The air was beginning to smell like fall. Someone was doing laundry somewhere, and the smell of detergent wafted on the breeze.

Someone else was smoking a cigarette, a clove cigarette, something I hadn't smelled in a long time. The smell triggered a sense memory back to one night in college and a club and dancing and drinking and the cramped backseat of a friend's car on the ride home that led to more than I was expecting that night and ended with a satisfied smoke of a clove cigarette in bed. I smiled at the memory. Smoking was a pleasure I still missed, some five years after quitting. But, as Carl Jung wrote, "Every form of addiction is bad, no matter whether the narcotic be alcohol or morphine or idealism." One addiction replaces another.

As I rounded the corner to my office on Main Street, I could see Cowboys Lounge was doing a good business down the street, the front door open, emitting sounds of laughter, music, the click of pool balls and clinking glasses. In the distance, I heard a car door slam. As I fished in my pockets for my keys, I heard Roscoe bark again, and I thought for a moment about heading down to Cowboys for a drink or two. *Maybe Amanda's there*, I thought.

As I fumbled with the keys in the front door lock, a thought started to nag at me.

The smell of a clove cigarette. The car door slamming. Roscoe barking a second time.

I started to turn, but it was too late.

I felt the whoosh of air behind me and saw the glint out of the corner of my eye, then a jarring impact on the back of my head snapped my neck forward and to the side. My vision did that closing-tunnel thing, but the tunnel opened back up when my knees hit the sidewalk.

I started to look up and back instinctively, but a set of large meaty hands pushed my shoulder blades forward, throwing me down to the ground. My cheek hit the sidewalk. Two quick kicks to my right side took the wind out of me, and I gasped for air. A hard toe kick to my thigh sent a shock of pain up and down my leg, numbing it. One hand pushed down on my left shoulder, and another hand grabbed a fistful of my hair and pushed my face into the sidewalk.

A raspy voice accompanied by bad breath whispered in my ear, "Be careful what you write about. You know what I'm talking about."

The hands let up, and there was another kick, not quite as hard, to my side, which nonetheless curled me up in pain.

"Stay down," the voice said. "Don't get up. Don't look back."

Through squinting eyes, I glanced around but not quick enough to get a full look at the figure that rounded the corner and walked away.

I stumbled to my feet, and I heard Roscoe bark again. I made my way to the corner of the building, peering cautiously around the edge, in case my attacker was waiting. He wasn't.

A car started in the distance, then a black SUV drove away down Fourth Street. A black Cadillac Escalade.

I had a rush of dizziness and braced myself against the building's wall.

I was bent to the right, still unable to pull myself up straight. I took several short breaths, but anything deeper brought an electric spasm of pain to my right side. A wave of dizziness passed over me as I lifted my head, and I was afraid I might pass out.

I made my way back to my office and grasped the door handle to steady myself. I lowered my head and took progressively deeper and slower breaths until I was well enough to move again. I finished the job of unlocking my door and went in. I locked the door behind me and eased myself into my chair.

I pulled a bottle of Four Roses whiskey out of the bottom drawer, grabbed an empty coffee mug, poured myself a short one and took a swallow. The whiskey made me feel better instantly, as the warmth radiated from my stomach to my sides where I had taken the kicks, out to my arms and down my legs, the right one of which I could now feel again.

My head was another matter. I had a splitting headache, and I gingerly reached to the back of my head, where a welt was growing. I pulled my hand away and looked for blood. Fortunately, there was none. I felt my cheek where it had hit the sidewalk, and I could feel a small mouse of a shiner developing. I popped two Tylenol in my mouth and washed them down with a slug of whiskey. I got up and went into a back break room that I shared with the neighboring financial adviser office. I took some ice out of the freezer, put it in a bag and alternated putting the bag on the back of my head and on my cheek. I sat back down at my desk, poured some more whiskey and let the Tylenol and ice take effect.

Just three days earlier, I was sitting in that very spot, depressed and bored, contemplating my life choices, a familiar, lonely cloud settling over me. I was in a rut, a laid-off cops-and-courts reporter wallowing for the past two years in a small town writing about city council meetings, school boards and Friday night football games, missing the action of crime scenes, homicides and police chases.

If I was being honest, despite the pain, for the first time in months, I was happy.

I got up and went over to the dropbox to see if there was another manila envelope. Nothing but the usual. I was almost disappointed. I opened X on my phone to see if I had another message from Mark Felt. Nothing.

I poured another drink, and I noticed my hand was shaking from the adrenaline.

I opened a new window on my laptop and typed in "Best tires for Cadillac Escalade." The first hit was a sponsored ad from a tire chain that recommended Pirelli Scorpions. All-season plus, 255 millimeters wide.

Now, for the first time, I was also scared. *Drop the whole thing*, I thought. *They know who I am, where I work, what I'm working on.* That goon easily could have just shot and killed me right then and there. He could have beaten me up a lot worse than he did. He very well could be the man who shot and killed Vern and Wanda Thompson, and he could do the same to me, anytime, anywhere. *Drop the whole thing*, I thought again.

When I was growing up, our local weekly newspaper ran a Latin phrase as its motto on the front page every week, "Qui tacet consentire videtur." Silence is consent. I always thought that was a good motto for a newspaper.

In the newspaper business, when you learn a piece of information, you have a simple choice: publish it or withhold it from your readers. It became my code. You either tell your readers what you know or you keep it a secret from them. When looked at that way, the decision was always an easy one.

I wasn't going to just drop the whole thing.

33

———

I awoke the next morning with my head still in pain. I downed two more Tylenol, took a hot-then-cold shower and had a quick breakfast of coffee and eggs. By the time I dressed, I was feeling better. My side was still sore and tender, and my leg now had a large purple welt, but I was functional.

From my house, I called Nick Ashley.

"How's it going?" Ashley asked.

"I've been better," I said.

"Oh?"

"Yeah, nothing major," I said with a chuckle. "Just a run-in with a mutual acquaintance."

"Who's that?"

"I think that same guy who paid you a visit."

"Oh. He threaten you, too?"

"You could say that."

"Big, muscular guy, bald head?"

"I actually don't know. He hit me from behind and held me down. I never got a look at him."

"He actually attacked you?"

"Did you happen to see what your guy was driving?"

"Sure did. It was a Cadillac Escalade."

"Black? Shiny, new?"

"Yep."

"Okay. Thanks, Nick."

I was about to hang up, then thought of something. "Oh, hey, Nick? One more thing. Did you create an X account with the name MarkFelt08081974 and send me a direct message?"

Ashley chuckled. "Nope, not me."

"Okay, just checking."

The bright morning outside was decidedly autumnal now. As I walked to my office, I passed by Harvey Taylor's place, and Roscoe greeted me, as usual. "Thanks for trying to warn me last night, old boy," I said.

On Fourth Street, I looked around on the ground along the side of the road, among the weeds and gravel. I spotted what I was looking for. A clove cigarette that I had smelled the night before. This is where he was parked, waiting for me, watching me. I looked for tire marks, and there were none. But I had a good idea what they were.

The funeral for the Thompsons was held Friday morning in the Stake Center of the Church of Jesus Christ of Latter-day Saints. The building was designed so that entire walls could be removed, and the middle section, which was used as a basketball court and function room, could be opened up and become part of the sanctuary. Folding chairs were assembled behind the sanctuary in rows of fifty. I estimated at least five hundred people were in attendance.

An LDS funeral is much like any other funeral, perhaps more efficient. It started right on time, which I appreciated. I noted, though, that when they sang "How great Thou art," they sang the whole damn song. Every verse. All ten minutes of it.

There were readings from the Bible, a eulogy, and words from the Thompsons' family, who tearfully recounted the Thompsons' life story and shared favorite memories. They talked about Vern's mischievousness and Wanda's famous mint brownies and sewing skills.

There were some readings from the Book of Mormon and some words about the mortal bodies and the celestial spirit that were off-putting, then many of the twenty-nine great-grandchildren came to the podium and sang about the eternal family.

Raised Catholic, I had long ago abandoned religion. I had written too many stories about senseless acts of destruction, kids with cancer, innocent bystanders shot by a stray bullet, apartment building fires killing bed-ridden seniors, too many abuses in the church and too much wrongdoing done in the name of religion.

I knew the LDS Church was considered by many Christian denomina-tions to be "not a real religion" and more like a cult, but to me, it was all the same. If you believed half the stuff in the Bible, Noah's ark, the burning bush, the Ten Commandments, why not believe that some guy in Upstate New York woke up in the middle of the night and dug up some golden tablets that told the story of Jesus in America preaching to the Native Americans? If you can believe in papal infallibility and transubstantiation, why not the notion of revelation? If you believe priests and nuns can't be married, and women can't hold church leadership positions, why not polygamy?

And if God was so goddamned omnibenevolent, how could he let two good people like Vern and Wanda Thompson get murdered senselessly in their own home?

These were my thoughts as the third verse of "How Great Thou Art" droned on.

At the end of the funeral, the caskets were rolled down the center of the sanctuary, and as they passed me, I thought about remains.

Aptly named.

These boxes contained all that remained of Vern and Wanda Thomp-son. This was all that remained of a person's living and working, farming, plowing fields, sewing, Sunday dinners, mint brownies, practical jokes, tears, joy, suffering, loving and raising kids. It was all now contained in a small wooden box being rolled down a converted basketball court on top of a contraption that resembled a cafeteria food cart.

I surreptitiously glanced at my watch. An hour and a half. *That's all you get*, I thought. The remembrance, the grieving, the summing up of an entire lifetime was sewn up in about ninety minutes.

In the next half hour, they'd be buried in a hole in the ground, and everyone who knew them will move on with their lives, doing their own living and working, suffering and enjoying, and the Thompsons would be but a distant memory.

That, more than anything, was what scared me: the idea of being nothing, of being so insignificant that even after a lifetime of living and doing, all that was left was a vague memory and a headstone with your name on it, slowly crumbling over time. Sure, I'd feel better if I were a believer, carrying a sense of certainty that I'd move on to the celestial world, reunited with my family. But I didn't believe in fairy tales anymore.

As the coffins were carted across the floor, I was struck by another thought that popped into my head involuntarily: *Is that it? Is that all there is to life?* I shuddered and shook my head, as if to remove the idea from my brain.

I recalled my own mother's funeral, and I suddenly felt utterly alone, the cloud heavy and dark, despite being surrounded by hundreds of people I knew.

I stuck around for a little bit afterward, eating "funeral potatoes," which the Mormons were famous for, and talking with some of the farmers.

I ran into Hernandez, who seemed eager to talk to me.

"What the heck happened to your face?" he asked, wincing in empathy.

"Lost a fight with a doorjamb."

I didn't think he believed me.

"So how's the investigation going?" I asked to change the subject.

"We're working on some things," Hernandez said, avoiding eye contact at the question, and I noted his cageyness. I was unsure whether to tell Hernandez what I knew. I wasn't sure myself whether the list of water rights had anything to do with the Thompson murders. Besides, I wasn't a police detective. That was Hernandez's job. Hernandez's job was justice; my job was the truth. We may have been going in the same direction, but we were traveling on different roads.

"Anything you're able to share?"

"Not yet," Hernandez said, looking down at his shoes, which made me think that he did indeed have something. That served to remind me, however much I liked Hernandez, police and journalists aren't on the same team, and it furthered my resolve to keep my own information close to my vest. "Not yet."

"Okay," I said with a tone that I meant to sound like I knew Hernandez had something and should share it.

Hernandez raised his eyes now and looked me in the eye. "But you'll be the first to know," he said.

"Keep me posted."

Hernandez cleared his throat, and I knew something was on his mind. I waited.

"I just want to make sure that stuff we talked about, the stuff I showed you, that's all off the record," Hernandez said.

"Of course. Which stuff in particular?"

Hernandez sighed, resigned to the fact that he wouldn't be able to just leave it at that with me.

"You remember that piece of paper we found at the scene? The one with the list of numbers and the Thompsons' address?"

"Yes." Now it was my turn to look at my shoes, avoiding eye contact with Hernandez. I tried to make it look like I was thinking, brow furrowed, rubbing my chin with my hand, but I wondered if Hernandez was just as perceptive and picked up on my cageyness. I hoped Hernandez wouldn't press me on what I knew about those numbers.

"Well, keep that under wraps," Hernandez said with a mix of command and pleading. "I shouldn't have shown that to you. It's part of police evidence. You write anything about it, it could jeopardize the investigation."

I looked back up, and the moment hung there, the two of us searching each other's eyes for a clue. I suspected that Hernandez might know, himself, what those numbers were, and I was tempted to ask him, and if so, what he thought of a possible connection with the murders, but I knew that would give away what I knew.

"Got it," I said instead.

We just stood there, looking everywhere but at each other.

"One other thing," I said. "Did you happen to find a clove cigarette at the scene of the Thompson murders?"

He was silent for too long, and his eyes shifted back and forth, as if reading something.

"How did you know that?"

My mind raced. I didn't want to tell him about my attacker the night before. "I thought I caught a glimpse of it from the photos you showed me on your iPad."

"That's all off the record, Phil," he said, unintentionally confirming it for me.

"I know, I know. I just wanted to confirm it."

He was silent again, and I could tell he was considering how much to tell me.

"Nothing definitive on it. We have no idea where it came from. Could have been someone driving by and tossed it out their car window."

"How did you find it?"

"Dan Wilde found it. He's good. He somehow spotted it in the front lawn."

"What's that?"

"Dan Wilde found it."

"Where did he find it?"

"In the front lawn."

"To the right of the driveway?"

"Um, let's see... Yeah, to the right of the driveway, as you're looking at the house from the street. In front of the house."

"That doesn't –" I cut myself off.

"Doesn't what?"

"Nothing, just thinking out loud."

"Okay, but remember, this is all off the record, Phil. You print any of it, and it'll get me in a world of trouble. State police are down here helping out, and they don't take kindly to sharing information with the media."

"I got it. Don't worry."

"Is that all?"

"For now. Thanks, Chief."

Like he said, it could have been some random person throwing it out their car window, but it was too much of a coincidence for me. Clove cigarettes aren't all that common, and now to have them at these two places, likely connected, I was pretty sure it wasn't a coincidence.

Just before I left the church, I turned and saw Hernandez pull out his notebook and make a note.

34

After the funeral, I made my way back to my office. Nothing in the dropbox. No new messages from Mark Felt.

Something still didn't feel right with Broten. I considered myself a good judge of character, and I found it hard to believe that Broten would be in on a scheme to help Childs build his massive city in the desert. But I had seen good men bend their ethics and morals before in order to stay in office. I had never held elected office, so I didn't know what it was like, but the desire to stay in office must be powerful. *For Broten to bend his ethics, Childs must be throwing money at Broten to keep him there*, I thought.

So I opened the Secretary of State's campaign finance portal and looked up the campaign finance reports for every year that Broten had run for election.

When Broten was elected to the county commission ten years earlier, the $96,000 PAC spending on the attack ads didn't show up on Broten's reports, but since his campaign didn't officially coordinate with the PAC on the attack ads, Broten didn't need to claim that $96,000 as a donation. But Broten did have donations of $5,000 each from Brad Childs, Fred Childs, Georgianne Childs, Luci Childs, the Idahoans for Idaho PAC, Summers Builders and the HBAPAC, among an assortment of smaller individual donations from citizens and businesses.

After that, Broten's campaigns for office over the years had the same lineup of $5,000 donations from the Childs family and business and the two PACS. He far outraised and outspent his opponents. More money flowed from the HBAPAC to the Idahoans for Idaho PAC, and the Idahoans for Idaho PAC had spent $50,000 on advertising. The Idahoans for Idaho report showed funds being spent on Broten's race.

I looked up Broten's subsequent races and found the same pattern up until the last race, the previous year.

Childs and his PACs disappeared from Broten's list of campaign contributions. Childs, HBAPAC and Idahoans for Idaho had donated to a few other candidates, but not a dime to Broten.

Broten's most recent reelection campaign last year showed nothing out of the ordinary, just the usual list of contributions from other Republican candidates, assorted individuals, a few out-of-state donations, family members and a couple of political action committees contributing relatively small amounts, $5,000 here and there. A mining company—the one testifying before the Natural Resources Committee—had donated $5,000, and a lumber mill in north Idaho donated $5,000.

I did not find any contributions from Brad Childs or Fred Childs or HBAPAC or Idahoans for Idaho in Broten's most recent reelection campaign.

I tried to piece it together.

Childs had helped Broten get elected to the county commission, after which Broten approved Childs's development for H-Bar Ranch.

Then Childs helped Broten get elected to the state legislature. Broten killed a study of the Basin 63 aquifer.

Now Childs was sitting in on a hearing on a bill that Broten supported as a state legislator that would allow Childs to use a series of water rights that were on a list found on the desk of Vern Thompson.

But Childs had stopped donating to Broten's campaign.

Someone had put the screws to Nick Ashley about one of those water rights out in the middle of the desert south of Fairview that Ashley and Vern Thompson were protesting.

That someone matched the description and drove the same Cadillac

Escalade as the goon who worked for Brad Childs and threatened the Ogatas.

I was pretty certain it was the same man who had "visited" me at my office and perhaps the same goon who had visited Vern and Wanda Thompson the night they were killed.

At this point, it could all be a coincidence with Vern and Wanda's murders. And the water rights might have nothing to do with anything and all these connections with Childs and his companies and PACs and businesses could just be a figment of my overhyped sense of skepticism. It could all mean nothing, just typical signs of how business is done.

But why in the hell was Broten helping Childs?

Money begets money, and greed begets more greed.

But greed didn't seem to be an answer for Broten. Broten was doing just fine between his practice and his role as a state legislator. Any land deal around H-Bar Ranch wouldn't benefit anyone other than Childs.

I used to play a game with my ex-fiancee Laura, where I would meet one of her friends or coworkers, and after a few minutes and a few details, I would put together a profile—rich kid from Brookline, parents divorced because her father cheated, now she has a daddy complex and tremendous trust issues, which explains why she second-guesses all of your decisions at work, and why she's not married, but has had a series of affairs with older men.

My accuracy would stun Laura.

I believed in the theory that humans are able to make an accurate assessment of people within the first minute of meeting them. So I got good at listening to my first impressions and allowed those thoughts to blossom.

My assessment of Broten was that he was upstanding, not like Childs, and he wouldn't throw in with a guy like Childs simply over a land deal. That nod that Broten threw toward Childs during the committee hearing suggested something else, a submission, subservience, an acknowledgment of a task performed that was expected, obliged. An obligation in exchange for something else. That's what was gnawing at me.

Lauren must have known more than she was telling me.

Just as you could make an accurate assessment of another person within one minute of meeting, you could detect a mutual attraction just as quickly. I was attracted to Lauren and I believed she felt the same. Lauren Broten seemed to be out of my league, but we had a certain ease the other day, comfort, a smile or just a connection that made me want to see her again. I sensed she had been holding back on me, that she knew more about whatever the connection was between her father and Brad Childs.

My phone rang, and it was Linda Davis calling.

"I made a couple of calls to my Democratic legislators after we talked yesterday," she said. "It's the good ol' boys club at work. You might want to look up House Bill 671 from last session. It explains how Brad Childs is going to get a hundred thousand people in and out of his little city in the desert."

"Thanks, Linda."

"But it didn't come from me," she said. "I don't want any part of this anymore."

"Understood."

After we hung up, I went to the state's legislative website, which contained a breakdown of all bills proposed during each session, listed by bill number with links to the bill summary, bill sponsors, full text of the legislation and how each vote went.

I scrolled down the list and clicked on House Bill 671. It was a bill to provide special funding, above and beyond the regular budget for the Idaho Transportation Department, for a new interchange on Interstate 84, at mile marker 67, halfway between the Blacks Creek and Mayfield exits. The estimated cost was $10 million.

I opened Google maps and found the location of the interchange. Just a quarter mile off the interstate at that location was H-Bar Ranch. That would solve Childs's road situation, and Childs was getting the state to pay for it. With an interchange just a quarter mile away, residents of Childs's development would have quick and easy access to the freeway and a fast drive into Boise.

The bill passed along party lines in both the House and the Senate. I checked the bill sponsor, Rep. Joe Foster, who also happened to be the chairman of the House Transportation Committee.

On a hunch, I checked the campaign finance report for Foster in the last election. Sure enough, there was the usual cadre of maximum individual campaign donations from the Childs family. I next looked up Idahoans for Idaho and had to dig down to one of their reports to see it spent $50,000 on Facebook ads in support of Joe Foster's campaign. Moving over to the campaign finance report for the Home Builders Association PAC, I found a $50,000 donation from HBAPAC to the Idahoans for Idaho PAC.

Broten had voted in favor of the bill. Even though Foster was carrying the interchange bill, surely Broten must have known about it.

I rubbed my eyes and stretched. I had a couple of dozen tabs open on my browser and as many bookmarks. Like my browser, my mind was a jumbled mess.

Just before I closed the tab for the Idahoans for Idaho PAC campaign finance report, the name of the registered agent caught my eye. Ted Dunlap, the name that kept coming up on Brad Childs's business licenses, water applications and political action committees.

I decided it was time to make an unannounced visit to the law office of Ted Dunlap.

35

———

Ted Dunlap's office was on the third floor of One Capital Center, a relatively nondescript fourteen-story concrete-and-glass office building at Main and 10th that used to be the tallest building in Boise when it went up in the 1970s. It still had some lingering cachet, but these days it held more of a sense of nostalgia, old money, faded glory and decay. It used to be nice, but Boise had since moved on.

The lobby and first-floor glassed offices were all dolled up, with modern bright-orange furniture, sisal rugs, funky light fixtures, sculpted artwork on the walls and dark-stained wood floors, but the decor just gave the feeling of lipstick on a pig, especially when I made my way to the third floor, with its bare, polished concrete hallway and eighties-patterned tiled carpet in the offices. I detected a faint odor of mildew and ammonia.

While the hallway had since been updated, Dunlap's office looked like it must have looked in 1976, a modest affair, just enough to hold a secretary at a front desk and, from what I could tell, another room where Dunlap kept his office. Two metal and black vinyl chairs flanking a dying fern on a black lacquer end table comprised the visitors' seating area, and two worn areas marked the untold dozens—hundreds—of pairs of feet that had scuffed the gold shag carpet in front of the chair to the right.

"Do you have an appointment?" the older, wizened secretary, who looked like she, too, had been original issue since 1976, asked me over her chained eyeglasses when I asked to see Mr. Dunlap.

"No, I was hoping to catch him free."

"I'll see if he's available. What's this regarding?"

I decided to take a chance, feeling for once like I wasn't the inferior player in this act. "I wanted to ask him about Brad Childs, Summers Builders, the Home Builders Association PAC and campaign contributions to John Broten."

"Have a seat, and I'll see if he's available," she said without batting an eye or taking a note, then entered an inner office door and closed it behind her. She had probably been very attractive in her day, another relic from a bygone Boise era.

I took a seat in the chair to the left, the one with the less-distinct scuffs in the carpet, and thought about the psychology of people choosing the chair on the right. I stared at the amateur-looking painting of the Sawtooth Mountains hanging in a cheap gold-painted frame hanging on the wall opposite the chairs. I thought I could make out the name "Dunlap" signed in the corner. Wife? Daughter?

After a half minute, the secretary emerged.

"He's busy at the moment, but if you can wait a little bit, he might be able to see you." Encouraging.

"I'll wait."

The secretary didn't offer me water or coffee. *Not that kind of place, I guess*, I thought.

I checked X. No new messages from Mark Felt. I checked email and my website analytics purely out of boredom.

After about a half hour, the inner office door opened, and what emerged was a fat, bald, mustachioed man wearing a rumpled brown suit, knit tie and a cheap polyester shirt starting to wear thin, not a good look since the man wasn't wearing an undershirt. His tiny brown wingtips were scuffed and looked like they were either purchased recently at a thrift store or were headed to one soon. Still, Ted Dunlap exuded some sort of confidence that only a mediocre white man with years of entitlement can pull off.

I stood up. Dunlap closed the door behind him and paused, looking me up and down, assessing me through squinted eyes that were black holes.

"Lunch?" he said as a smile began to creep over his face.

I looked at my watch. It was two o'clock and I had already had my lunch. I was about to say as much, when Dunlap began to walk past me.

"'Cause that's where I'm going, and if you want to talk to me about Brad Childs, that's the only place you're going to do it," he said and reached for the door. For such a heavy man, Dunlap moved gracefully on his small feet, as if he had been a dancer or an athlete in a previous life. The secretary sat bored, staring out the window, not paying her boss any attention as he exited the office. I followed.

"You like Raymond's?" Dunlap asked in the elevator ride down, referring to a posh steakhouse a couple of blocks away. I had eaten there once, but my paycheck wouldn't allow many return visits.

"Uh, yeah, nice place."

"Good, because that's where we're going."

Out on the sidewalk, Dunlap walked quickly, and I lengthened my stride to keep up.

"So you're the fella that bought the *Fremont Herald* from Gus Haggard?"

The question surprised me. *How the hell did he know that?* I wondered, as my mind raced to recall whether I had even identified myself to the secretary as being with the *Fremont Herald*. It gave me the feeling of being exposed again, on the defensive, that Dunlap knew more than I, giving him the advantage, likely a calculated move.

"Yes," I said, trying not to sound surprised.

"Good folks, Gus and Janie. Did some work for them one time. Good man, that Gus. Retired Navy, if I recall."

"Oh, I didn't know that."

Dunlap gave me an assessing sidelong glance.

"How long have you owned the paper?"

"Two years now."

"Mmm. How's business?"

"Pretty good. Circulation's up, ads are up. Can't complain." I never wanted to let on that I was doing well and never wanted to sound like I was bragging.

"What brought you out to Idaho?"

"Looking for a change. I got laid off, and my fiancée left me. Needed a change of scenery." My abrupt confession to a complete stranger surprised me. But for some reason, I had an affinity for this graceful, brusque fat man striding beside me.

"Well, you got it, didn't you?" Dunlap smiled at me.

"I guess so," I said, sharing the smile.

Dunlap entered Raymond's and nodded at the girl in a tight-fitting short black dress at the front desk.

"Good afternoon, Mr. Dunlap," she said.

"Ashleigh, you're looking gorgeous today," Dunlap said casually as he turned immediately left into the bar area and nodded at the young, trim bartender who had a handlebar mustache and was wearing a red velvet vest over a crisp white dress shirt, bow tie and a sleeve garter.

"Mr. Dunlap," the bartender said.

Dunlap waved and held up two fingers at the bartender, who said, "Right away."

Dunlap casually tapped the bar twice with an open palm as he strode to a back table with a "reserved" sign on it next to a wall of windows looking out onto the street. Dunlap's grace was cut short only by his concerted effort to squeak himself into the space between the booth and the table. But once situated, he lounged casually, as I eased myself into the seat across from him.

"They need to space this out a bit," Dunlap complained.

"Yeah," I said, pretending I had had trouble, too, as I pulled my reporter's notebook out of my back pocket, put it on the table and fished in my breast pocket for a pen.

"No, no, no," Dunlap said. "Put that away. Put that away. I'll talk to you but not on the record. This is just between two men."

I reluctantly put the notebook back in my back pocket.

The bartender arrived and placed two old-fashioneds on the table.

"The usual, Mr. Dunlap?"

"Yes," Dunlap said, then turned to me. "You?"

"Nothing for me, thanks."

"No?" Dunlap said. "I'm buying."

"No, I'm good, thank you. I ate already."

"Suit yourself."

"Very good," the bartender said and went away.

I sipped my drink, and Dunlap took a gulp. It was the best drink I had ever tasted. So this was what it was like to have money. The whiskey relaxed me, made me comfortable talking to Dunlap.

"So how long have you known Brad Childs?" I asked.

"Not yet." Dunlap lifted a palm off the table at me. "Not yet."

Dunlap took another gulp of his drink and looked around the room. I did the same.

"I like coming here this time of day, after the lunch rush, before the dinner crowd," Dunlap said, nodding to the open room, which held only a few people in the bar area and the adjoining restaurant. "The staff is cleaning up, getting ready for tonight, folding napkins, laying silverware, inspecting wineglasses. Makes me feel like I'm part of a family." I knew that feeling and understood it.

"It's quiet this time of year, especially," Dunlap said.

"I suppose," I said. "I don't come here often."

Dunlap turned back to face me and straightened himself. He smiled and chuckled. "No, I guess not. That's good. That's good," he said, almost to himself. "You should see this place on a Friday night during the session. It's quite a scene. Full of legislators and lobbyists, friends and hangers-on. Used to be even crazier, back in the day."

"I can imagine," I said.

Dunlap took another drink and settled back in the booth.

"I'm easing out of the business," Dunlap said unexpectedly.

"What is your business? If you don't mind me asking," I said.

This drew a hearty laugh from Dunlap, catching the attention of a couple of diners at a table in the dining room.

"Excellent question, Philip." I liked that he called me Philip and not Phil. "Excellent question. You don't really know me at all, do you?"

"No, I just know your name shows up on a lot of documents connected with Brad Childs."

That sobered Dunlap, and he looked irritated. "Patience, Philip. Don't interrogate me. Enjoy your drink, for God's sake."

I sat back sheepishly and took another sip.

"I'm a lawyer, as I'm sure you're aware," Dunlap said. "But over the years I've managed to expand my business and my offerings to other areas than just the practice of law. And now I'm getting ready to retire—from most of my business dealings. I'll still keep a hand in, but I'm removing myself from other parts of my business. It seems I've developed a conscience as I've grown older. Perhaps that's why Mr. Childs and I parted ways."

It was my turn now to show my irritation, annoyed at Dunlap's cryptic speech. Dunlap noticed my impatience.

"All right, all right," Dunlap said. "You're a man of straightforwardness. Of course you are. You're a journalist."

Dunlap finished his drink and pointed at the bartender, who nodded.

"Did you know I started out as a defense attorney, with the public defender's office?"

"No."

"No, not many people do. I was, as they say, idealistic, when I first started out. It didn't last long, though. As I came to know my clients, I began to feel that they deserved everything they got for their incredibly stupid decisions in life. Have you ever noticed that? Bad things happen to people who make poor decisions in life. Not a good frame of mind for a defense attorney to be in, as you can imagine. Still, I did well, managed my cases, made connections, got friendly with prosecutors. Prosecutors who went on to work for the attorney general's office. Prosecutors who went on to become county commissioners, state legislators, corporate attorneys, lobbyists. I developed a good network of players who were rising through the ranks, and I found myself with connections from one end of the state to the other. From the third floor of the capitol all the way down to the basement."

The bartender brought Dunlap another drink, while I still worked on my first. Following right behind the bartender was a cute waitress delivering a porterhouse steak and a baked potato, which Dunlap tucked into right away and continued speaking in between greasy bites.

"I quit the public defender's office and opened my own practice. At first, I kept my hand in defense work, but that morphed into pleading down DUI and domestic violence cases for state legislators. That gave me a reputation as a fixer, someone to go to, someone to rely on to be discreet."

Dunlap chewed on a massive bite of steak and washed it down with a swig of old-fashioned. I felt like a priest in a confessional.

"They come back into town in December to do their leadership elections, about a month before the session starts. That's usually when they reach out to me, line things up for when they're back in town."

"Legislators?" I said.

"Yes, sorry, the legislators."

"What do you mean, 'line things up'?"

Dunlap laughed quietly. "It meant just about anything," he said, looking again back into the bar area and dining room, casually waving his steak knife. "Oh, how they looked forward to coming back to Boise for the session. They lived in Rexburg or White Bird, Jerome and Blanchard, boring little towns with boring little Mormon populations, spending three hours in church on Sunday. I imagined them sitting there in church listening to the sermon, all the while thinking about their plans for what they'd do once they came to Boise for the session, their taxpayer-funded apartments, lobbyist-funded dinners. They'd tell their wives that they wouldn't be able to make it home that weekend because they had work to do." Dunlap chuckled. "Their work was here," he said, pointing his steak knife over his shoulder. "These rooms would be packed. That bar would be lined with attractive young women—and attractive young men, depending on the legislator."

I leaned forward. "Prostitutes?"

"Mm-hmm." Dunlap nodded casually, his mouth full of baked potatoes. He swallowed and said, "This place was a hive of activity during the session, a regular den of iniquity. You wouldn't believe some of these legislators, high and mighty in the statehouse, arguing against abortion, passing laws against birth control, railing against sex education in schools, taking the moral high ground, and then come Friday, they'd be in here like a dog in heat picking out their companion for the evening." He took another drink and laughed again. "God, they were like teenagers with their parents out of town. Grown men, for God's sake." He took another bite of potato on top of a piece of steak and shook his head. "Disgusting, really. I never understood it. They come here to Boise for the session like it was Las Vegas. What happens in Vegas stays in Vegas. The biggest hypocrites were the ones who'd pass laws banning same-sex marriage on Thursday, then leave here Friday night with a fair-haired boy of nineteen. Sad, really."

I looked around the room, imagining the scene. I admitted to myself I was shocked, and it took a lot to shock me. I didn't think Dunlap was blowing smoke. It was like a secret world that I didn't want to know existed. I took another sip, feeling tipsy already on what must have been 100 proof whiskey, and looked appraisingly at Dunlap, who was finishing off his lunch, wiping his mouth with his napkin and reaching for his second drink.

"And you'd set all this up? Like a pimp?"

Dunlap threw down his napkin, offended at the accusation. "No. I just made phone calls, let everyone know what the game was, where the game was, what the rules were. I didn't run the boys and girls. I just let them know when and where the business would be."

"For a fee?"

"Oh, please. Don't make me regret taking you in my confidence. I thought you were a man of the world. Don't be so pious."

I smiled. "Fine."

My concession in turn allowed Dunlap to be contrite. "You're right, though," Dunlap said. "It's a nasty business, and I did grow tired of it. That's why, like I said, I'm removing myself from that part of my business dealings. Besides, the world has changed. Time is passing me by. I'm a dinosaur, in a lot of ways. Things are different these days. It was a chapter of my life that's closing, and I'm fine with it."

"So was John Broten one of your clients?"

Dunlap laughed and shook his head. "No. Mr. Broten was ... ungettable. He was your consummate Boy Scout, Philip. He had no vices, no weaknesses. I befriended him." Dunlap paused, swirled his drink and took a contemplative sip. "I liked him. I like him. He's a good man. I was very sorry when his wife died."

"So what's your connection to Childs?"

"Hmm," Dunlap said. "Brass tacks. Another part of my business, which I intend to continue, is used as a front for other businesses. I register a business under my name, file all the paperwork, do the legal, notarize it. Mr. Childs—Fred Childs, the father—first came to me to file a business license for a company that he wanted to establish to develop some land in Meridian, but he didn't want anyone to know it was his company—for various reasons, having to do with the city, the neighbors and competitors. I have to say, it's pretty common practice now, but Fred Childs, he was the one who started it. It caught on, and I've done it for dozens of businesses. It's relatively lucrative for the amount of work it requires, perfect for a man entering his golden years."

"Same goes for campaign donations from PACs?" I said.

Dunlap let out another one of his loud guffaws, and he raised his glass to me. "Well done, my boy. You have done your homework. You're halfway there, aren't you?"

"I think so."

"So, yes, that was part of the work I was doing for Fred Childs—a good man as well, I should tell you."

"But not his son?"

"Hmm." Dunlap's mood changed again, and he fished the cherry out of his first drink and popped it in his mouth. He wiped his fat fingers on the napkin in front of him. "The son is another story. Another story, altogether. He and I have parted ways."

"Is it because of Broten?"

"In part, yes. I just don't like the man. I don't like the way he does business. It's one thing to help someone with their vices; it's another to exploit them."

"You're being cryptic again," I said.

"So I am. Brad Childs got his hooks into Broten early on, helped him get elected to the county commission. This was before I was associated with him. I was dealing mostly with his father on land deals at the time, but I saw what was going on. Fred asked me to help out, keep it above board and under control."

"That's when Childs dropped the ad campaign against Linda Davis," I said.

"Yes. I came in and said, 'This is too much.' Linda's a good woman. She didn't deserve that kind of treatment."

"But by then, it was too late. It still worked."

"Correct. And Broten got elected, which wasn't a bad result."

"The ends justified the means."

"Let's just say the ends were acceptable," Dunlap said. "And like I said, Broten was a good man. Is a good man."

"And then Brad Childs needed Broten in the legislature," I said.

"Which was more in my wheelhouse," Dunlap added. "I liked Broten and found that I could actually get behind his campaign. So we set up the PACs to make it not easy to trace back to Brad Childs, which you've obviously done, and funneled money into Broten's campaign. He got elected, then he got reelected. I approached Broten a few times to see if I could be of other service to him," Dunlap said, waving a pudgy hand toward the bar. He shook his head with a frown. "Nothing doing. He wasn't interested. I think he was still mourning his wife a little bit. I think he still is. But like I said, he's a good man. He has two daughters, and I think he's just an upstanding citizen."

"So what happened?"

"When he realized what I was offering him, that's when I think it was the beginning of when things started to go wrong. He got wise to what kind of a person I was, what kind of a person Brad Childs was, and he started to try to dissociate himself from Mr. Childs. And from me. Perhaps that was also the beginning of the end for my involvement in all of this, seeing myself through John Broten's eyes."

"But Broten knew that Childs had paid for those attack ads," I said. "He must have known what he was like."

Dunlap chuckled and finished his drink. He chuckled some more and glanced coyly at me, considering. "You don't know the half of it, my boy." Dunlap slid his empty glass to the edge of the table, and the bartender arrived with another drink, quietly removing the empty glass, as I continued to sip at my first drink.

I didn't know what he meant by that, and I sensed that Dunlap was pausing to let me try to figure it out.

"You mean creating these front companies to buy up water rights," I conjectured.

"Yes, that was the son's primary focus, from what I could tell," Dunlap said. "He had me do a lot of those. I'd set up the business, then that business would apply for water rights or transfer water rights."

"How many?"

"Oh, I don't know, Philip, maybe a couple dozen. Maybe more. I don't really keep track, and I do similar applications for others as well."

"And did you know Childs was putting the water rights all together so that he could build H-Bar Ranch?"

Dunlap took another drink and nodded contemplatively. "Ah, see, here's what you need to understand, my boy. The reason people come to me is because I don't pay too close attention. I don't ask too many questions, and I don't look too closely at the businesses. Frankly, I don't really care. I don't waste a single brain cell on any of that. The service I provide is completely legal and above board. And it's strictly transactional. I file paperwork; they write a check. It's as simple as that. Anything beyond that is beyond my interest."

"So that's not why you parted ways with Brad Childs?"

Dunlap looked down at his drink, then back up at me, squinting, his head cocked to the side, assessing me. I could sense Dunlap was considering telling me something more, and I knew enough to keep my mouth shut.

"Brad Childs has several other businesses, some of which I set up for him," Dunlap said finally. "They have my name on them. One of those businesses is a photo studio on Chinden that Brad Childs owns. Somehow, and I don't know how, John Broten discovered what kind of business is conducted in that studio, in the back room."

Dunlap took a gulp of his drink, and I kept silent.

"I have to admit, even I was shocked by what was going on in that little photo studio," he said. "I'm not a technologically advanced person. I still have a flip phone, and I'm not familiar with all that goes on on the internet. I know some people are into that kind of thing, get addicted to that kind of thing, end up just looking at that stuff on the internet and nothing else. It actually cuts into the real business that goes on here. You'd be surprised at how business dropped off. Some legislators would rather just go back to their rooms with a laptop for the night than have a companion from the bar. Safer that way, I guess."

Dunlap waved his hand as if to shake the thought.

"C'est la vie," he said. "To each his own, I say. Who am I to judge? Anyway, I never even really gave it much thought. Like I said, I'm an old-fashioned sort of man, stuck in my old ways. I'm a throwback, an antique. That stuff was a mystery to me. I knew that kind of stuff existed, but I never thought much about it, let alone how it got made. I suppose it has to get made somewhere. So why not in the back of a dumpy little photo studio in good old Boise, Idaho?"

I sat there, stunned once again. I had my hand on my drink but didn't move.

"Brad Childs tried to bring me into that business, but when he showed me what he was producing..." Dunlap trailed off, shook his head, took another drink. "I won't bore you with the details, Philip, but I was never aware before of the appetite some men have for looking at that sort of thing." He shuddered. "There was nothing illegal, mind you. No minors or anything like that. I would have turned him in in a heartbeat if there was anything like that going on. Still, I wanted no part of it. He tried to tell me it was no different from arranging dates, but I didn't see it that way."

I found my voice, but it was scratchy and weak. "And that's when you parted ways with Childs."

"Yes. And really when I realized it was time to retire. The world is passing me by, Philip, and I was done. Of course, it's been a lengthy process to extricate myself from all of Childs's businesses, as you can imagine. But that's the work that's consuming me now, as I file paperwork, transfer ownership, that kind of thing. I have to say, Childs has been amicable, recognizing that I'm retiring, not suspecting that I'm doing it because I want nothing to do with him any longer. That I'm disgusted by him."

"So why are you telling me all this?"

Dunlap smiled and softened. "I don't really know, Philip. I like you. I liked you as soon as I saw you. I'm a good judge of character, and I could tell right away I could talk to you. I think I needed to tell someone. Maybe I secretly want him found out, caught, I don't know. I go on instincts a lot of the time, and my instinct told me to tell you. When you came into my office and my secretary said you were there to talk about Childs, campaign contributions and John Broten, it felt like a sign from the gods." He held up both hands and looked to the ceiling, and I couldn't tell if he was being sincere or putting me on.

Just as Dunlap finished his third drink, the bartender came to the table holding the check and a pen. Barely looking, Dunlap grabbed the pen and signed his name on the check.

"Thank you, Mr. Dunlap. Great to see you again," the bartender said and walked away.

Dunlap scooched out of the booth and stood up gracefully and steadily, as if he were a man who had not just had three 100-proof old-fashioneds.

I finally downed the rest of my first drink and stood up, not feeling nearly as steady as Dunlap appeared to be.

I took a twenty-dollar bill out of my pocket and put it on the table.

Dunlap looked at it and smiled, and the thought occurred to me that perhaps it wasn't enough money for the cost of the drink.

"That's not necessary, Philip."

"Yes, it is."

"A man of ethics. My goodness, that's so refreshing." He slapped me on the shoulder. "So refreshing."

"Well, thanks for the chat, Mr. Dunlap."

"You can call me Ted," Dunlap said, extending his hand. We shook and made our way to the front door. Dunlap tapped the bar twice with his palm, his ring making a hard sound on the bartop, and waved to the bartender.

"Have a great day, Mr. Dunlap," the bartender said.

Dunlap paused at the front desk to take a mint and kiss the hand of the girl in the tight-fitting black dress.

"Thanks for coming in, Mr. Dunlap," she said. "We'll see you next time."

On the sidewalk out front, Dunlap looked me up and down appraisingly again, just as he had done in his office.

I thought of something and kicked myself for not thinking of it earlier.

"Ted," I said, trying out the familiarity. "What I don't get, though, is why Childs stopped making campaign contributions to Broten. He didn't help him out at all with the last election."

Dunlap looked down and rubbed his chin. "No." Dunlap looked back up at me, squinting, with a look that suggested he wasn't going to say more.

"But Broten is still helping Childs. He's trying to get a bill passed to change water laws over place of use and point of diversion rules."

Dunlap paused, and I wasn't sure if he was going to say anything. "I can honestly say, Philip, that I don't really know. I could speculate—and I have my theories—but I don't like speculating, especially with something like that. That's going to have to be something you find out for yourself. I'm sorry."

I said nothing, contemplating whether to keep pressing.

"Good luck, Philip."

We shook hands again and went our separate ways.

The answer was always out there somewhere, just waiting to be found.

36

———————

When I opened the door to the Broten Law Firm on the seventh floor of the Hoff Building, Lauren Broten was standing at the front desk, speaking with the secretary.

"Hello, Philip," she said and appeared to be happy to see me. "What a nice surprise. What brings you around?"

"I had a couple more questions for you."

"Sure, come on back," she said.

She led me back to her office, but this time, instead of sitting in the lounge area of her office, Lauren sat at her desk, directing me to one of the hard-backed chairs in front of it. She didn't offer coffee or water. She placed her folded hands on her desk.

I pulled out my notebook.

"Does your firm do work for Brad Childs?"

Her eyes narrowed. "No, but even if we did, I can't discuss our clients."

"If your firm doesn't do work for Brad Childs, what's the connection, then?"

"Who says there's a connection?"

"Brad Childs has been helping your father get elected going back to the county commission."

"Like I said, Philip, that has to do with my father's political life, and he keeps that separate from the law firm."

"But you suggested I talk to Summers Builders."

"No, I didn't. I suggested Oscar Mason. You brought up Summers Builders, not me."

"I find it hard to believe that you didn't know anything about Brad Childs."

"I didn't say that."

I let out a small sigh and looked her in the eye, trying to convey my feeling of frustration and my desire to tell her to just tell me everything. I decided to try a different tack.

"What do you know about H-Bar Ranch?"

"Nothing."

"Your father seemed to know about it when I asked him."

"I thought you said you were here to see me, not my father."

"Well, I just find it odd that your father knows about H-Bar Ranch but you don't."

"I don't know all of his business, Philip, and he doesn't know all of mine. What makes you think he knows anything about that development anyway?"

"I thought you didn't know anything about H-Bar Ranch."

"I don't."

"Then how do you know it's a development?"

"Look, Philip," Lauren said, irritated. "Are you working on a story that you want to ask me questions about?"

"I'm just trying to figure something out."

"Such as?"

I realized that I was expecting her to tell me everything, but I hadn't been doing the same with her. I decided to come clean with all that I knew.

"I know that Childs helped your father get elected to the county commission, and shortly thereafter, your father helped to get Childs's H-Bar Ranch approved. By the way, what Childs did to Linda Davis was pretty despicable, but we'll save that for another conversation. After county commission, Childs helped your father get elected to the state legislature, where your father helped to kill a study of Basin 63, which Oscar Mason and PFS Resources seemed to know about, and PFS Resources was doing work for Brad Childs. It turns out that H-Bar Ranch is a lot bigger than first proposed—about fifty thousand houses bigger—but there's one problem: Childs doesn't have the water rights for it. So he starts buying up old, senior water rights all over the valley, enough to supply water—coincidentally—to fifty thousand houses. But state law says he's got to use those water rights in the place he's getting the water. So he tries to get the law changed so he can put all those water rights together in one place—H-Bar Ranch."

Lauren smiled and looked pleased.

"Well?" She held up her hands at Philip. "There you go. It sounds like you've got your story. You can leave me out of it completely. As for my father, people donate to campaigns all the time, and my father has voted on hundreds of bills."

"But there's one more piece that doesn't make sense."

"What's that?"

"Why is your father helping Childs now?"

"I don't know what you mean."

"It's clear that your father is helping Childs get this bill through that would allow him to consolidate all of his water rights and use them at H-Bar Ranch. But I don't know why. Childs isn't donating to his campaign anymore. And I don't think your father is corrupt. I don't think he's getting a piece of H-Bar Ranch or a kickback."

Lauren looked blankly at Philip.

"So why is your father helping Childs?"

"I don't know what you mean."

"I think you do."

"I don't."

"What does Childs have on your father?"

Lauren's back straightened, her eyes rounded and her mouth opened. Her hand reached up to her neck, and she closed the collar of her blouse.

"Excuse me?" she asked defiantly.

"If it's not campaign contributions and it's not kickbacks, why is your father doing whatever Childs wants him to do?"

"You've got your story. Why don't you just stick with that and leave my father out of it? I don't know what you're talking about. My father has nothing to do with what you're working on." Her voice quavered, and her blouse fluttered at her chest.

"I think he does, but I just can't figure out why."

"I have no idea what you're talking about."

"It must be that he's being forced, Lauren. Is that it? If so, then why? What does Childs have on your father that he's making him do all this?"

"Damn it," she said, her eyes now blazing hot, her hands clenched in fists on the desk. "Just stick with the damn water story, Philip. Don't drag my father into this. Just drop it."

"Just drop it."

"Drop the part about any connection between my father and Childs. There's nothing there."

We held a glance, and I searched her eyes for the message she was sending.

Lauren's phone, which was sitting on her desk, began to buzz, and she picked it up. She looked at who was calling and let out a quiet expletive.

"This is Lauren," she said in a rough voice. She visibly tensed and turned away from me. "I'll be right there," she said, her voice changing again to yet another tone, this one somehow older, wearier, angrier. She hung up and turned to me.

"I have to go," she said coolly without looking at me, as if I wasn't even there. Lauren was somewhere else, someone else now. She hurriedly closed her laptop and gathered her things.

"Sure," I said. "Is everything okay?"

Lauren looked at me briefly, absently, with an air of irritation.

"Please," she said with a faint eye roll. She continued to pack her things up, then looked up at me again. "Like I said, just drop it," she said this time more as a command than a recommendation. "Just stick with the story you're working on and don't complicate things."

Her tone was off-putting but at the same time served as a kind of confirmation. I didn't say anything, just sat there watching her, wanting to help her.

"I'll see you out," Lauren said, standing up.

We walked silently past the secretary and to the front door.

I began to open the door, then stopped. "You sure you don't need any help?"

Lauren rolled her eyes. "Jesus."

I began to think of the other night with Lauren at the Grove Hotel bar, our knees touching under the table, and I felt something more than just a desire to get a scoop, to get the story, to find out the answers for the sake of finding out the answers. I felt something else.

"Won't you let me help you?" I said in a tone that I could see had an effect on her, and I thought for a second she might give in.

"Not now, Philip." I couldn't tell if she meant I could help later or if she meant it in a scolding way.

We stood there for a moment, and then she took in a sharp breath and gave a quick shake of her head.

"I've got to go," she said. "Now, please."

I left reluctantly and made my way to the elevator and out of the building. Down on the street, I looked at my watch: 5:30. I had to make a decision.

37

I jogged to my car and quickly pulled it into a space on Eighth Street in view of the parking lot behind the Hoff Building. After about five minutes, Lauren emerged from the side door of the Hoff Building and made her way to the lot. She got into a white Volvo station wagon, quickly started it, pulled out of her space and squealed the tires slightly as she turned the car around toward Eighth Street and out.

I put my car in gear and followed her. Lauren circled the block and turned right on Idaho Street, away from downtown. I kept a couple of car lengths behind her. Traffic was busy, as people were leaving work and heading back to their cookie-cutter houses in Meridian or Eagle. Lauren's shiny white car was easy to spot, and the traffic lights on Idaho Street were timed, so once we hit a green light, it was steady driving down the line. She turned left onto 16th Street, which then took a ninety-degree right-hand curve at the Cabana Inn and became Main Street. I had to speed up to keep up with her there, and my tires squealed on the sharp turn.

Main Street led to the Interstate 84 connector and onto I-84, and I was worried that I'd have to try to follow her on the open highway during rush-hour traffic. But then her brake lights flashed, and she pulled to the right and turned onto 18th Street in front of the Admiral Lounge, a strip club that was practically a Boise institution that had its heyday in the eighties, back in Boise's Wild West days, when hitting a strip club after work was a thing.

Lauren's car tilted and she sped into a sharp left turn into the alley behind a used car lot next to the Admiral. I pulled into the alley behind the car lot and parked, just able to see Lauren's car, which was now parked in the alley behind the Admiral, next to a set of concrete stairs leading up to a black metal door. There were several cars in the Admiral parking lot, a mix of Toyota Tacomas, F-150s, a Mercedes and even a Porsche Carrera 911, suggesting a good crowd on a Thursday night. Maybe Boise's Wild West days weren't completely over.

Lauren got out of the car, climbed the stairs, opened the door and entered like she was entering the back door of her own home, as if she had entered this door hundreds of times before.

I waited. The marquee billboard in front of the Admiral announced auditions daily, happy hour five to seven, amateur Tuesdays, hot women, cold beer. I had never been to the Admiral. I had been to my share of strip clubs in my younger days, and it somehow seemed perfectly acceptable then. Now, though, whether because of my advancing years or because of changing times, going to a strip club seemed ridiculous.

Sitting in my car, I tempered my urge to go inside to see what was happening with the rationale that I didn't want to miss Lauren when she came out. Fortunately, my internal struggle didn't last long, and the door opened after just a few minutes.

Lauren emerged from the building with another woman. She was slightly younger than Lauren, heavily made up and had frizzy, obviously dyed blonde hair with dark roots showing and she was wearing a long over-coat draped over her shoulders.

Her feet and legs were bare. She was moving slowly, shuffling and wobbly, as if the solidity of the ground beneath her were suspect. She held onto the stairs' metal railing as she descended, then lurched a hand forward to the car to steady herself, as Lauren guided her to the backseat, where the woman lay down. Lauren slammed the backseat door, and I imagined her huff as I detected an eye roll.

Lauren got in the driver's seat, and the car proceeded down the alley away from me. I started my car and followed Lauren's car on Main Street as she headed back toward the city. She eventually turned south onto 9th Street away from downtown, toward the Boise Depot, an iconic landmark high on a hill looking straight down Capitol Boulevard to the state capitol building. The road climbed and took a sharp left turn onto Federal Way. Traffic thinned, and Federal Way entered an older part of Boise that hadn't yet been developed.

A few houses that probably had been respectable in the seventies gave way to run-down shacks, a couple of scattered, decaying office buildings and a gas station. Up ahead, Lauren's brake lights went on, and she steered her Volvo to the right into the parking lot of the Federal Arms Motel, a motor inn preserved from the 1950s, a row of green-and-white connected rooms on a single story with doors opening to a common walkway that served as a front porch looking out onto Federal Way. The sun was now starting to set, and lights were popping on in the city below. The lights of the city and the foothills beyond it provided a spectacular view, and I wondered how this part of town had not yet been turned into upscale condos and apartment buildings.

I drove past the motel, turned right and right again into a narrow alleyway behind a convenience store that was next to the motel. I was in position to see Lauren enter the motel office, and after a few minutes she returned to the car, pulled the woman from the backseat and practically carried her to unit number five.

After a half hour, Lauren emerged from the room and made her way to the convenience store, then returned to the room with three bags of groceries. I figured the woman was bedding down for the night or more. After another half hour Lauren emerged again and made her way to her car, started it up and pulled onto Federal Way.

I followed.

38

Lauren made her way down Federal Way back toward the city and descended Capitol Boulevard. The foothills were still visible in the dying daylight, but the lights of the city were now on full display, and traffic was returning to the city for evening festivities.

Lauren retraced her route from the Admiral, but she kept going straight on 27th Street, across Fairview Avenue and across Main Street, through the West End, a residential neighborhood of hundred-year-old houses, nice but not as exclusive as its favored cousin, the North End neighborhood.

At State Street, Lauren turned left, then made a quick right onto 28th Street after St. Mary's Church and school. This became another residential street, busier, with Lowell Elementary School on the left, next to Lowell Pool, an above-ground art deco city pool built in the 1950s.

Across the street, on the right side of the road were less-nice, smaller one-story houses fronting the busier 28th Street. Lauren's car pulled to the side of the road in front of one of the houses, and I turned left into the small parking lot of the swimming pool. I watched as Lauren got out of her car and looked up and down the street, not noticing my nondescript tan Honda Civic.

Lauren used a key to enter a cute, tidy blue bungalow with black shutters that reminded me of New England. Lights went on inside the house, and I caught glimpses of Lauren moving about among the rooms. After fifteen minutes, Lauren came out of the house carrying a small overnight bag. She turned on the porch light before closing the front door, which she locked. She threw the bag in the back of her car, got in the driver's side, started the car, looked both ways and made a U-turn to head back down 28th Street toward State Street. She nervously glanced in the rearview mirror as she passed by my parked car.

I surmised that Lauren was returning to the Federal Arms Motel with the overnight bag, which I assumed contained the belongings of the woman Lauren had left there.

Rather than follow Lauren, I got out of my car. Once I was certain that Lauren had turned left onto State Street and was safely out of sight, I walked the short distance to the blue bungalow.

Next to the front door attached to the wall was an old-style black mailbox, which I tilted open and saw a collection of mail. I pulled the assortment out and shuffled past the junk mail labeled "current resident" until I found a power bill with a name on it.

The envelope was addressed to Cindy Broten. I quickly returned the mail to the box and made my way back to my car.

I pointed my car in the direction of the Admiral.

39

———————

The Admiral was a sad, run-down affair with an anteroom enclosed by plywood simply painted black, where a large, seemingly annoyed bouncer took my ten-dollar cover charge and granted me access to the main room through a black curtain that appeared to be a bedsheet stapled to the doorframe.

The room was as I expected: a bar to the right and a long, narrow stage running perpendicular into the middle of the room, with three poles and a couple dozen chairs around the stage. A series of curtained cubicles ran along the south wall to the left, and a dozen or so tables were scattered throughout the room.

Three women were on stage dancing to "Pour Some Sugar on Me," while a couple other women were on the floor giving lap dances. A woman emerged from one of the cubicles putting her bra back on.

The place was nearly filled with an eclectic arrangement of college kids whooping it up, a group of young men probably on a bachelor party, a couple of young men in suits and an odd, sad assortment of older solo men in various states of dishevelment and hygiene, sitting bleary-eyed with fist-fuls of dollar bills that they probably couldn't afford to lose.

I found a couple of empty chairs at the far end of the bar, a good location to see the entire room with a view of the front door and close to a door to a back hallway, near where I figured the steel door that Lauren had used earlier was located. The bartender was an attractive, dark-haired, dark-eyed woman, about my age, fully clothed in tight jean shorts and a soft gray T-shirt knotted above a pale white stomach. She had a sleeve tattoo and a piercing in her eyebrow. She seemed bored, and I wondered if dancers graduated to bartender. She placed a cocktail napkin down in front of me and didn't say anything.

I ordered a gin and tonic, and the woman turned to make my drink. I took a long look at her pale, toned thighs and half-cheeks peeking out from under her jean shorts until I noticed she was looking at me in the mirror behind the bar and caught me checking her out. When our eyes met, she gave me a smile.

Now that I was there, I wasn't really sure what to do. I didn't really have a plan, only my instinct to see with my own eyes what I was writing about, just like going to Perry's farm.

"Nine dollars," the bartender said as she set the drink down in front of me.

I tried not to make a face at the price, peeled off a ten and a five and placed them on the bar. She smiled at me. Fortunately, the drink was strong, likely a business calculation, and as I sipped it, I tried not to think about the fact that I had dropped twenty-five dollars in five minutes and hadn't even put any dollar bills in any G-strings.

As I was counting heads and multiplying by cover charges and ten-dollar drinks, the door behind me opened, and a short wiry man with a sharp-angled face, cold blue eyes and a wispy mustache walked through it.

About six months earlier, I had written a story about a Fremont family whose house had burned down while they were on a camping trip. While they were gone, the town had pulled together, raised money and collected housewares and furniture to replace what had been destroyed in the fire. The local burnout fund donated $500 to make sure they had a place to stay temporarily. A friend had called them as the family was driving home to tell them the bad news about the fire. As the family pulled into their street, they were greeted by about fifty people, most of them complete strangers, who were there to offer help and donations.

The mother, Shelly, worked at the front desk of one of the elementary schools. The father, Dave, was a guard at the prison.

The man who walked through the back hallway door at the Admiral was Dave.

Dave was dressed like he could be one of the customers: polo shirt and distressed denim jeans, but his demeanor and the way he scanned the room with watchful eyes told me something else. When Dave's glance passed over me, he did a double-take and smiled.

"Phil?" He came over, shook my hand and sat down next to me. Dave glanced over at the pretty bartender and gave a slight nod. The bartender set to work making a seven and seven.

"Hi, Dave." I made no secret that I was happy to see him and was genuinely relieved to see a familiar face. Like many of the subjects I wrote about, I developed a fondness and respect for Dave, his stoicism in the face of the fire and his calm resoluteness to the situation. I could tell that Dave could be a mean son of a bitch if he needed to be, and I admired that, slight as he was, he exuded that toughness without saying a word.

"What are you doing here?" I asked.

"Working," Dave said as the bartender brought his drink and Dave took a sip.

"You're not working at the prison anymore?"

"Oh yeah, I'm still there. This is just a little something on the side. They got us working four tens at the prison," Dave said, referring to four days of ten-hour shifts. "So I got a little extra time on the side. This is a good chance to pick up a little extra money. The insurance company is still nickel-and-diming us on the fire. We'll get what we're due, but in the meantime, we gotta make ends meet, so I picked up a little side hustle."

"What, security?"

"Yeah, some of the boys here can get a little rowdy. Some get handsy with the girls. So I just roam around acting like a customer and step in when I need to."

"Huh, interesting. I had no idea."

"Say," Dave said, punching my arm playfully. "What are you doing here, more importantly?"

A bare-breasted young woman who looked like she was barely out of high school, wearing a pink thong, walked past and smiled and winked at me, and I could feel myself blushing.

"Ha. Yeah. Well, I'm sort of working, too," I said.

"You writing something about the Admiral?" Dave asked guardedly.

"No, nothing like that," I said reassuringly. "In fact, I'm not really sure what I'm working on. I'm just trying to figure something out."

I could tell Dave was skeptical, but after I had published the story about the house fire, Dave had called me the next day and thanked me for doing such a good job on the article. For a reporter, there's no greater feeling than that feeling of relief when a source calls to tell you that the article you wrote about them was good. In particular, Dave had thanked me for not putting anything in the story about the troubles their son was having at school and with some of the neighborhood kids. Shelly had told me a little more than she probably should have, and Dave appreciated how I had left that part out. So I knew that Dave knew he could trust me.

"Okay," Dave said tentatively.

"You know a woman named Cindy who works here?"

"Yeah." Dave chuckled. "Oh yeah, I know her. We had a little trouble with her tonight. In fact –" Dave stopped and looked at me. "You writing about her?"

"No, I'm not writing anything right now. Like I said, I'm just trying to gather information. And this is all off the record, Dave."

"Well," Dave said hesitantly, "I don't know what her deal is. I think she comes from money. At least it seems that way."

"So why does she dance here?"

"I don't know. Other than I think she's got a drug problem. Or maybe she just likes it. She's good at it. Real nice body, too. Guys love her. They call ahead to see if she's working."

"You said she's got a drug problem? Like meth?"

"Yeah, I think she was doing that for a while but she's switched over to oxy. I'm not sure but I think she might be getting into heroin. That's getting cheaper now than oxy. See it all the time at the prison these days."

"That doesn't sound good," I said.

"No. She's a good kid. But she was so strung out tonight. They had to call her family to come get her. I think it was her sister. She's come to get her before."

"You know her last name?"

"No, we don't much use last names around here."

"Who called her family to come get her?"

"The manager."

"He knows the family?"

"I guess so. The sister has come here before to come get her, but usually it's some other guy comes to pick her up."

"Who's that?

"Guy by the name of Eddie Travers. Big guy, bald, lots of muscles."

"What?" My mind was racing to try to put the connection together. "He drive a Cadillac Escalade?"

"Yeah, you know him?" Dave asked suspiciously.

"I think so, unfortunately," I said, reflexively rubbing the lump on the back of my head.

"You sure you're not writing about this?" Dave said. "I like you, Phil. And I appreciate that story you wrote about us. But if you're fucking with me, I ain't going to be too happy. I need this job right now, and I don't want to mess it up."

"Honest, Dave, I'm just trying to figure something out. I don't even know if I have a story or not. I'd never let anything get back to you anyway. You know you can trust me. I don't work that way. I don't write stuff like that."

"All right," Dave said somewhat apologetically. "Yeah, Travers is a crazy motherfucker. Big dude, lots of muscles. Always carrying. Scary guy. A little off his rocker."

"He work here?"

"Sort of. He comes in from time to time, like I said to come pick up Cindy. He seems to push the manager around a bit. Seems like Eddie works for someone else, and maybe the manager works for him, too, or knows him. Connected somehow. I don't know. I don't stick my nose in where it doesn't belong. Especially with that guy."

"What kind of work is Travers doing?"

"Damned if I know," Dave said. "I don't want to know. I'm just waiting for the day I see him at my other job," he said, referring to the prison. We sat and sipped our drinks as I tried to process this new information.

"So why does he come in to pick up Cindy?"

"He'll pick her up sometimes in the middle of a shift, take her somewhere, then bring her back."

"Where does he take her?"

"I don't know. I don't want to know. He'll just come in, give her a nod. She grabs her things and off they go out the back door."

"Drugs?"

"Probably."

"Prostitution?"

"Maybe, but I don't think so. Like I said, Phil, I don't want to know."

Dave downed the rest of his drink and set the glass down on the bar and looked over my shoulder toward the back door.

In a low voice, Dave said, "Well, speak of the devil."

40

I kept my back turned to the door, but I surmised Travers had walked in through the door behind me. I worked on my drink and waited for Travers to enter my right line of vision. Travers stepped forward a few paces into the room, with his back turned a quarter to me, giving me an opportunity to assess him. Light bounced off his shiny bald head and disappeared in the folds around his thick neck. His bulging eyebrows shaded uncharacteristically tiny sharp eyes. His flat nose looked like it had been broken maybe more than once. Thin, taut lips seemed out of place on the bulging features of his face and made a horizontal line over a bulbous, dimpled chin. I thought he might have been a good-looking guy before steroids. His black V-neck T-shirt was tight around his chest, shoulders and massive arms, which were veined, hairless and bigger than my legs. A hint of a hard belly pushed against his T-shirt, which hung loosely just below his waist, no doubt concealing whatever handgun was holstered at his belt. Maybe the same gun that killed Vern and Wanda Thompson. His distressed denim jeans had those ridiculous-looking embroidered back pockets. The jeans were flared and frayed over urban cowboy boots, likely holding another concealed weapon.

Dave tapped me on the knee as a way of saying goodbye, cleared his throat and stood up. I turned back to the bar, afraid Travers might see me, but I could see the two men reflected in the mirror behind the bar. Dave strolled over to Travers, and I could hear Travers ask, "Is she here?" I heard Dave explain Cindy's absence. Travers showed Dave no friendliness and barely recognition. Travers looked at Dave with cold hard eyes and treated him like a servant. I involuntarily shivered.

While they were talking, I took the opportunity to steal away. I nodded to the bartender, who gave me an inviting smile and nod. The bouncer grunted as I made my way out the door. Once outside, my shoulders released their tension, and I exhaled a deep breath and inhaled the crisp fall night air.

I quickly made my way around the corner of the building and looked back into the alleyway. Parked in the lot was a shiny black Escalade with a license plate PMPD UP. I jogged over to my car, started it up and parked myself in the alleyway across the street where I had been before. I had a clear sightline to the Escalade. I waited, hoping that Travers wasn't staying for a drink. While I was waiting, I grabbed my camera bag out of the trunk.

I replaced the standard lens with the long lens. I placed the bag and smaller lens on the floor of the passenger side and placed the camera on the seat next to me. I shuddered thinking about Travers and the possibility that it was he who had shot and killed Vern and Wanda Thompson. That black Escalade may have been parked in the driveway while Travers was inside trying to intimidate Vern into dropping his water protest, just as he had threatened Nick Ashley.

Vern, not knowing Travers had a gun, grabs a fireplace poker and tells Travers to get out of his house. Travers, spooked or mad at the upraised poker, goes for his gun and pulls the trigger. Wanda runs in, spooking Travers a second time, causing him to squeeze the trigger again.

Whether Travers felt remorse for the elderly couple, married fifty-three years, I couldn't say. Or maybe he was relieved or proud that he could report back to Childs that he wouldn't have to worry about that protest one way or the other. Maybe it was Travers's first time killing someone. Probably not. If it had been, he'd be scared, jumping at shadows, not driving around still doing his job like nothing had happened. He'd be lying low. Travers was not lying low, and that made me nervous, especially now knowing he was probably the one who had attacked me at my office the previous night.

I shot a couple of photos of the Escalade, especially the license plate.

I then remembered the tires. I got out of my car and ran to the Escalade, hoping Travers wouldn't emerge. I crouched at the back of the passenger side of the car, shielded from the Admiral door in case it opened. I checked the tire there. Pirelli Scorpion all-season plus, 255 millimeters wide. I pulled out my phone and snapped a couple of photos of the tire and the tread, stepped back and shot a photo of the Escalade.

I ran back to my car, scared as hell that Travers would come out and catch me.

I caught my breath and reached for my camera again. I had the camera raised in position when Travers came out of the Admiral, and I took a couple more photos with Travers in the frame.

41

———————

Travers got in his Escalade and pulled out of the Admiral parking lot. I followed, staying two car lengths back, which was a challenge as Travers drove just under the speed limit.

He headed west on Main Street, and when he turned right onto 27th Street, I realized he was heading for Cindy's house, and I now knew why Lauren had not taken Cindy home but to the Federal Arms instead. When we got to 28th Street, I pulled into the parking lot of the city pool and watched as Travers pulled over in front of Cindy's house. Travers walked to the side of the house, then onto the front porch, where he looked in the window, his hands shielding his eyes. Travers banged on the door a couple of times, then looked up and down the street, realizing he had banged a little too loudly. Travers walked around to the other side of the house and disappeared, reemerging on the opposite side.

Apparently satisfied that Cindy wasn't home, he returned to his Escalade and pulled a fast U-turn back down 28th Street.

I had to hustle to catch up and barely made the light at State Street. Travers went back down 27th to Main, where he turned right, went through another light, then veered onto Chinden Boulevard. Chinden, a mashup of "China Garden," harkening back to Boise's vibrant Chinese population before racism forced most of them all out of Idaho, was now a long, ugly drag of used car dealerships, gas stations and small businesses struggling to survive in strip malls and random fifty-year-old buildings patched up and painted just enough to stay standing.

We drove past microbreweries, a steakhouse with a braying horse statue on top of it, past a motel, a florist and an Army Navy store. Travers slowed down and turned right into a small parking lot of a dingy 1980s strip mall that glowed blue from the fluorescent lights in the canopy that covered the cracked walkway. I pulled into the alley behind a Mexican restaurant, whose parking lot was empty even though it was Friday night. The alley connected to the strip mall, and I was able to pull ahead just enough and in time to see Travers enter Porter Portraits, a photo studio whose two front windows flanking a glass door were curtained with red velvet drapes behind displays of wedding photos and high school senior portraits. Next to the photo studio was the darkened office for Summers Builders. I drew in a breath and snapped a few frames of the storefront.

After several minutes, Travers came out of the studio carrying a manila envelope and got back in his car. He pulled out of the parking lot quickly and headed back down Chinden.

Travers made his way back toward the city and toward the state capitol building, which shone brightly on the right. Travers made his way through the North End and down Harrison Boulevard, a long strip of stately old houses separated by a tree lawn median that drew thousands of trick-or-treaters on Halloween.

Harrison Boulevard turned into Bogus Basin Road, which climbed sixteen miles and two thousand feet up to the local ski area, and I was concerned he might be headed that way. But Travers turned right onto Curling Drive at Simplot Hill, a tall grassy slope, popular for sledding in the winter. The hill was owned by the Simplot family, the farming family that had been selling potatoes to McDonald's since the early days. The Simplots used to own a house at the top that they had donated to the state to be used as the governor's mansion. As it turned out, the governor at the time was married to one of the Simplot daughters, but the marriage didn't take. The governor never moved into the house, and rather than pay for the upkeep, the Simplots simply demolished the house, planting a giant flag-pole in its place.

I followed Travers up Curling Drive and onto Braemere Drive past Crane Creek Country Club. Braemere climbed steadily into the foothills, lined with houses that were at the time the mansions of Boise, populated by society's upper crust, the Simplots, the Morrisons, the Knudsens, the magnates of their day and their progeny. As the houses aged, they became more accessible to Boise's more run-of-the-mill millionaires, the trial lawyers, financial advisers, orthopedic surgeons and power company executives. After them came the professors, judges and middle managers, teachers even. So the elite moved farther up the hill, building newer, bigger, fancier houses along the way.

Driving up Braemere was like looking at the geological record of Boise's social ladder, its layers of affluence laid one on top of the other like the exposed walls of a deep river canyon.

If the bottom of Braemere was the oldest and poorest layer, the freshest layer, the very top rung of Boise's social ladder, was Nines Ridge Lane, a secluded stretch of just a few houses situated on a ridge overlooking downtown, whose lights now blinked and glowed, suggesting a bigger city than it really was.

Everything on Nines Ridge Lane, even the view, was aspirational.

I made sure to stay well behind Travers for fear of being spotted on the lightly traveled street. Nines Ridge Lane was gated, and Travers leaned out his window and punched in the code, which opened the gate and granted him entrance. I did a U-turn and parked on Braemere, facing downhill, got out of my car and strolled to Nines Ridge on foot, walking past the gate on the sidewalk. Travers's Escalade was parked in front of a low, sleek, modern house of white stucco and black trim with massive uncurtained plate glass windows in the back and front so that, from the street, I could see straight through the house to the city lights below.

I was afraid of getting too close to the house, assuming that a guy like Childs in a house like this would have security cameras and an alarm system. So I trotted back to my car, opened the trunk and took out my camera, which still had the 80-200m zoom lens that I usually used for football games.

I took up a position across the street from Childs's house and zoomed the camera lens directly into the living room. I watched as Travers handed Brad Childs the manila envelope he had picked up at the photo studio.

Childs set his drink down on a coffee table and opened the envelope. He pulled out several sheets and looked them over and nodded. Childs's back was to me, close to the window, close enough for me to see the sheets he pulled from the envelope were photographs, close enough for me to just barely make out what they were photographs of but not who was in them. Knowing what I knew, though, about that photo studio and who Travers was looking for, I safely assumed who was in the photos. Childs returned the photos to the envelope, handed it back to Travers, picked up his glass, took a sip and said a few words to Travers. Travers nodded and started to turn toward the front door.

I hurried back to my car.

42

I slumped down in the driver's seat of my car and adjusted my mirror to see Travers's Escalade pull through the gate, back onto Braemere Drive from Nines Ridge Lane and pass me down the hill. I left my headlights off and didn't even start my car, putting it in neutral and letting gravity pull the car down the hill silently, well behind Travers. As soon as Travers's vehicle came into sight around a curve, I would slow and let the Escalade disappear, making sure I never entered Travers's rearview mirror.

Travers made his way back down to Bogus Basin Road, and I started my engine and was able to keep myself lost among the other cars on the road at that time of night.

I followed Travers through the North End, then skirted the west side of downtown, under the overpass for I-84, which had once been a homeless encampment but was now a skate park that was bustling on this Friday night. Travers took River Street back over to Ninth Street and Capitol Boulevard, and I was concerned that Travers knew where Lauren and Cindy were holed up at Federal Arms.

But instead of turning left onto Federal Way, Travers stayed straight on Capitol Boulevard and onto Vista Avenue, which led to the airport.

After a mile or so, Travers turned onto Kootenai Street into a quiet residential neighborhood known as The Bench. It was just that: a bench elevated above the city, and the houses here were nice in their day, the suburbs of Boise, a mishmash of colonials with postage-stamp-size yards all the way up to brick mansions with sprawling lawns.

Travers turned right onto Owyhee Street and pulled over.

I passed Travers and pulled over in front of a massive pickup truck as cover. I could still see Travers's car in my sideview mirror, and I watched as he got out holding the manila envelope as he crossed the street and walked toward the corner property, a brick house surrounded by a brick wall topped with sharp wrought-iron finials.

Travers pressed a buzzer on the brick gateway at the sidewalk and waited.

After a half minute, the gate buzzed, and Travers opened the wrought-iron gate. Once Travers was through the gateway, I hustled out of my car and made my way to the alleyway on the north side of the property. The brick wall was only five feet tall, but the house was obscured by a heavy layer of trees and bushes surrounding the property. I was able to peek through an opening among the trees and bushes that gave me a view of Travers standing and waiting at the front entryway.

The man who opened the front door was John Broten.

He greeted Travers and let him in. I walked around to the back of the property to the guesthouse, which was bigger than most of the houses on the block. The detached three-car garage with living quarters above was as big as the other houses in the neighborhood. It was certainly bigger than my tiny abode in Fremont.

Broten's property was immaculately landscaped with a sprawling golf-course-quality lawn, Japanese maples, pine trees, flower beds, even a small footbridge over a burbling canal running downhill from a rock waterfall. I walked around the property entirely and decided to stay on the street, about a half block away within view of the Escalade parked near the front gate.

Travers wasn't inside for long. When he emerged from the house, I could see that he was no longer holding the manila envelope as he made his way to the Escalade. I tucked myself behind a utility pole, as Travers paused at his driver's side door and looked in my direction. I waited until I heard the car door slam, and the Escalade started up and pulled away.

I wasn't interested in following Travers anymore. The Federal Arms wasn't far away.

43

———————

As I expected, Lauren's white Volvo was parked in front of unit five at the Federal Arms. Lights were still on inside the room, and sheer curtains slightly obscured what was going on inside. Lauren's silhouette passed by the window from time to time, and she was talking animatedly. At one point, she was talking on her phone. After about an hour, the lights went out. Lauren did not emerge. I waited another hour before determining Lauren was staying the night. I pulled my car onto a side street under the cover of some pine trees next to a squat office building in the shadows of a streetlamp and parked. I walked over to the nearby convenience store, used the bathroom and bought some food, including a cold premade turkey bacon wrap that looked relatively safe. I avoided conversation with the overly friendly female clerk who expertly and pertly asked me, "How's your night going?" I answered tersely, declined my receipt and left. I ate my dinner in my car and settled in for the night.

I pulled out my phone and sent an email to Chief Hernandez, attaching the photos of the Escalade and tires, with a note, "Hey, Chief. Here's a Cadillac Escalade with tires that match that tire track you found in the Thompsons' driveway. Might be something."

When I was in college, when I worked as a security guard on the overnight shift at a county-run nursing home, I learned to sleep while sitting up. My partner and I would alternate patrolling the grounds in one-hour shifts, and I would use my hour in the security office to sleep, sitting in my chair, leaning against a filing cabinet. My internal clock got very good at knowing when one hour was done, and it was time to wake up before my partner returned from patrol.

I practiced that now, snoozing one hour in my car, waking up to confirm the Volvo was still there, going back to sleep for an hour and so on through the night.

Just before dawn, while it was still dark, I did some deep breathing to wake myself up and chugged a half liter of water. I walked over to the convenience store, where fortunately, the talkative overnight clerk had already been replaced by a pimply faced, sullen young man who was not interested in me in the least. I used the bathroom, washed my hands and splashed cold water on my face and combed my hair. A cup of hot coffee and a breakfast sandwich back at the car, and I was as good as new.

The curtains to unit five were drawn, but I could now see a sliver of light turned on where the curtains didn't quite meet. After a few minutes, a disheveled Lauren stumbled out of the room and headed to the convenience store. She came back with two coffees and a couple of bags of food. She knocked on the door with her foot and the door opened. I rolled down my window and waited.

It was a clear crisp fall morning, and the smell of the pine trees above me mingled with the smell of fresh-cut grass as the sky was just threatening to turn light and the birds were just beginning to chirp. It was still dark enough that the streetlights cast shadows on the still-quiet Saturday morning streets.

The door to unit five opened, and Lauren walked out, her hair wet from a fresh shower. She walked past her car and across the parking lot. She looked both ways and crossed Federal Way to a walking path on the other side.

She walked a hundred feet or so and stopped at an overlook, leaned on the railing and looked across the valley to the city lights across the way.

I quietly got out of my car and made my way across the street to where

Lauren was. I stopped behind her and a little to her right. I looked past her toward the city. The lights were still on downtown, and they shimmered against the foothills behind.

Among the foothills, I realized I could see the tree-lined neighborhoods wending their way up Braemere, and the lights and trees gave way to what must be Nines Ridge Lane, and if I used my imagination, I could pick out a light that might belong to Childs's house.

As I stood there in my own reverie, Lauren turned and faced me. She didn't seem surprised to see me in the least, as if she were expecting me, as if our meeting were prearranged. She didn't seem happy to see me or sad to see me. She didn't seem to have any emotion at all. She looked drained and empty.

"How is she?" I said finally.

"Who?" Lauren said, almost defiantly.

"Your sister."

Lauren opened her mouth as if to say something, likely in protest, but then thought better of it. She looked down, then back up at me.

"She's fine."

"Travers is looking for her."

"I'm sure he is," she said.

"Can I talk to her?"

"What are you going to do?" she asked me, her voice now cold, hard.

"I just want to ask her a few questions."

"And then what?"

"I don't know. I'm still figuring it out. I don't have all the answers yet."

I paused again, and Lauren said nothing.

"Let's talk to Cindy," I said in a voice that I thought might sound soothing. "After all, she's the reason your father's being blackmailed."

Lauren drew in a sharp breath.

"You're just caught in the middle of all this, Lauren," I said. I put my hands on her arms, just below her shoulders, and gently moved my thumbs over her sweater. "Let me help you."

Her shoulders relaxed, and she looked into my eyes. The sun was now starting to come up over the horizon. Lauren looked past me to the motel. She looked tired, resigned.

"Fine."

I followed her quietly across the street and the parking lot, as she pulled a key out of her pocket. She knocked softly on the door to unit five before turning the key in the lock and opening the door. She stepped inside and I followed.

The smell of clove cigarettes hit me as soon as I walked in the door.

44

Cindy was sitting on the bed, wearing a white camisole that barely covered her lower parts. She made no effort to cover herself up. She looked like hell, with swollen eyes and puffy cheeks, and her voice was hoarse like an old woman with a two-pack-a-day habit for fifty years. Cindy took a drag from a thin, brown cigarette that I recognized and flicked the ashes into a slightly filled can of Diet Coke that sizzled when she tapped her cigarette on the opening.

"Who the hell is he?" Cindy croaked.

"Cindy," Lauren said in a calming tone.

"Who the hell is he?" Cindy yelled, and Lauren closed the door.

"He's a reporter with the –"

"A reporter? Are you fucking kidding me, Lauren? You brought a reporter here?"

"I didn't bring him. He found us. And if he could find us, someone else could, too."

"Eddie?" Cindy said derisively.

"Yes, Eddie."

"Who cares?"

"I do, Cindy. Listen, this is Philip Chandler. He already knows what's going on." She looked at me. "At least I think he knows."

"Yeah, right. What do you think you know?" she said to me.

"I know you were there the night your boyfriend beat me up," I said.

Cindy let out a dismissive rush of air between her lips.

"I know you were there the night Eddie Travers shot and killed Vern and Wanda Thompson."

That got her attention, and Lauren's attention, too.

Lauren spoke up.

"What are you talking about?"

"Vern and Wanda Thompson were shot and killed Monday night at their house in Fremont, while you and I were at city council, and I think Eddie Travers was the one who killed them, and I think Cindy was sitting out in his Escalade while he was inside shooting them."

"Cindy?"

"How the hell would you know that?"

"Police found a clove cigarette outside the house, in the front lawn, where the passenger side of the car would be, and I'm willing to bet that if they're able to get DNA off it, it's going to come back as a match to you. Just like the clove cigarette that you were smoking while you were waiting for me at my house Thursday night. The same cigarette you were smoking while your boyfriend followed me to my office and gave me a hell of a beating. The exact same kind of cigarette you're smoking right now."

"Cindy?"

Cindy nervously shifted, and her hand shook as she stubbed out the cigarette on the top of the soda can and threw the stub inside.

"I didn't know he was going to beat you up. I'm sorry."

"What about the Thompsons?" Lauren asked.

"He doesn't exactly tell me what he's up to, you know," Cindy said. "I had no idea what the hell he was doing. He just said we're going for a ride, said he's gotta take care of something, talk to a couple of old people down in Fremont. I didn't know what he was doing. And I didn't exactly have any choice, you know?"

"What happened?" Lauren said, her voice rising and shaking.

"He went inside the house, and I waited in the car. He was in there for a long time, then I heard these gunshots, like two or three shots, and then Eddie came outside, all sweating and nervous and amped up. He said we're getting the hell out of there and told me to keep my mouth shut. He didn't tell me anything. And I didn't ask. Then I saw the news the next day and figured out what happened."

"Jesus, Cindy. You're a witness to a murder, for God's sake. An accessory, even."

"I had nothing to do with it, Lauren. I was just sitting in the goddamn car, for Christ's sake."

"Try and tell that to the police."

"Is that what you're going to do? Call the police? Call the cops on me? Turn me in?"

Lauren turned away from Cindy and ran her hands through her hair.

"I don't know. I don't know what I'm going to do. Jesus."

"Lauren," I said. "Can I talk to you outside?"

Cindy stood up and started pacing nervously. She picked up her phone and looked at it, then threw it down on the bed. I opened the door, and Lauren and I went outside onto the small walkway in front of the room.

"Lauren, you're going to have to call the police."

"I can't."

"She's a witness to a murder. If what she says is true, she'll probably avoid any serious trouble. Maybe charges of not reporting a crime to police or something like that."

"I can't."

"But look, it'll all be over. It'll all be out in the open. She'll be able to get the help she needs, and Childs won't have anything over your father anymore."

"It would kill her. It would probably kill my father, too."

"No it won't, for God's sake. Just call the police and end this whole thing."

"I can't, Philip. I can't do that to her."

"Then I will."

"You wouldn't."

"Now that I know, I can't keep it a secret. I'm not going to be charged with concealing evidence or not reporting a crime."

Lauren visibly deflated, and she turned slightly, her left arm falling to her side and her right hand running through her hair.

"Let me talk to my father first. I can't just call the police without letting him know. Let me talk to him and then I'll call the police."

She looked deep into my eyes, and I couldn't help myself.

"Fine," I said. "But I'm going with you."

45

Lauren went back in the room and told Cindy to stay put and keep calm. She left her some cash, grabbed her purse and walked to her car without even acknowledging me. She got in her car, and I ran over to mine, pulling out quickly to catch up.

We drove the short distance to her father's house, and we parked in a paved area off the back alley next to the garage.

Lauren led me along a flagstone path that wound through the immaculately landscaped backyard and over a small footbridge that crossed a stream. Dew glistened on the grass, and the morning held the promise of a day of leisure, reading the paper on the back porch over a cup of coffee with the prospect of a lazy weekend of nothing to do ahead.

Lauren glanced back just once to make sure I was still there. We entered the house through a back door that opened onto a mudroom that had a bench and coat hooks and shelves that held hats and boots and coats, as if it were a country cottage. Lauren set her purse down on the bench and hung her keys on a hook almost automatically.

"Dad," she called out as we entered a massive kitchen, gleaming with white cabinets, black marble countertops, and shiny stainless steel appliances. It looked like it had never been used but staged for a magazine shoot.

Lauren paused, listening, and I could hear floorboards creak with approaching footsteps.

"Hi, Lauren," John Broten said, then stopped short when he saw me. Broten looked at me, then at Lauren, back to me, then back to Lauren.

"What the hell is he doing here?" Broten said angrily.

"He'd like to talk to you, Dad," Lauren said calmly, her voice visibly soothing her father.

"About what?" Broten said.

"Everything," Lauren said, the single word full of meaning.

Broten blinked.

"He knows everything," Lauren said.

"You told him?" Broten said, sounding hurt and betrayed. I suddenly felt awkward standing in his kitchen.

"No, Dad, he figured it out on his own. And if he can figure it out, someone else could, too."

Broten looked again at me, looking me up and down, as if appraising me, still angrily, condescendingly, affronted that I would be standing here in his home, invading his gleaming, spotless kitchen. I instinctively knew to stay silent, let Lauren keep the lead.

"Dad," Lauren said softly.

Broten looked back at Lauren, then back at me.

"What are you going to do?" Broten said to me with a sneer. "You going to write about this? You're going to write a story about me, about all this? What do you want? You want money? You're here to get money from me? How much?"

"Dad," Lauren said again, less softly, as if a command.

I stepped forward.

"I don't know what I'm going to do just yet, Mr. Broten, but I didn't come here for money," I said, my voice sounding odd even to me echoing among the kitchen walls. "I'm not a blackmailer. I'm a journalist. Blackmailers may be the kind of people you deal with, but that's not who I am. I just came here to ask you some questions."

Broten's shoulders slumped and his face lost its anger and became drawn, tired, older, showing the weight of his burden. He looked at Lauren, who nodded.

"It's fine, Dad," Lauren said in a tone that struck me as commanding, in control.

"All right," Broten said finally, and he turned and waved his hand for us to follow. He led us through the kitchen and into a great room that was as big as my tiny house in Fremont. It was painted pale blue and held over-stuffed furniture and had a large stone fireplace and a massive blue-and-cream oriental rug on the floor. Like the kitchen, it looked like no one lived there, as if it was made up for a movie set. On the far end of the room, Broten opened a heavy oak door to a study and entered, with Lauren and me in tow.

This was where Broten spent his time. It had signs of life, of being used, lived in. It was a large room with high ceilings and dark wood paneling, and one wall was consumed by shelves of books. A collection of a sofa and armchairs surrounded a large coffee table and faced a smaller brick fireplace to the left. To the right, the back wall held tall windows, nearly to the twelve-foot ceiling, framed by heavy maroon fabric drapes and covered by sheer inner curtains. Despite the light that the windows let in, the room had a gloomy feel, a pall like a funeral parlor. In a corner was a bar set with a dozen half-empty bottles of liquor.

In front of the windows was a large antique desk, complete with leather blotter. Two antique chairs faced the desk, and a new modern office chair was behind it, its back to the windows. A half-empty glass of amber liquid sat on the desk, which was messy with files, newspapers and law books.

On top of the mess was a manila envelope that I recognized as the one Travers had delivered the night before.

Broten made his way to his chair behind the desk, and Lauren sat in one of the chairs in front of him. I remained standing. Broten seemed to regain some of his composure, sitting in a familiar spot, remembering who he was, his importance, his power.

"I don't know what you want, Chandler, or what you think you're going to do," Broten said, with a little more energy and confidence. "But I assure you, whatever you think you know, if you print any of it, it's not going to go well for you. I'll sue you for libel so fast –"

"Even if what I print is true, Mr. Broten?" I interrupted.

"Even if it's true, Mr. Chandler," Broten said. "How do you think that will go for you? Do you have money in the bank to defend yourself? Got enough to hire a lawyer for a year or two?"

"No. No, I haven't."

Broten seemed to soften.

"Besides," Broten said, looking over at Lauren, "you don't want to bring any other trouble on yourself. Whatever you think you know, you probably don't know the half of it. And I don't think you want to find out."

"I think I already know everything."

"Really? I highly doubt that."

"What I couldn't figure out was what Childs had on you," I said. "Sure, he got you elected to the county commission with those attack ads against Linda Davis. And I suppose that and some campaign donations bought him some goodwill to get his H-Bar Ranch development approved. But putting in that clause in the development agreement that allowed him to expand it as far as he wanted was sneaky and risky. Maybe you were okay with that on principle. Maybe not. Maybe you got that done for him in exchange for his help getting you elected to the legislature. Once you got into the legislature, you didn't need to kowtow to him anymore. Clearly business is good, money's not an issue, reelection in your district was safe as mother's milk. So why then, I kept thinking, why would you kill a water study of Basin 63? And then you led the charge in changing the state's place of use and point of diversion water laws for him. You also voted for that interchange so his H-Bar Ranch would have easy access to the freeway. I can see how Childs could buy off the Idaho Liberty Coalition. That's easy. But what about you, Mr. Broten? I thought, could it be a kickback, once the deal is done?"

"I don't take bribes or kickbacks," Broten said indignantly.

"No. That's what I figured. That's not the kind of person you are and not the kind of person who needs it. And there was something else in that nod you gave him in the committee hearing. An agreement that you've done what he's asked of you. That you held up your end of the bargain. That's when I started to think that Childs must have something on you, something he's holding over your head, threatening you with."

Broten and Lauren waited.

"And then I followed your daughter last night," I said. "To the Admiral,"

I said, looking at Lauren, who gave no expression. "And I learned about Cindy. She has troubles, as you're well aware. Dances at the Admiral, which I'm sure you don't want public. But it's worse than that, isn't it? Drugs of different varieties over the years. Meth, heroin, oxy, which not only got her messed up, but her addiction got her into other trouble that Childs was able to use against her. You'd do anything to protect her, like kill water studies and get state water laws changed. And I'm not going to ask to see proof, Mr. Broten, I don't want to see it, but I'm willing to bet I know what kind of photos are in that manila envelope that Eddie Travers dropped off last night," I said, pointing to the desk.

"Dad?" Lauren said.

Broten snapped up and reflexively reached out and pulled the envelope under his arm.

"And then there's the matter of Vern and Wanda Thompson," I said, not wanting to slow down.

"Who are they?" Broten said.

I scoffed. "Maybe you're the one who doesn't know the half of it, Mr. Broten."

"What are you talking about?"

"They were just some nice old farm couple down in Fremont who made the mistake of filing a protest against Childs's water rights, and Childs sent his goon Eddie Travers, the same goon who was standing right here in this room last night, Broten. Childs sent Travers down to put a scare into Vern and Wanda Thompson to get them to drop their water protest, just like he did to Nick Ashley. But old Vern Thompson decided to put up a fight, and Travers put a bullet in him and then put another one in Mrs. Thompson. That's what you get for messing around with Childs."

"Jesus," Broten said, rubbing his face with his hands.

My phone buzzed in my pocket, but I ignored it.

"And I've got more bad news for you, Mr. Broten. Your daughter Cindy was sitting in Eddie's Escalade outside the house when it happened."

"What?" He looked from me over to Lauren, who just looked down and turned away. "Is this true, Lauren?"

"I'm afraid so, Dad," she said without looking up.

"How could you let this happen?"

Now Lauren looked up, her face red, with tears beginning to well in her eyes.

"Don't you dare," she growled. "You can't keep putting this on me. I can't take it anymore. I can't watch her every minute of the day. I'm tired of it. It's too much. She's too much. I can't take care of her or protect her anymore, Dad. I'm done."

The room fell silent except for the ticking of a clock somewhere in the room.

"I'm sorry, Lauren," Broten whispered barely audible, and he lowered his head.

Lauren turned toward the fireplace and cried quietly, wiping her eyes and sniffling.

"I don't know what to do with her anymore," Broten said to me without looking at me. His voice was soft, tired but calm and clear. "Lauren knows. We've tried everything. We've tried to help her. Paid for rehab, sent her to school, sent her to Europe, resorts, therapy, counselors." He was still looking down at his desk. "Their mother died when they were young. I guess Lauren was old enough to handle it. Cindy wasn't. She was never right after that. Angry, free-spirited, rebellious, vengeful. It was like she was taking revenge on the world, on herself. We've tried everything."

The room was still. The clock measured out a few more ticks.

"What do you expect me to do?" Broten said.

"Quit enabling your daughter, for starters," I said, almost to myself.

Broten looked up quickly. "Excuse me?" Broten said indignantly.

"Cut her loose, for God's sake," I said. "Let her go. The only way she's ever going to get better is if she hits rock bottom and decides to pull herself out of it. But she's not going to get there if you pay for her house to live in, send her on European vacations, pay for her treatments and come rescue her every time she gets strung out. Look what you're doing to your other daughter." Someone I now realized I cared about. "What about her? Don't you give a damn about her?"

"Who the hell do you think you are?" Broten said, slamming his hand on his desk. "Don't tell me what to do with my family."

My shoulders slumped, and I looked down and rubbed the welt on the back of my head. I looked back up at Broten and held my hands out, palms up.

"I didn't come here to tell you what to do," I said. "I came here to get answers about what's going on. I'm just writing a story about two good people who were murdered, possibly three, and it's because of Brad Childs and his plans to steal other people's water so he can build a city in the middle of the desert. I don't care what you do, Broten, but if you ask me, you'd be doing yourself a favor if you cut your daughter loose."

"I can't do that," Broten said. "Not now. This whole business is almost over. Once this bill passes, I'm out, I'm done. I won't run for another term. I'll retire. It'll be all over. And I can focus on helping Cindy. Childs agreed. This is it."

"Childs," I spat out with disdain. "You made a deal with the devil, Broten. Talk about ruining lives. If you let her go, Childs has nothing on you anymore. Kill the bill, tell Childs to go to hell. Call the police. It'll be painful, there will be some embarrassment, but it truly will be over, and you'll be done with it all."

Broten looked up at me, now calm again, resolute.

"I can't. I won't. She'd never forgive me. I won't do it."

"Mr. Broten, the Thompsons are dead, Alan Garry is dead, and you're moaning over your messed-up daughter. I'm sorry your wife died, but this is an awfully long mourning period. And it's an awfully long trail of pain and suffering because of it. Maybe focus on helping your other daughter for a change. If you don't, she'll be the one to never forgive you."

For the first time, Broten looked scared, afraid of being connected to the Thompson murders, Alan Garry's death, the blackmail.

I sighed, turned and paced the room, trying to figure out what to do. I had been saying all along that I wasn't sure what I was working on, whether I was going to write a story, what I was going to do, and now it came down to this. The time for waffling was over. I was either going to have to do something myself or drop it. The idea of dropping it was unfathomable. I could walk away right now and never look back. Leave them all to their sordid dealings. But I knew there was no way I could just ignore what I knew. No way I could do nothing. I was starting to think about leads and headlines and layouts.

"Philip," Lauren said suddenly, her voice soft and steady, again with a tone of command. "Just expose Childs's scheme without dragging my family into it. Write about the water rights, H-Bar Ranch, but just leave out the part about my father and my sister."

I involuntarily chuckled.

"That would only get me so far," I said. "That leaves me with only half the story."

"That will be enough," Lauren said in an odd way that I couldn't tell if she was pleading or demanding. "It will have to be enough," she said, her voice not as soft but just as steady.

I paused, appraising Lauren.

My phone buzzed again. My mind wandered, trying to think who might be trying to get a hold of me so desperately early on a Saturday morning. I was tempted to look, but I ignored it for now.

"Besides," Lauren said, "you don't even really have this part of the story." She pointed a hand in the direction of the desk, her father and the manila envelope under his arm.

I looked at her, puzzled, but some sort of light began to turn on in my mind, like a dimmer switch slowly going up.

"You have everything else, Philip," Lauren said. "Don't you see? You have the records of water rights. You've been out to H-Bar. You have the legislation. The water study. For God's sake, you have enough right now to write your story. But that's all you really have. Anything about blackmail, my father, my sister, whatever's in that manila envelope. You have no proof of any of it. Certainly nothing you could write in a story that you could publish. You have the rest. Write that."

"How can I write a story without explaining all of this?" I said, waving a hand in the direction of Broten and the manila envelope.

"My father is acting out of principle," Lauren said matter-of-factly. "Just like he's said publicly, on the record. Just like you already have."

"But I know the truth," I said angrily.

"But you can't report it," Lauren said. "Not without proof. You can't write what you think you know. You can only write what you can prove to be true."

I looked over at Broten and the desk and the manila envelope under his arm. Broten now sat up straighter, his eyes still red but dry now. A look of confusion passed over his face.

My brow furrowed, and then I smiled. She was right. I looked back at Lauren, who was stone-faced.

My mind raced. The light that was going on in my head now came on completely. I laughed.

"You came down to Fremont to see Bernie and you stopped by my office, just like you said."

"Correct."

"And you were actually hoping I wouldn't be there."

"Correct."

"So it would be the perfect opportunity for you to put an envelope with F9 Development's business license in my dropbox."

"Yes."

"And you're Mark Felt."

"Yes."

"Who's Mark Felt?" John Broten asked. "What is he talking about?" he asked Lauren.

"Your daughter's been feeding me tips anonymously all along, Mr. Broten, letting me know about Brad Childs's plans. All so that it would look like I was just some nosy reporter. And she did a good job of it, too, until I got too close to what Childs was holding over your head." I turned back to Lauren.

"You tipped me off to the study of Basin 63, led me to H-Bar Ranch, the attack ads against Linda Davis."

Lauren nodded her head at each item. "Yes."

"Mark Felt. I should have figured it out when you told me about reading *All the President's Men*," I said derisively. I thought of that night at the bar with her. "I should have known I was being played."

"Philip," Lauren said, sounding exhausted. "Just write what you have."

Lauren had drawn me in as close as possible so that I could expose Childs but not close enough to expose the Brotens. It was the only way to extricate themselves from Childs without letting Childs know it was them. It was the only way to expose Childs without him using what he had on Cindy.

Lauren hadn't intended for me to find out about Cindy, but she was right that I couldn't write about her. Knowing is one thing; writing about it is another. It would all be speculation. And all I could write was about Childs, the water rights and H-Bar Ranch. If I wrote all that I knew about Childs's scheme, it would leave the Brotens innocent and out of it. Childs would be exposed, but it wouldn't be the Brotens who exposed him. She had led me down the path to report what Childs was doing, just not why Broten was helping him. I could and would report Childs's whole plan, thus exposing him without forcing Broten to oppose him and without running the risk of Childs exposing Broten's secret about Cindy.

"Chandler," Broten said suddenly, his voice one of command, as if he had pulled himself together and reminded himself that he was a powerful state senator and attorney.

He reached over to a ledger on his desk, opened it, and began writing in it. He folded the page, then tore out what was now clear to me was a check. He held it up and shook it at me.

"Here," he said.

I walked over to him and took the check. It was made out to me in the amount of fifty thousand dollars.

For a moment I considered putting it in my pocket. It was almost double what I was paying myself out of the business per year, and I immediately thought about what I could do with the money.

"Take it, and don't write a word about any of this," Broten said. "Lauren shouldn't have told you anything. She means well, but I can handle this. I can handle Childs. I don't need you to write some story exposing all this. Take that and drop the whole thing."

I held the check in front of me, and I realized my mouth was half-open, and I must have looked like some country bumpkin in the face of so much money.

"That's all you have to do," Broten said. "Just do nothing. Go back to writing about city council meetings and whatever else they do in Fremont. Just go back to what you were doing, ignore all this, and everyone's happy."

Almost as if on autopilot, I watched my hands as they tore the check down the middle, then again and again, calmly and deliberately. I set the pieces down on Broten's desk.

"That's not who I am, Mr. Broten," I said.

Broten's face turned red, and he was about to say something, when Lauren's phone buzzed.

She picked it up and looked at a text message.

"Oh my God," she said.

"What is it?" Broten said. "Is it Cindy?"

"She just texted me. She said she's tired of waiting around. She said she needs a fix. She called Eddie. He's coming to get her."

46

———

Broten stood up, and Lauren hit a button on her phone and held it up to her ear.

After a few seconds, Lauren spoke. "Cindy, call me back. Do not go with Eddie. I will come get you. Just call me back and tell me where you are."

She hung up the phone and looked at her father, neither knowing what to do or say.

My own phone buzzed again, and this time I pulled it out of my pocket.

It was a text message from Chief Hernandez.

"Call me. Now."

I looked at Lauren. "Hold on," I said. "I have to take this. Give me a minute. I'll be right back."

I exited the study, apparently through the wrong door, not the way I had entered, and found myself in an ornate foyer between a grand staircase and the massive wooden front door where Broten had received Eddie Travers the night before.

I hit the speed dial for John Hernandez.

"Where are you?" Hernandez said, sounding annoyed.

"I'm working," I said, not wanting to disclose I was at Broten's house. "I can't talk long, Chief. I'm kind of in the middle of something."

"Where the hell did you get those photos you sent me last night?"

"I took them."

"Geez, Phil. Now you're caught up in this."

"What do you mean?"

"Do you know the guy you took photos of?"

"I think I know who it is," I said guardedly. I looked back at the door to the study, anxious to get back to Lauren.

"Does the name Eddie Travers sound familiar?" Hernandez said.

"Yeah, I think that's the guy," I said. "Look, Chief, I gotta –"

"Listen, Phil, you've got to keep those photos to yourself. Delete them. Pretend you never sent them to me. Delete them off your phone, delete them out of your sent email. I'm going to do the same."

"But, Chief –"

"I'm conducting a police investigation, Philip. Don't interfere with it. Do you understand?"

"Fine," I said. I had no intention of deleting those photos, but I wanted to get him off the phone and get back to Lauren.

"And for God's sake, stay the hell away from that guy. I can't tell you too much, but trust me, he's dangerous."

I scratched the welt on the back of my head and thought briefly about telling Hernandez what happened but thought better of it. "I will."

Hernandez sighed. "Look, I'll fill you in later," he said in a more conciliatory tone. "But for now, just do what I say."

"Fine, Chief, will do," I said quickly and hung up.

When I returned to the study, Broten was standing by the fireplace sipping from a glass.

Lauren was not there.

47

"She's gone," Broten said, pointing his glass toward the back door. "Went to look for Cindy."

He must have grown accustomed to this, having Lauren do this kind of thing, rescue Cindy, chase her down, take care of this part of the business and keep him out of it. I briefly considered sharing those thoughts with him and giving my opinion of him, but I was thinking of Lauren right now.

I rushed through the door, through the living room and spotless kitchen and out the back door, across the immaculate lawn to the driveway, which sat empty, except for my own car.

I looked both ways up and down the alley but could see no sign of Lauren's car.

I jumped in my own car and headed back to the Federal Arms. There was no sign of Cindy, Lauren or Eddie Travers. I knocked on the door to unit five, knowing there would be no answer.

I headed back through downtown, briefly passing by the Hoff Building parking lot. Lauren's car wasn't there. I continued on to the Admiral, naively expecting it to be open on a Saturday morning. There was only one car in the parking lot, a blue Ford Mustang, perhaps left there by a customer the night before. I pulled into the parking lot, got out of my car and tried the front door, which was locked. I scurried around to the back alley, where I had seen

Lauren take Cindy out the back door. I climbed the stairs and knocked on the door. I waited and knocked again. I tried the door, but it was locked.

I got back in my car and drove over to 28th Street and Cindy's house. Again, no signs of life there.

I was at a complete loss, feeling hopeless and impotent.

I called Lauren's cell phone, and my call went straight to voicemail.

"Lauren, it's me, Philip. Please call me back. Let me help you. Just call me back."

I sat in my car for several minutes, looking down at my phone, willing it to ring.

I decided to make the rounds all over again, back to the Admiral, past the Hoff Building parking lot, back up to the Federal Arms, where a maid was now cleaning unit five. I drove past Broten's house and down the alley, but Lauren's car wasn't there.

I tried a long shot and drove back out to the photo studio on Chinden Boulevard. No sign of Travers's Cadillac Escalade.

Becoming desperate, I made my way back up Braemere Drive up to Nines Ridge Lane, which now looked different in the daylight, more plastic, fake somehow in the harsh sunlight.

Travers's black Escalade wasn't there, but a white Ford F-150 was parked in front in its place.

From the sidewalk, I could see inside the house and saw Childs with two men, one bearded and perhaps even bigger than Travers and the other short and squat. Childs led them out of the living room, to the east end of the house toward the garage. I waited several minutes but saw no sign of Travers. Someone from a neighboring house opened their front door and emerged, and I walked back to my car, not wanting to get the police called on me.

I drove back downtown, not knowing what else to do. I called Lauren's number again and it went to voicemail.

Reluctantly, I decided to drive back to Fremont.

It was just as Lauren had said. It was time to just write the story. The story I already had.

As I drove back to Fremont, I formulated the story in my head, putting together the puzzle pieces I had, the pieces I could prove and back up with documents, thinking about headlines and ledes.

I parked in front of my house and walked the three blocks to my office. When Roscoe barked, I didn't welcome it. "Shut up," I mumbled at him. Roscoe stopped and sat, perhaps sensing my displeasure.

I spent the day in my office dumping my notes into a Word document, and the story began to take shape.

By late afternoon, I allowed myself a couple of shots of Four Roses, and as the sun began to set, I rubbed my face and thought of Lauren.

I called her again, left another voicemail.

I finished my story on the water rights and H-Bar Ranch. I included the Thompsons' murder in it, the list of water rights, their connection to Childs and H-Bar Ranch, and just as Lauren had said, I left out anything about blackmail, Cindy or Eddie Travers. I used Broten's original statement from the committee hearing that the state shouldn't pick winners and losers and stood on his original principle of the free market.

It would have to be enough.

I stayed at my office late into the night, taking sips of whiskey and fact-checking my story. I printed it out double-spaced, marking in red pen every fact, number, data point, anything that could be challenged and verified, and triple-checked each one. Once a fact was checked and verified, I put a checkmark next to it.

I had to be very careful how I wrote it. Childs's threat of a libel suit was no idle threat. I laid down facts and only facts, one after another, each one completely true, verifiable and undeniable.

By one a.m., I was exhausted but satisfied with my story.

I texted Lauren one more time, "Please call me or just text me and let me know you're all right."

I stumbled home and went to bed.

It was a short sleep, though, as my phone began to buzz just after sunrise.

I quickly picked it up, hoping it was Lauren, but the caller ID read "Chief Hernandez."

"We found Travers," he said loudly.

It sounded like Hernandez was outdoors. I could hear the wind blowing, people talking, cars driving by, radio traffic.

"You caught Travers?" I said, my voice gravelly, my head groggy.

"We got him all right."

"Did he tell you anything?"

"He didn't say a thing."

"Of course not."

"He didn't say a thing because his body and his car are at the bottom of Lucky Peak Canyon."

"He's dead?"

"You know Suicide Bridge?" Hernandez asked. "That bridge where that mom drove herself and her three kids off the cliff a couple of years ago?"

"Yeah, I remember it."

"That's where he did it. Drove off that same spot."

"I'm on my way," I said, my adrenaline kicking up a notch.

"And, Philip? One more thing."

"Yeah?"

"There's a dead woman in the car with him."

48

Just to the east of Boise, on State Highway 21, the Lucky Peak Bridge spanned 432 feet across the Mores Creek inlet to Lucky Peak Reservoir.

It had been the site of several suicide attempts, so many that it earned the nickname "Suicide Bridge."

On the east side of that bridge, off to the left as you drove down Highway 21, there was a small parking area looking down into the canyon below. This parking area was unprotected from the cliffside. No Jersey barrier, no rocks, no guardrail, just a straight unimpeded plunge two hundred feet into Lucky Peak Reservoir.

The spot had been the site of at least two suicides in the previous ten years, a despondent mother with her three young children, another a heartbroken young man whose girlfriend had broken up with him.

After the suicide of the mother with her three young children, there had been talk of putting up some sort of barrier at the cliff's edge, boulders, a fence, a Jersey barrier, anything. But nothing had been done about it.

It remained an open invitation.

The drive out to the Lucky Peak Bridge was incongruously gorgeous, and I couldn't quite square the thought of this picture-perfect, crisp fall morning with the ugliness of the situation.

When I got to the bridge about twenty minutes later, an officer was slowing cars down right before the bridge. On the other side, police cars, fire engines, rescue trucks and ambulances lined Highway 21. I passed the lineup and parked my car in the first available opening, about one hundred yards down the road.

I grabbed my camera, threw the strap over my neck, pulled out my notebook and pen and started walking toward the scene. I had learned long ago that to gain access to an area, just look and act like you belong there. It helps to actually believe you belong there, too.

As I approached, I started taking photos of what I could, knowing I could be stopped at any second.

When Hernandez spotted me, he was visibly angry.

"For God's sake, Phil," Hernandez said, putting a hand on the camera and pushing the lens to the side. "Put that thing down. This is an active scene. Back," he barked, drawing the looks of the others at the scene, and pointed behind me, walking with me. "You're not here for work."

I did as I was told but held my camera up in the air and fired off a couple more shots, in part just out of defiance.

Hernandez led me to the back of a police SUV, shielded from the wind and out of earshot of the other police and rescue workers. Hernandez looked around, then back at me.

"All right. Spill it," Hernandez said, pulling his own notebook out of his pocket.

"Spill what?" I said.

"Look, goddammit," Hernandez said. I had never heard Hernandez swear before. "I like you, Phil, but so help me God, I'll throw you in the back of my car and take you to jail right now. Anyone else and you'd be in handcuffs right now."

"Why?"

"Are you serious? You send me photos of a guy who might be connected to a double homicide in my town and who is now at the bottom of Lucky Peak Reservoir. Now tell me what the heck is going on." Heck was more like it, and I could tell Hernandez was calming down.

I was hesitant to talk, in part because I didn't have my whole story straight, and in part because I didn't want to blow my scoop. I knew that anything I told Hernandez could be fair game for another reporter. I didn't want to tell Hernandez everything I had, but I knew I was going to have to talk. I knew telling at least part of the truth would work.

"I've been looking into land sales in the desert out by where the Thompsons live. You know, that's what Vern told me the last time we spoke. I started hearing about this guy Eddie Travers driving around in a Cadillac Escalade, putting the screws to people, threatening them, trying to buy up their land. A family by the name of Ogata was one of them. I think he might have something to do with that explosion at Nick Ashley's. And then I got jumped at the office the other night by a guy I'm pretty sure was Travers."

"Travers jumped you at your office?"

"I'm pretty sure it was him. I caught him out of the corner of my eye, and then I saw his Escalade pull away."

"You didn't report it?"

"No," I said sheepishly.

"Geez, Phil. What night was this?"

"Thursday."

"Time?"

"About 9:30."

"Tell me what happened."

"I was unlocking the door to my office, and this guy came up behind me, punched me in the back of the head, pushed me down, punched me a couple more times in the side and kicked me in the leg. He said, 'Be careful what you write about.'"

"All right, so how the hell did you get photos of him?"

"I was driving around Boise last night, and I spotted the Escalade, and I followed him and took those photos when Travers stopped at a convenience store, and I sent them to you."

"You just happened to spot the Escalade?"

"Yep," I said, and I knew he knew I was lying, but he let it pass.

"Right. Did you confront him?"

"No, I just took the photos of him. I followed him some more but then I lost him downtown. And that was it."

Hernandez sighed, ran a hand through his hair and turned to the cliff.

"And now he's at the bottom of Lucky Peak Reservoir," he said almost to himself.

"Any ID on the woman?" I asked, even though I already knew who it was.

"We think so. We're still pulling the bodies out of the car. It was under five or six feet of water, and we had to call the dive team out, which took a while. We've got a wallet with a driver's license, but we've called family to positively ID."

It was then that Lauren Broten's white Volvo pulled up.

49

───────

Lauren parked haphazardly across the road, carelessly crossed the road toward me and Hernandez, her eyes red, her face drawn, as if she already knew what she was about to experience.

"Is it Cindy?" she asked Hernandez, not even acknowledging me. "Is it my sister?"

"Come with me," Hernandez said soothingly, putting an arm around her shoulder and walking her away from me, toward the cliff's edge.

I stood back, but I could see Hernandez motion to another officer, who handed a small black-and-gold pocketbook to Hernandez. Hernandez opened it and pulled out a driver's license and handed it to Lauren.

Lauren fell to her knees and let out a low, long wail, a noise I had heard too many times at crime scenes before, mothers wailing for their dead children, wives for their dead husbands. It was animalistic, almost not human, somewhere between "No" and a guttural growl, and it always gave me a chill to hear it but always from a distance. Now, though, I felt the pain myself, and I wanted to cry.

A couple of EMTs moved over to her and knelt beside her, holding her up and rubbing her back. I instinctively moved toward Lauren, wanting to hold her in my arms and console her. I got about halfway, when a state police trooper held out a chiseled forearm across my chest.

"Hold up. This is a crime scene. Media staging is back there," he said, pointing to a cordoned area about a hundred yards down the road.

"But I'm –" I suddenly didn't know what to say. I'm what? A friend? An insider? No, I was just a reporter.

"Back there, buddy, come on," the trooper said, this time a little more forcefully, this time with his hand on my chest and giving a little nudge.

"Chief," I yelled out to Hernandez.

Hernandez's head snapped around, and he gave it a frustrated shake and made his way over to me.

"It's all right," Hernandez said to the trooper.

"Sorry, Chief, this is our scene," the trooper said. "Not your jurisdiction."

Hernandez looked like he was about to say something to the trooper but then thought better of it. He looked at me and held up his hands, as if to say, "Nothing I can do."

"Come on," the trooper said, turning me around toward the media area.

When I turned around, standing there before me was Brad Childs.

"What the hell is he doing here?" Childs said to the trooper.

"Sorry, Mr. Childs," the trooper said. "I was just escorting him out."

"Any comment on this alleged suicide?" I asked, emphasizing the word *alleged*, as I pulled my notebook out of my pocket.

Childs didn't say anything, just looked at me with a sneer.

"How about the homicides of the Thompsons?"

"I've told police everything I know," Childs said.

"Really?" I said.

Childs stepped forward and got in my face. Quietly, he said, "Be careful what you write about." It's what Travers had whispered in my ear the night he attacked me.

And then he stepped back and smiled.

That's when I heard Lauren's voice behind me.

"You did this," she yelled at Childs. "You're responsible for this. You killed her. You did this." She was bordering on hysteria, and she was violently pointing her finger at Childs's face as she got closer.

Childs, for the first time, looked frightened, and he backed away.

The trooper at my side stood between Childs and Lauren, and two more troopers jumped in to hold Lauren back. She continued to scream, "You did this," as the troopers pulled her back and put her in the back of an ambulance, where I could still hear her screaming.

"I'm sorry about that, Mr. Childs," the trooper said.

"Sorry? Mr. Childs?" I said incredulously. "What the hell is this? Why aren't you interrogating him?"

"Get him the hell out of here," Childs said to the trooper.

"Come on, buddy, let's go," the trooper said as he grabbed my shoulder and started pushing me back.

"Why the hell are you taking orders from him?" I said as the trooper pushed harder.

"Hold on," Hernandez said. "I got it."

Hernandez put his arm around my waist and walked me toward the media staging area.

"What the hell, Chief?" I said.

"Nothing I can do, Phil. He's right. It's out of my jurisdiction now. State police are handling it from here on out."

About halfway to the media staging area, Hernandez stopped.

"What's going on?" I asked him.

"You remember that slip of paper with the numbers on them?"

"Yes."

"I figured out those were water rights applications."

"How did you figure that out?"

"I'm not as dumb as you think I am, Philip. It sounds like you figured that out, too?"

"I did but I wasn't sure they had anything to do with the murders."

"Well, I figured out those applications were filed by Brad Childs. It took some digging, but I put it together eventually. I went out to his office and talked to him, and when I did, I spotted this guy, Eddie Travers," he said, pointing his thumb back at the cliff's edge. "I took a look at his car, the Escalade, along with the tires. Pirelli Scorpions. I noticed he had a gun peeping out from under his jeans, so I looked him up, and turns out he didn't have a concealed carry permit. I was getting ready to bust him just for illegal carry, search him, see if he had a gun that matched the gun that killed the Thompsons. I've been keeping an eye on him, with the possibility of bringing him in. I asked Brad Childs a few questions about Travers, how long he had worked for him, whether he knew anything about the Thompsons, where I could find him."

"What did he tell you?"

"Not much, said he'd never heard of the Thompsons, said he hadn't known Travers for very long."

"So what the hell is he doing down here now?"

"He was the one who called the police," Hernandez said.

"What?"

"He said Travers had left him a suicide note, admitting he had killed Vern and Wanda Thompson. Travers wrote he felt guilty about it, was afraid the police were going to find him, and in his letter to Childs he said he was going to go out and kill himself."

"Did he say why he killed them?" I asked.

"Childs said Travers admitted he had gone out to talk to the Thompsons about putting together some sort of land deal with them. He said Travers was going behind his back. Travers was going to take the land Childs owned—the land associated with those water rights applications on the piece of paper—and put them together with land that Vern Thompson owned around there and do some sort of development of his own. But something went wrong. Vern got mad or something over the deal, picked up a fireplace poker and came at Travers. Travers said he got scared, pulled out his gun and started shooting."

"That's what Childs told you?" I asked, trying not to sound incredulous. "You believe him?"

"That's what the suicide letter says."

"You saw the letter?"

"Childs gave it to us this morning. It was written on a computer, printed out and signed by Travers."

"It was at Childs's house?"

"He called us out there early this morning. Showed us the letter, which he said Travers dropped through the mail slot. Childs said he was concerned for the welfare of his employee, and he wanted us to go out and find him. He said he called us as soon as he found the letter.

"And then this morning, we got the call from a fisherman who spotted the car in the water," Hernandez said.

When we got to the media staging area, a group of reporters and cameras were crammed into a cordoned-off pen, and Hernandez ushered me into it, where I felt like we were a bunch of herded cattle.

As Hernandez approached the group, reporters began shouting out questions, to which Hernandez held up a hand. "I'm not taking questions, guys. Someone will be over in a bit to get you more information." And then he walked away.

Eventually, the crowd of reporters dissipated, especially after they were told that the bodies had been removed from the vehicle already and taken by boat to the boat launch area, loaded in an ambulance and taken to the coroner's office. The vehicle wouldn't be hauled up until the next morning.

Once they got a canned statement from the state police and enough B-roll footage, the reporters left the scene to get their stories ready for the news and the paper the next day.

I was still there when a trooper came by and took down the yellow police tape that had served as the media staging area pen.

Most of the police cars, ambulances and fire trucks had left the scene, and I made my way over to the cliff's edge, where Hernandez was still standing, looking down.

"I guess that wraps it all up nice and neat," I said to Hernandez.

"Yeah, nice and neat," he said in a way that wasn't convincing.

"Is Childs that well connected?"

"Apparently so."

"You believe all of what he said?"

"Doesn't matter what I believe. Only what I can prove."

50

———————

On Monday, the coroner's office delivered the bombshell: the woman in the car with Travers was Cindy Broten, the daughter of prominent Republican lawmaker John Broten.

John Broten stayed silent for the first couple of days, not taking reporters' phone calls, which resulted in "Broten could not be reached for comment" in the news stories.

On Wednesday, he finally held a brief press conference, at which he read a statement that his daughter had had a troubled life and had fallen in with the wrong people. He didn't take any questions, ending the conference with the statement, "Please respect my family's privacy in this difficult time."

I called Lauren several times, but it went straight to voicemail each time.

The family held a private ceremony, and only a brief one-paragraph obituary appeared in the paper.

The official police explanation was that Cindy Broten was Travers's girl-friend, and he had taken her with him. They had both died of blunt force trauma, ostensibly from the impact of the Escalade in the bottom of the canyon.

Part of me expected the Brotens to finally speak up now about Cindy and the blackmail from Childs, but as their silence continued, it became clear the Brotens decided they still didn't want the scandal of their daughter made public.

I ended up publishing my story on water rights and H-Bar Ranch the following week.

My story of declining water tables, dried-up wells and a major change in the state's 150-year-old water law took up the whole front page and four pages inside.

Massive development soaks up

water rights, could change state law

It was a sixty-point bold, six-column, double-decker headline.

Once the public knew what was going on, I thought naively, my story would surely stop the change in water law, trigger the current county commissioners to reconsider the development agreement with Childs and shut down H-Bar Ranch. I ordered an extra thousand copies, made my deliveries and waited for the phone to ring from the store managers telling me they had sold out and to bring more papers.

But my phone didn't ring.

My phone didn't ring that afternoon, the next day or the day after that.

When I checked on my single-copy sales, there were still dozens of copies left. My stack of a thousand extra copies sat in my office, mocking me.

Apparently, massive development and water rights wasn't the right headline to attract any sort of attention from the public.

All that week, no call, no change—no indication anyone would try to stop Childs's plans for H-Bar Ranch. No one apparently was interested in water rights, place of use laws and massive developments in the middle of the desert. I did get a couple of emails from readers and comments about what a great story it was. Bernie Samstone admitted it was too long and he didn't read it all. Nor did I receive any calls from lawyers, neither Brad Childs's lawyers nor John Broten's.

No response from the county commissioners about the development agreement. Nothing from state legislators about approving a study of Basin 63 or putting a halt to the change in water laws. Nothing from the Department of Water Resources.

Childs's development eventually would get built. Ogata would sell out to Childs, who later would be successful, with the help of the Idaho Liberty Coalition, in changing place of use and point of diversion laws. Broten would vote for the bill in the Natural Resources Committee, but then quietly vote against the bill when it reached the Senate floor, an act of quiet, meaningless defiance. It would overwhelmingly pass the Senate, then the House, with the usual supermajority partisan split, so Broten's "no" vote would have little effect other than a couple of sideways glances from his Republican colleagues, who would carry the bill on the floor, loyally reading from scripts prepared by the Idaho Liberty Coalition.

Despite his assurances, Broten wouldn't retire right away. To the contrary, Broten would end up running for governor a couple of years later, eventually dropping out of the Republican primary and endorsing the man who would go on to become governor. Lauren would serve as his campaign manager. After dropping out, he would go back to his law practice, eventually being appointed district court judge by the governor he had endorsed.

I never heard from Lauren again, and I wondered if her only interest in me was to expose Childs or whether it was just too painful to see me again.

Ted Dunlap would eventually retire, although his retirement would not be met by articles in the newspaper or celebrations in the State Bar law journal.

The investigation into the murder of Wanda and Vern Thompson wrapped up, and the investigation closed, solved with the simple explanation that Eddie Travers had killed them both then killed himself out of guilt, taking Cindy Broten with him.

The family of Alan Garry would continue believing he had died in a tragic car accident on a desert highway doing what he loved: researching water. A GoFundMe campaign would raise $100,000 for Garry's family, and on the one-year anniversary of his death, a small memorial consisting of a cross and some flowers would sprout up at the site of the crash. Eventually, over time, that memorial would get swept away in the wave of development that would come and be supplanted by a new, wider road leading into a high-end subdivision.

With a narcissistic flair, Childs would name his little city in the desert Childs Springs. Eventually, Boise would become like most western cities such as Salt Lake, Phoenix and Denver, spreading like a pool of suburban vomit on the desert floor, and in just a couple of decades, Childs Springs would be a bustling suburb of Boise, not too far away, just off the now-expanded freeway with its own interchange, home to a couple hundred thousand residents who drove to work in the morning with the sun to their backs and home in the evening with the setting sun behind them, unburdened by the blinding sun in their eyes, a fate suffered by those living on the west side of Boise. Why more developers hadn't discovered this eastside amenity earlier, I didn't know. I had to hand it to Childs to foresee this future and capitalize on it.

Wells would run dry for several homes, farms and ranches downstream from Childs's development. But without a study of Basin 63, and with the entitlements Childs had been able to secure for his development, there was nothing anyone could do about it. The farmers and ranchers simply sold their land, some to Childs, some to other developers, who eventually would fill the land with houses. The existing homes and subdivisions would be forced to join Childs's development—and pay to hook into his water. Eventually, the landscape would be a long, continuous strip of ugly subdivisions nestled along the congested interstate that would be expanded to eight lanes and still backed up at every rush hour.

As I sat in my office that Tuesday evening foreseeing the eventualities, the cloud began to settle in again.

I had done my job, but sometimes that was all I could do. I had done what was right, even if the rest of the world didn't. That didn't make the situation any more palatable.

The setting sun glared into my office's front window, and I didn't seem to have the energy to get up and pull the shades.

I pulled the bottle of Four Roses from my desk drawer, poured a cup and took a long swallow. The streetlight outside my office clicked on, and its light eventually replaced the light of the sun, which slowly fell behind the horizon.

The stack of untouched, unsold papers cast a long shadow across my desk.

ALSO BY SCOTT MCINTOSH

Philip Chandler Thrillers

Basin 63

To find out more about Scott's books, visit:

WriterScottMcIntosh.com

ABOUT THE AUTHOR

Scott McIntosh is a journalist with three decades in the news business and dozens of state and national writing awards to his credit. He has been a reporter, editor and newspaper owner, with stints in New Mexico; Rochester, New York; Cleveland; San Francisco; and Idaho. He is currently the opinion editor for the *Idaho Statesman* in Boise, Idaho, where he lives with his wife, Nicola. They have two adult sons.

To find out more about Scott's books, visit:
WriterScottMcIntosh.com